The Triple Alliance of Dallington Place
Book Two in the Series

Sophie Cloud

The Triple Alliance of Dallington Place
Book Two in the Series

Olympia Publishers
London

www.olympiapublishers.com
OLYMPIA PAPERBACK EDITION

Copyright © Sophie Cloud 2024

The right of Sophie Cloud to be identified as author of
this work has been asserted in accordance with sections 77 and 78 of the
Copyright, Designs and Patents Act 1988.

All Rights Reserved

No reproduction, copy or transmission of this publication
may be made without written permission.
No paragraph of this publication may be reproduced,
copied or transmitted save with the written permission of the publisher, or in
accordance with the provisions
of the Copyright Act 1956 (as amended).

Any person who commits any unauthorised act in relation to
this publication may be liable to criminal
prosecution and civil claims for damage.

A CIP catalogue record for this title is
available from the British Library.

ISBN: 978-1-80074-005-1

This is a work of fiction.
Names, characters, places and incidents originate from the writer's imagination.
Any resemblance to actual persons, living or dead, is purely coincidental.

First Published in 2024

Olympia Publishers
Tallis House
2 Tallis Street
London
EC4Y 0AB

Printed in Great Britain

In loving memory of Alan

'If there is one lily there is hope.'

Introduction

Dallington Place Prisoner Of War Camp
March 1940

The horses were gone, the 'Legend of Hades' was upon us. The lines where the race track had been were now being used as a walkway between the camps. Every time a lily shoot appeared on the grass, as quickly as it appeared on the ground ready to flourish, it was stomped out by military boots.

'Show them some mercy,' said Colonel Shaddock. 'Efficiency is the key.'

'Just get the job done,' Commanding Officer Harding had ordered.

The Italian Prisoners of War had arrived at Dallington Place. It was quite unrecognisable. Clean, stark and rather a desolate place now. Kathryn had taken down the good drapes and replaced them with a dark green, standard curtain that the army used. The only place untouched by the military was her beloved sitting room which was out of bounds, even to the army officers. All Kathryn's original furniture had been sent to Endelwise Manor for safe keeping by the Fitch family. It had taken a month to move everything and Kathryn was exhausted. Today she had turned Sebastien's restaurant into a refectory. Many more army surplus seats had been installed and also some long benches at the side of the room for staff. The sign over the doorway had been removed and was now called the "Refectory". This had upset both Kathryn and Dawson.

Every single horse had been found a new home. Dawn had cried non-stop as Reggie was re-stabled at the local farm for now. Lily was living at Endelwise Manor with her grandparents to keep her safe for the time being. There were too many army trucks and boisterous men around. Dawn had promised Kathryn she would stay on a few extra weeks to help her with adjusting to life at Dallington Place as a Prisoner of War camp. Then she would move back to Norfolk too. Kathryn could not will herself to say it. She sighed when someone mentioned it.

'Prisoner of War Camp.' Dawson felt the same, so kept himself largely to himself. He was agog at all these Italian men and felt uncomfortable to talk to them as yet. Although he was retired he enjoyed helping Kathryn with light duties. It wasn't in his nature to sit back and let others work hard around him. He happily made Kathryn pots of tea and cleaned the motor cars the best he could. At the end of each day he would shuffle happily back to his cottage in the knowledge that he had kept out of people's way, contributing to the hardworking lifestyle Dallington Place required.

People from the village were surprised that Kathryn had stayed on, as her home was rapidly transformed into a Prisoner of War camp, but she stubbornly ignored the criticisms and disapproving looks. She was jolly well not going to move back to her mother's old cottage in the village that her friends suggested would be more suitable for her safe being. Kathryn saw this as moving backwards in life and she felt this was simply unacceptable. She could have moved into Willow Tree Cottage and she almost relented, but she felt the memories of the first years of married life were too strong there. Besides, she had already rented it out to a land agent, and the money was very welcome. She would stay put and people would have to lump it, she thought stoically.

Dallington Place resembled a stark military base, a place of scorn and hardship now. She embraced the challenge of getting to know all the military men, although having them living beside her was not easy. But she could do this – she had to do this. There was no alternative.

Kathryn missed Ernest and Sebastien very much as they were away fighting for their country, in France. She seldom saw Roberta either, as she was working for the telephone exchange in London. When she wasn't doing that, she was volunteering with the ambulance service.

At least Mr Montgomery was here, Kathryn thought. She felt safe with him nearby. The cuckoos were amongst them with their watchful eyes and they were outnumbered.

Part One

Chapter One
1940 The Italians

Kathryn watched her prize horse The Legend of Hades, his flanks having moved passed the young shoots of the lime tree buds with slippery synchronicity, slowly, easily. His chestnut coat shimmering in the foggy atmosphere. Sinking his hooves in the damp grass, dew like tears lingered gingerly on the long blades of grass where the race track once stood. Now overgrown, unkempt, trodden on. Her "Legend of Hades", her dearest horse, was now slinking passed her. Pilot was long gone now. It was Italian Prisoner of War boots not hooves taking over. Treading on private land and sleeping in their newly built Nissen huts, just next to the stable block. Like unwilling cuckoos, these Italian men were making their nests in a habitat foreign and unwelcoming. Kathryn knew it wasn't their fault but she couldn't help feeling resentful.

Dawn led The Legend of Hades into his horsebox without a turn of her head towards Kathryn. Dawn knew Kathryn was watching her from the sitting room and would know she would be crying discreetly, saying her private goodbyes to her loyal horse. Her small hands gripped the heavy army surplus curtains as she peeped out at her daughter-in-law completing her final equestrian duty at Dallington Place. There would be no more equestrian duties for a while. For how long the horses would be gone, Kathryn had no idea. The future was changing again.

***

1939 — Six months previously

'My name is Mrs Marjorie Wright. I am here to speak to my son Sebastien,' she stated boldly.

Dawson, open-mouthed and flustered by the surprise appearance of such a wilful looking woman, led her quickly into Kathryn's study. Clearing his throat nervously, he wondered where Kathryn was at this precise moment.

'If you would be so kind and wait here, Mrs Wright, I will find out where Mrs McAlister is,' he said, shutting the study door and quickly putting on his overcoat. It was folded neatly under the coat stand where he always kept it. He set off outside and down to the Nissen huts. He hoped at least Mr Montgomery would know where she was at this time of day.

Jorie watched him from the window and raised an eyebrow at the name "Mrs McAlister". Was that her husband's name, she wondered. She looked about to find a suitable place to sit down. There was a comfortable chair next to the chaise by the small and open unlit fire. It was cold; she didn't want to sit down.

As she crossed the room, she thought perhaps she should sit on a leather-bound chair by a desk but it looked rather official, with silver framed photographs placed neatly between an expensive silver pen and diary. Above, on the wall, were some larger photographs hung against the pretty silver and white wallpaper. She peered at them. Her brow wrinkled as her eyesight was not what it used to be.

There was a picture of a triumphant win on the race track which Jorie presumed was taken here at Dallington Place. The grainy picture caught her eye as she admired the beautiful racehorse. Pilot's nostrils were flared and he looked prideful at his triumph. There was a good-looking man and a woman grinning from ear to ear in the centre and underneath the embossed writing it said, "Kathryn and Alexander with Pilot, Dallington Races – 1935". This was Kathryn and her husband, Jorie surmised.

Below it was another even larger photograph, a picture of a large bustling crowd, and in large gold writing it read, "The opening of Dallington Races. May 1935." The crowds were waving enthusiastically and with triumphant exuberance. The ladies and gentlemen were beautifully attired and Dallington Place was obviously the place to be seen then.

Aristocracy and monied people alike milled about in a smaller photo which was entitled "Mr Kipling opens the races". Beside Mr Kipling Jorie could see a young man she knew to be Sebastien. His wide smirking grin as so recognisable. She sniffed under her breath and said quietly to herself, 'Very impressive,' admiring how successful Kathryn Beaumont had become.

Just then she heard footsteps at the door to the study. She immediately sat down on the leatherbound chair and watched the oak door open slowly. Her eyes moistening with tears, she was suddenly overcome with emotion.

Where had all those years gone, and what had become of Sebastien, she thought. It had been too many years and she was sorry for that. To see Sebastien after all this time would be such a shock, and she gripped the warm leather on the arms for comfort, digging her fingernails in nervously wondering who was going to enter the room. To her relief, it was the old man again.

'Mrs McAlister will see you in the orangery, please follow me,' Dawson instructed, oblivious to her panic and her emotional state. Jorie dutifully followed him outside.

***

May 1940

The newly built Nissen huts that were placed next to the stables were Mr Montgomery's pride and joy. He had the idea to install them rather than let the men sleep at Dallington Place for now. Kathryn would have felt unsafe and outnumbered in her home if it wasn't for Mr Montgomery's good idea. Neat in rows, made from corrugated iron, they were visible from Kathryn's bedroom. She thought them ugly but understood their necessity. There were twenty men to each Nissen hut. They were as functional as they were plain.

The early May morning mist had started to clear and Kathryn yawned sleepily. A fight had broken out in the night between two Italian men and Kathryn had to call the Home Guard at two o'clock in the morning as she was frightened for her own safety. Instinctively hearing the terrible rumpus coming from the Nissen huts and not being able to get hold of Mr Montgomery for reassurance, she called the Home Guard.

More manpower was needed than just the camp guards. The Home Guards arrived in no time at all, cheerfully helping sort out the problems, but Kathryn had failed to return to sleep. Wondering if perhaps it would be a sensible idea to have some men from the Home Guard stay on the camp premises, this thought churned over in her mind. Local men, she thought, that were sensitive to her predicament here. Men that had known Dallington Place as a family run manor house, not Prisoner of War camp.

Mr Montgomery, now working alongside Kathryn, had begun to live with his new wife Agnes, in Dallington village. Mr Montgomery had suggested she gather more friends around her, perhaps to live with her at

Dallington Place. Now Kathryn was ready to agree and seeing how capable the Home Guard were in restoring order, she thought that perhaps it was wise that a couple of the Home Guards be installed here, perhaps in Dawson's cottage. She knew it was foolhardy to be alone. Several of the camp guards that slept in a separate Nissen hut were, of course, watching the men, but she needed more solidarity around her at night at Dallington Place, people she knew.

The captains and the commander who took over her daily life during the day were something she was stubbornly getting used to, although they irritated her. They respectfully called her ma'am and she always returned their politeness, but she was well aware they thought she shouldn't be living here. Digging in her heels, she had balked at the idea of any more security around her at night. But now she would have to relent. There were decisions to be made this morning. It was difficult enough knowing she was a distraction to the men. There was embarrassing talk in the village too, that she was brazen and impudent to stay on with so many unruly men around. And perhaps the villagers were right.

Mr Montgomery was right though, she needed more friends around her.

Dressing fast, she ran down the main staircase passing some officers on her way down. They saluted her good morning and she nodded politely in reply. Picking up the telephone in her study, she dialled her friend Petra's number.

'It's fine, really it is,' Petra's breathy but firm voice replied excitedly down the line. 'I can stay with you for a couple of months and really I agree, you need more women around you. Some solidarity!' she stated happily.

'Thank you so much, how can I ever thank you enough!' cried Kathryn, her eyes moistening with joyful tears. She hadn't realised how much she had been soldiering on alone and to have a good friend immediately come to her aid was fantastic news. She knew she was tired, but a heavy burden lifted off her shoulders as soon as Petra had agreed to stay.

'It would be my pleasure, please don't think I am doing you a favour, I should say the opposite is true... You see, I have been pondering a sabbatical for quite a while and the healthy country air will do me wonders. Besides, Pearl is here, at Throgmorton Street. I think you need to build an army of women around you, Kathryn. Some camaraderie, I should say,' she stated boldly, as if she was going into battle.

Smiling, Kathryn asked her, 'Do you speak any Italian by any chance?'

having suddenly remembered that Petra had travelled to Italy a few years ago on a summer's teaching post.

'Yes, my Italian's not bad at all, a little rusty perhaps but I can improve it!'

'Oh yes, of course, I will never forget what a genius you are and a life saver!' Kathryn quipped, and laughed loudly. She hadn't laughed for quite some time and she was enjoying talking to her dear friend.

Kathryn suddenly heard a commotion outside and she was brought down to earth with a bump. Saying her goodbyes to Petra, she placed down the receiver and walked over to the large bay windows. The sun had begun to shine and she squinted to see the line of small lime trees she had planted yesterday. It was the middle of May and there was still no sign of her orange lilies. Kathryn watched, mesmerised by a line of prisoners marching past her. She then watched Colonel Shaddock march closely past the window, ready to perform an inspection of the prisoners. She looked at each and every man, standing to attention, and what caught her eye was the expression on their faces. They didn't seem necessarily sad, and Kathryn was aware that the conditions were good at Dallington Place compared to other camps, but each and every man, emperor or ordinary gentleman, had a look of defeat. Kathryn had seen that look on Bertram's face, many years ago, and it was as if the life was sucked out of them. She shuddered. No wonder the orange lilies were not taking bud; nothing and no one was given enough oxygen to breathe, she thought.

Striding over to turn off the study light, hands on her hips, she stopped to admire the pictures of Dallington races and her beloved horses, Pilot and Hades. A tear pricked her eye. Wiping it away as it threatened to fall down her cheeks, she heard a knock at the door. It was Mr Montgomery. He stood before her, legs astride territorially, and he was still wearing his riding breeches. She was surprised he wasn't in his uniform but happily so, as the uniforms just reminded her of her fear for the safety of Ernest and Sebastien.

'Sorry, about the commotion, ma'am, the inspection I fear was too near your study. I saw you from the lawn. It's a sorry sight, I'm afraid, the men have no idea how to march.'

'Good morning, Mr Montgomery, and please, you must call me Kathryn. You did a fine job rounding up the prisoners, but we mustn't be too hard on them, they are far from home. Just as my Ernest and Sebastien are. I just hope they have someone kind like you beside them.'

'Thank you, ma'am… Kathryn, I mean. Men need a feminine view of things sometimes. You have quite the point there.'

'Thank you, Mr Montgomery, but I fear the men would rather I left.'

'Well, I think that would be a grave mistake, if I'm not talking out of turn,' Mr Montgomery stated shyly.

Kathryn, realising she had an ally in him, turned off the light quickly. 'Would you like to join me for breakfast? It's just myself, but you are most welcome,' she asked warmly.

'Thank you, Kathryn, I would very much like that,' he replied, following her to the dining room.

***

Flicking through the newspaper, Kathryn's thoughts turned to Sebastien and Ernest. Most days she tried to limit how much she worried about them, and if she fretted much more, she felt she would become ill. Twice a day, morning and evening, she would think on them and send them her love. Those days when they were all together at Dallington Place were bliss, she mused, placing down her cup of tea to pour another.

She slunked in the armchair by the large open fire of the breakfast room and closed her eyes for a moment. She pictured the boys at the breakfast table, when Sebastien had first arrived at Dallington Place. The two young men, bantering over eggs and bacon, and her, having to calm them both down. How she had eyed him suspiciously, this sudden cuckoo amongst them. Now she would give almost anything to have them back right this minute. She even managed a smile when she remembered the day Dawson had allowed Sebastien to take the motor car without her permission, and how they had to tow it out of the ditch. Now she wished she could go back in time and just laugh about it. Dawson seemed to enjoy himself, anyway. Where was he, she wondered, having not seen him about this morning. She decided to look for him and as she went to fetch her camel coat from upstairs, she almost bumped into Lettie who jumped down the bottom two stairs.

'Morning, ma'am, I do beg your pardon. I realised I have left the beef stew in the oven. Would you like a pot of tea?' she called, rushing towards the back staircase.

'Yes please, Lettie, two cups. I'll take one to Mr Montgomery and one to Dawson, if I can find him,' Kathryn called after her, though she wasn't sure if she had heard her. She could see how rushed off her feet Lettie was. She was going to have to interview for some more kitchen staff.

Just as she was pulling on her camel coat quickly and looking for her galoshes, Mr Montgomery opened the front door.

'The weather is turning and my feet are hurting something terrible,' he said, wincing and sitting down on a velvet chair that had seen better days.

'I was just about to bring you some tea. By the way, have you seen Dawson this morning?' Kathryn asked him, worrying that he might be poorly today.

'Last seen chatting to Colonel Shaddock by the fountain. He was with me earlier, pottering about in the garden shed. He keeps tidying everything away and I'm forever looking for my tools,' Mr Montgomery explained with a sly grin. 'He told me he was going to put his feet up for an hour and listen to Churchill on the radio.'

Kathryn shot Mr Montgomery a knowing look. 'Well, he has been pottering about here too, hiding everything. I cannot find my galoshes anywhere!' she said, giggling at the old man's antics. 'Mind you, I don't blame him, he thinks the prisoners are going to steal from us.'

'I think, Kathryn, everything has been taken from us, with regards to Dallington Place, I mean,' Mr Montgomery stated wisely, sipping his tea, his sore and numb feet recovering at last.

'You are right there, Mr Montgomery,' Kathryn said, reflecting on their current circumstances and biting her lower lip nervously. Mr Montgomery said his momentary goodbyes and Kathryn ran up the stairs to change into something more practical, so she could help out in the vegetable garden. Maybe she could recover the garden tools too.

***

The skies had cleared by lunchtime and sipping on her third hot cup of tea of the day, she knelt back on the cool grass and surveyed her progress. She had neatly planted ten rows of carrots and her back ached. Mr Montgomery was on his way to chat to her, carrying his own tea, and he waved as he walked towards her. She waved back and smiled as he stopped to speak to Colonel Shaddock who was standing outside a Nissen hut. Her fingerless gloves aiding her to hold on to the boiling liquid, she reminded herself to buy some new ones this week as there were holes in these. Mr Montgomery, carrying a shovel that he had taken from Colonel Shaddock, came and stood beside her.

'Kathryn, I do think we need some more manpower here. You and I cannot do all this work between us,' he said, placing his shovel down on the overturned soil.

'Do you have any news from the Grant Office? I wrote to them last week asking for assistance, but I haven't heard from them yet. I stated that we have to feed one hundred and fifty men, as well as my own staff here. Our food is barely stretching, how do they expect Dallington Place to be run as a Prisoner of War Camp on such a meagre budget, with little manpower for the workload that needs to be done as soon as possible. It's overwhelming, Mr Montgomery,' she explained wearily.

'We need to make this land work for us, Kathryn, and we need more farm labourers and machinery,' he said with his hand on his chin, deep in thought.

Standing up and pulling off her gloves, she put her hands on her hips. 'Land girls, Mr Montgomery, that's what we need! A better ratio of women to men.'

Mr Montgomery smiled with approval of Kathryn's suggestion and with that smile of confidence from him, Kathryn took off for the house to chase up the Grant Office.

Chapter Two
Petra's Arrival

Sweet damask stripped from our walls.
Our Rosebuds flock to our halls.
What makes our grass grow?
Blood and soil,
Blood and soil.

Stare him in the eye, our Italians.
Everyman and Emperor.
Men of War.
It was our home
But not anymore.

Kathryn had had a late night. There had been a meeting in the Dallington Village Hall and it had carried on well past midnight. Margaret Byers, the church administrator, had decided to step down and the villagers were looking for a new secretary and a member of Parliament to stand for East Grinstead to represent them. Mr Mullins, the farmer's son from nearby Deepdene, had great ambitions in the political arena, shadowing the local MP for Lewes recently. Everybody expected him to put himself up for this potential role but he was having second thoughts about pursuing a seat in London.

Earlier on in the week, Margaret Byers had telephoned Kathryn to help with the church flowers on a Sunday but she had also dropped a bombshell, enquiring whether she would consider standing as an MP herself. Kathryn had shrunk back in horror at this suggestion. Political ambitions were not something she had any aspirations for, at all. She had enough to do at Dallington Place. Rumours were rife that the village wanted a woman to stand and Kathryn was flattered to be asked, but she declined as she didn't have the time or energy to take on a political role.

'Everybody respects you here Kathryn, and it would cease the tut-

tutting you are receiving with your stubbornness in staying on at Dallington Place. And with all those Italians,' Margaret added.

This had put Kathryn's back up. She knew with all her heart that Devlin wouldn't have stood for her to be bullied out of the place he bought for them. The place she loved more than anywhere in the world. It was out of respect for his memory that she was fighting to stay on here and she didn't like the insinuations that it was out of some flighty air of stubbornness. What business was it of anybody else's where she lived, she thought. So she politely declined Margaret Byers' kind offer. If the villagers could be so condescending to her and think they had a say in where she lived, she wasn't going to further stir the pot and work for them. She agreed to arranging the church flowers, though, as her mother had enjoyed this relaxing task and in her memory she would continue this family tradition.

But she had an idea. She knew William Lovat enjoyed his politics, as he had recently become involved in the local parish council in nearby Bexhill-on-Sea, where he and Geraldine had moved to. They had fallen in love with Bexhill during the time William was designing and commissioning an aircraft hangar there. They had loved it so much, living by the sea, they had decided to live there permanently. Kathryn missed them dreadfully, but the meeting would be a good excuse for her and Geraldine to catch up, so she let them know about the meeting immediately. Wishing she could bring them back to Dallington would be a wish too far, but any excuse to see them would be marvellous, she mused. Occasionally Geraldine would visit Kathryn whilst William busied himself with the local council in Bexhill. It wasn't often enough, so picking up the telephone, she called Geraldine excitedly.

The village hall was crowded and hot, and finding it hard to concentrate on what the speaker at the front was saying, Kathryn scanned the room for William and Geraldine. She couldn't see them and found her mind wandering to earlier on in the evening. She had asked Dawson to clean the motor car for her, her Jaguar SS100, recently purchased from Doctor Laraby. She wanted to show up at the town hall in something smart and the proud buy made her feel confident and glamorous. She thought about how she had bought it from Doctor Laraby, who after a few weeks of driving found it didn't suit him. It was too ostentatious for him whilst doing his rounds. It was too noticeable and he found his patients recognised him too often and would try to flag him down in the middle of the street to keep him talking about their ailments. When Doctor Laraby had visited Dallington Place a couple of weeks ago to check on Dawson's arthritis, he had complained of the attention to Dawson and herself.

'Now what am I going to do with it?' he said, in mock exasperation, holding up his hands to Kathryn with a wry smile, guessing somewhat perhaps she might rather like it for herself.

For a cut price and after dipping into some of the savings that Alexander had left her, she happily bought the car, even driving Doctor Laraby home so she could claim her car there and then. Smiling to herself and then looking down in embarrassment, hoping no one had seen her looking so smug, she looked at the letter from Ernest that Mr Manslake, the postman, had just delivered. As soon as she had seen Mr Manslake cycling up the drive, she had wound down the window in a hurry to take the post, on the way to the meeting. She placed the letter on the dashboard for safekeeping as she proudly waved goodbye to him, as he stared at the new motor car with approval.

She secretly loved the attention her Jaguar SS100 was getting, with its shiny silver paintwork making it extremely flashy in the May sunshine. She felt glamorous and modern on her way to the village hall.

Her hands were itching to open the letter as it sat in her lap, as she waited in the hall car park. She was early and as she turned off the engine, she was just about to rip open the envelope when Margaret Byers tapped on the window. Startled, she wound it down quickly. Margaret seem harried.

'Kathryn, the meeting is starting early, there's not many seats left, do hurry up!' she cried, turning her back on Kathryn and starting down the path towards the hall.

Jumping out of the motor car, Kathryn followed Margaret down the path, clutching Ernest's letter.

The hall was full and Kathryn was one of the last there, so she had to sit at the back. She searched the room for Geraldine and William, found them and waved. Geraldine gave her a mock look of disapproval and tapped her wristwatch. Kathryn smiled back and shrugged. She had no idea why she had got the incorrect time for a meeting. Perhaps Lettie had taken down the time incorrectly when Margaret had called yesterday with the details of the meeting. Feeling guilty for overwhelming the young cook with other duties, Kathryn shut her eyes for a moment, and waited patiently for the meeting to begin.

The speaker introduced Margaret Byers to the stage and Kathryn opened her eyes and listened intently to what she was about to say.

'Ladies and Gentlemen, we have quite a few notices to get through tonight and I'm sure you want to be home for supper and not too late. As you know,' Margaret said, 'I will be stepping down this week and we have been very busy looking for my replacement. We have had much deliberation through this decision process and although there were many strong candidates, we would wholeheartedly like to introduce the winner. I have to add that I strongly agree with the decision and I fought hard for this particular lady myself.'

Clearing her throat nervously, letting the audience hold their breath in anticipation, Margaret Byers took a white card from the desk in front of her and read it slowly, aloud. 'With quite a few impressive radical ideas of her own, I would therefore like to introduce Marjorie Wright.'

Kathryn's mouth opened wide with shock and she could see Geraldine turning around to get her attention.

How on earth? thought Kathryn. How had she managed to get herself this position so quickly. Jorie had turned up at Dallington Place only a few months ago and now she was going to become Political Secretary for East Grinstead and maybe work her way up to be a Member of Parliament in a few years, if she was popular. Kathryn knew Jorie was a hard worker from what she had learnt about her through Bertram's letters all those years ago and this woman could make anything a success, but returning to Dallington village after a year, and then within a few months winning a seat in the village – now that was a surprise. She felt almost as if Jorie was treading on her toes. Jorie would now be mixing in the same circles and entwined in their lives.

Seeing the effervescent Jorie by the entrance door, busily shaking people's hands as they congratulated her on her triumphant win, Kathryn braced herself to greet her.

'Kathryn, my dear, we really must meet for lunch.' Jorie started reaching forward to kiss her on her cheek. Just as Kathryn was about to answer, a man shoved in front of her, obviously not able to contain his excitement at meeting the good looking American, Marjorie Wright.

'I know your husband Giles,' he shouted over the noise of the bustling hall and simultaneously treading back on Kathryn's toes. Kathryn winced and smiled weakly back at Jorie, who mouthed, 'I will telephone you!'

Kathryn waited for Geraldine and William to file out behind her, as they had become caught up signing the members' register.

'Can you believe that?' said William, putting his arm around two of the three of his favourite women in the whole world. 'I'm dying to see your new motor car, Kathryn,' he said, hurrying the women along. Kathryn looped her arm through Geraldine's as William walked on ahead, making a beeline for the Jaguar, once he had spied it from afar.

'Well Marjorie Wright has firmly got her feet under the table here in Dallington then,' said Geraldine, as bemused as Kathryn was.

'I heard a man say that he knew her husband, Giles. Who is he, do you know?' asked Kathryn, eager to find out, her brow furrowing with intrigue.

'I will have William to investigate, she must surely use her married name sometimes,' replied Geraldine, equally intrigued.

***

At last, in her warm and comfortable bed with only her side lamp illuminating the room, she had made sure the curtains were shut tight. She could hear a loud commotion coming from the Nissen huts. Getting out of bed and looking towards the camp, she could see lights flickering on and off through the mist. The Italian Prisoners of War had lights out at ten o'clock sharp and they should all have been sound asleep. She could hear crunching sounds on the gravel below her window and presumed this was Colonel Shaddock and a few other British officers who had overseen the nightly round up of men. She tried to crane her neck to see more clearly below her and then she heard the British men raise their voices.

She sighed. All she wanted to do was to read Ernest's letter, so she stopped listening to the men and firmly shut the curtains again. It was their job to worry, she thought. She had had enough of all this rumpus. It was nothing to do with her. Jumping straight back into bed, she tore open the envelope and unfolded the letter in haste.

Absorbing the first few lines Ernest had written, and drawing her knees up to her chest, she began to relax. She put her hands over her ears and continued to read.

It read:

8th April 1940

Abbeville,
France

Dearest Mamma,

I hope you like the poem I have written below. We, the rifle regiment, are staying in a village called Ballecourt not far from Abbeville. We are protecting the locals as much as we can. Sebastien and I even met the French Resistance in a local tavern the other night. I will tell you all about it when I see you, as I am not allowed to write about it in this letter.

Spring is here and is blossoming into Summer and the two worlds one of peace and the other of destruction, seem to merge into one. Some towns and villages are burnt out. Cathedrals, some raided shops and copses and woods either burnt down or chopped down, and then three miles away, there are beautiful villages untouched, as yet. With chocolate box houses, gardens with honeysuckle, blueberry vines and silver grasses. A relaxing place to be with the humming of the bees and wild honeysuckle in the hedgerows. We smell a scent most divine and then we return to Ballecourt where there is a smell of acrid smoke, burnt out crops and destruction in the village.

If you thought about it too much, it would destroy you. One's head and heart couldn't take it in and make sense of it all. I understand why Bertram was the way he was now. Sort of detached. Sebastien and I talked about that yesterday.

Sebastien seems sullen and not his usual jovial self. He misses Lily but he never mentions Dawn. I talk about Roberta all the time to him but he looks at me rather scornfully as if love is a waste of time for him. He doesn't want to know about anybody else's happiness. I don't think he loves Dawn anymore. Please don't repeat this, although I know you wouldn't. It would break Dawn's heart, I fear.

Our lorries were stopped in their tracks yesterday. They were lined up at the end of Ballecourt and we couldn't move as Schneider tanks have moved into the village and we were blocked in. What comforting beasts they are. But I feel safe here now. We are billeted to a farmhouse that is reasonably comfortable.

Sebastien, I can tell, is restless and wants to return home now!

We got word we will be here for another month or so and then perhaps we can have some leave. I cannot wait to see you Mamma and be back to Dallington Place.

I have to go now as we have a rifle inspection.

We will be home as soon as possible. Please tell Roberta that I love her and I am proud of her helping Petra at Throgmorton Street, doing her bit for the war effort. I miss her so much, too much, I think. So bye bye for now.

Your loving son,
Ernest x
I have written a poem for you. It is called 'The Marigold.'

The Marigold by Ernest Wright

Morning has broken, silence a thing of the past.
Marigolds, that bloom in France.
Mourning as they bend their saffron head.
As once abundant and thriving as once a
Beautiful English rose,
Scarcity this time of war.
As the dew settles on each petal like a tear,
I will hold you dear.
Where villagers find a gilded hand of friendship
To applause the cause, the Resistance will come and go.
For the high times and the low,
The tall hedges, the wild flowers grow.
Marigolds, your leaves lend an ear.

Cold till you fold.
Burnt out villages,
Desolate land, fan out through France.
Look askance, from left to right,
Not one blade of grass,
Untrodden from an enemy boot.
Fighting with brilliance are we.
We will come home, you will see.

Placing the letter back in its envelope and content that Ernest and Sebastien were safe, she turned down the lamp and snuggled under the bed sheets. Petra was arriving early in the morning and she wanted to be up early to greet her herself in her new motor car. She knew Dawson had kindly washed it for her this morning. Feeling content now, more than she had in a long time, that the boys were safe, though she did feel somewhat despondent that the glamour had gone from Dallington Place. With a glimpse of the old days with Petra arriving tomorrow and her new motor car adding a splash of glamour in these austere times, life was not so bad.

***

Petra was early. Her embroidered bag at her feet, she waited patiently for Kathryn to arrive. The 11.07 from Victoria was five minutes ahead of time, uncharacteristically. Normally there could be a hold up at the Darton crossing, where the line was cordoned off for ten minutes occasionally to let the sheep cross from nearby farms. But not today.

Kathryn honked the horn and waved as she drew up beside the station, spying Petra in her usual plumage. Her turquoise and brown belted jacket caught the light and a slim pencil skirt showed off her feminine figure. Her long grey hair she wore loose today and she looked almost girlish. Petra ran over to the car, her neatly laced, flat brogues were the only sensible thing about her. Reaching out for Kathryn as she slid into the sumptuous leather seats of the beautiful Jaguar motor car, she kissed her warmly on both cheeks.

'I can't tell you how excited I am, Kathryn. To be in the country with you and have a rest from London! The bombs have been shattering my nerves,' she stated, seeing how well the country living suited her friend. 'And you know, I think you have lost weight, if that's possible, and still as beautiful as ever!' she cried, throwing her handbag over the back seat.

'No, I am not beautiful, my friend,' she answered back, aware Petra was treating her precious motor car like an old truck. Giggling, Kathryn shot Petra a look 'What, in my old green trousers and grubby gardening sweater?' she exclaimed, looking down for a moment as she started the engine. This was her daily uniform at Dallington Place now and Petra had better get used to it, she thought, slapping her friend playfully on the knee and turning left at the main road for home. 'You had better get used to me looking like this!' she continued as Petra raised an eyebrow.

'What nonsense, there's not a man I dare say is not in love with you in all of Sussex,' Petra said knowingly. 'Even if you are all in green!'

'Just you see what awaits you,' Kathryn said smugly as she put her foot on the brake, noting the absent sheep from earlier were now huddling together, blocking the road ahead.

'So what of the Italians, are they a pleasant bunch?' Petra asked naively.

'Do you mean the one hundred men or so that inhabit the Nissen huts on my lawn?' Kathryn said resentfully.

Petra let out a small whistle as she wound down the window to inspect the sheep.

'Poor devils!' mused Petra, looking to see who was in charge of this flock of sheep.

Kathryn shot Petra a look of mock horror. 'What about us? It's an intrusion, you know,' she said, starting to move the motor car slowly as the sheep were routed off to the side of the road.

'Well, I bet there are some handsome ones,' stated Petra, trying to stir the pot, with a twinkle in her eye.

'Well, you know I haven't been bothered to look, but maybe you are right. I should look, as there's not a decent looking man in the area I could call fanciable.'

'You know what, Kathryn, it's a good thing I turned up when I did, if only to keep you from maidenhood or spinsterhood,' Petra said proudly as she nudged her friend in the ribs.

As they pulled up into the stables at Dallington Place, Kathryn could see Petra was agog. She noticed the beauty of the lawn had long gone. She could understand what Kathryn had been trying to explain. No fine horses roaming in the nearby field. No orange lilies bobbing near Bertram's memorial bench or by the front door. Just men scattered around in uniform. As Kathryn opened the motor car's door, she could hear shouts coming from the far end of the lawn and as she took off towards the vegetable plot, there was Mr Montgomery on his back, his legs splayed and clearly unconscious with a huge cut above his right eye.

Chapter Three
Jorie's Story, England 1939

Jorie had been disappointed that Sebastien wasn't living at Dallington Place when she first visited a year ago. She and Kathryn had eyed each other suspiciously as they sat together in the sitting room. Their lives were so entwined through Bertram, they could have been sisters. With long pauses and awkward silences, it was clear they were very different. Kathryn was as friendly and as helpful as possible but she felt put out that this woman had called in on her at home without notice, which had put Kathryn at a disadvantage.

'Do you know when he will be returning from France?' Jorie had asked her, genuinely concerned for Sebastien's safety.

'I'm afraid I do not,' Kathryn had stated, sipping her tea and crossing her legs nervously, trying to get comfortable.

This woman sitting before her was very attractive. With her wide, darting, bright blue eyes and beautiful shoulder length hair, she made Kathryn feel inferior, especially as she had been out gardening in the rain this morning. She was sure her hair was a wild bird's nest and sadly she hadn't seen a hairdresser in months. Jorie was the type that could wake up looking beautiful, Kathryn was sure, and she was well aware that she was not of this ilk. Impossibly tall against Kathryn's lack of height, Jorie wore a pair of jodhpurs that fitted like a glove, and the silk scarf at her neck gave her an air of relaxed sophistication. Kathryn always felt she never looked relaxed herself, with a little wrinkle at her brow and her hair always too wild, especially like today.

'How long have you been in England, may I ask?' Kathryn had said, extremely curious.

'Actually, a couple of years, Kathryn. I was working for the Suffragette movement in Westminster when I first arrived and then I met my husband, Giles, in Chelsea.'

Kathryn was surprised for this independent-spirited woman had married another Englishman and moved, lock, stock and barrel, to London.

'I should have visited Sebastien sooner, I know, but time just flew, what with work and meeting Giles and the beginning of the war. I just hadn't found the right time to visit Dallington Place. You see, Giles has a meeting in Brighton today so I thought I would try on an off chance to see if Sebastien would see me. I should have written, I know how rude this must seem,' Jorie explained, embarrassed by her lack of foresight.

'No, I understand, perhaps you thought Sebastien may not wish to see you?' Kathryn said quietly, now empathic to Jorie's situation. She knew Sebastien wasn't always easy and could brush people and situations off when it suited him.

'It's been a long time,' Jorie explained, 'because of the way he left Santa Anna. I was angry with him you see. I was also mourning the loss of Bertram so I wasn't thinking straight at the time. I had lost a bab…'

The words trailed away as she looked momentary distracted by some voices outside the window. It was a child's voice that had caught her attention.

Kathryn nodded sympathetically, going to the window to beckon Lily and Dawn to come inside. Jorie looked up at Kathryn, unclear as to whether she knew what she had meant about the "baby".

'Dawn's here. Would you like to see her and May Lilian, Sebastien's daughter? We call her Lily,' Kathryn said proudly.

'I would like that very much, but I feel I may be overwhelmed if I see them,' Jorie said, beginning to look upset and close to tears.

'But you have come all this way, not to see them would be such a shame,' Kathryn said, imploring her to change her mind.

'Perhaps another time, Kathryn. I really should be going, would your man take me back to the station? Giles will be waiting for me in Brighton to return home. He is a man of habit and if I'm not at home, he will be very upset. We have plans, you see.'

'Yes of course, but don't you at least want to say hello before you go? You can always return and spend longer with them another time,' Kathryn reiterated, surprised at Jorie's coldness towards the girls. To leave without seeing them and to ignore them seemed rude.

'Like I said, Kathryn, I really don't want to make a fuss and it was Sebastien that I came to see,' Jorie explained, speaking too matter-of-factly and snapping her handbag shut.

'Right you are then,' Kathryn said, backing down, her pleas ignored and she rose to see her out, just as Dawn knocked on the door and called out to Kathryn. Jorie resembled a frightened rabbit, caught in the glare of the headlights of a motor car, so Kathryn instinctively rushed over to the door to prevent Dawn from entering.

'I'm just having a meeting, dear, I will be with you in ten minutes,' Kathryn said whispering to Dawn, blocking her from the view inside the study.

Lily called out for Kathryn as Dawn was applying her make up at the hall table. Kathryn kissed the little girl on the cheek, and promised to meet her in the kitchen so they could bake cakes together. Excited, Lily slipped away to find Lettie down in the kitchen and to get ready for Kathryn to join her. Kathryn knew she would be rushing to find her little apron and helping Lettie make her a cup of tea.

'Dawson will drive you to Lingfield station but I hope you will return and see us all. Sebastien will be home I should think in the next couple of months,' Kathryn explained, relieved to spy Dawn making her way down across the lawn to the Nissen huts. Kathryn decided she didn't like Jorie at all. She seemed cool and detached and why, she wondered, did she want to see Sebastien after all this time?

***

1940

'How is he?' Kathryn asked Dr Laraby, shutting the door so Lily couldn't see poor Mr Montgomery lying on his bed in such a state.

Kathryn had kindly put him in the master suite that Alexander had used, next to Kathryn's suite of rooms.

'The best bedroom at Dallington Place,' Alexander had boasted. He had felt for a man of his age and stature it was the most suitable. With large bay windows and high ceilings, and a rich red curtain that pulled all the way across, it would enable him, in the mornings, to stand in his dressing gown and admire the view of the horse and rider statue as well as the vast amounts of lawn, and a birds-eye vantage point of the race track. Lost in thought for a moment of Alexander, and brushing away a moment of sadness, her attention wandered back to Mr Montgomery.

'He will recover, albeit with a little bit of a headache but he will be fine. The cut above his eye will close quite rapidly, I should say, if he rests,' explained Dr Laraby.

'Do you think he tripped or was pushed over by an Italian, Dr Laraby?' Kathryn asked, concerned.

'Well, he was quite dehydrated and it may have been exhaustion, which could have initiated the fall, so let him rest. Perhaps more help is needed here?' Dr Laraby asked, aware that the whole family were experiencing an enormous change in Dallington Place.

Kathryn nodded, clutching her address book to call Mr Montgomery's wife.

'Don't you worry. I wouldn't like to speculate on how it happened. He will be fine, so please don't fret. But I think a few days of bed rest and some more staff working alongside him in future, he will be as right as rain,' said the kind doctor, shutting his medical case firmly shut.

'Yes, you are right, and it's something we have recently discussed. We are just awaiting the government's help on that. You see, he doesn't like to ask Dawson because of his age. Mr Montgomery has been taking on too much alone, I fear,' Kathryn explained, wishing they had all acted sooner.

After saying goodbye to Dr Laraby Kathryn thought it was a good idea to have a word with Dawn. She needed to pull her weight a little more. Mr Montgomery needed her help even though the horses had been sent away and she was spending much of her time in London. The stables still needed cleaning and painting, ready to be turned into bathrooms for the prisoners of war. Kathryn decided she would discuss this with her tonight; she would have to persuade her and how she wished Geraldine was here more often. Geraldine was good at this sort of thing, she mused. Still, Kathryn was proud of her dear friend, now married to the Member of Parliament for Bexhill-on-Sea.

Just as she was about to venture back inside the house, feeling a chill from the south wind, something unusual caught her eye. As Kathryn watched the branches of the tall tree stir, a precursor to the storm that was predicted, she looked away from the skyline and down towards the vegetable garden. By the Nissen huts she could see the men were being rounded up in a rather undignified fashion. Two officers were reprimanding some men, shouting and marching up and down along the huts. The shouting gave her a sharp headache, and as she turned towards the stables she saw something colourful lurking in the sky.

The sun was momentarily shining brightly and as Kathryn shielded her eyes, squinting and holding her hand up to her forehead, she saw a hot air balloon rising over a copse and travelling along the line of the river, a resplendent, bright red balloon. Kathryn could just make out there were four or five people in the basket below and they were waving frantically. Kathryn thought how brave they were, especially as an enemy aeroplane could appear at any time. Only yesterday, British Hawker Hunter aeroplanes were flying over on exercise, making their way back to RAF base "Manston" in Kent. It would have been disastrous if the balloon had become entangled with them.

Dawn was walking away from the Nissen huts towards the house when she saw Kathryn standing looking skyward. Following Kathryn's gaze, she too caught sight of the balloon.

'Wowza, look at that,' she said loudly, letting out a long whistle, shielding her eyes but trying to prise them open to take in the glorious sight. Kathryn smiled at Dawn's choice of word.

'I can't wait to do that, where do I sign up?' Dawn said, now catching up to Kathryn and giving her a friendly nudge.

'So glamorous, yet foolhardy I should say,' Kathryn replied, enjoying the beautiful, vulnerable magic craft gliding up towards the clouds.

'I wonder who they are!' said Dawn, now beginning to feel bored and yawning, as she gestured to Kathryn that she was going back into the house.

'I would just love to know and to meet them,' Kathryn replied, enthralled by this rarity.

'You sure say, it would make a change from this rabble here!' Dawn exclaimed, agreeing with Kathryn. 'At least some of the Italians are handsome!' she cried, now pulling a cigarette out of its packet.

'Dawn, I need to ask you to help me more. We can't let Mr Montgomery do the lion's share of the work,' Kathryn said with her brow wrinkling more than usual.

'Sure thing,' Dawn answered flippantly, taking a slow drag from her cigarette.

'No, Dawn, I mean... really help,' Kathryn said, beginning to feel irritated.

'Well, the horses were my thing, and now they are gone. I get so bored in the country and I just love London,' she answered, stomping her half-finished cigarette into the ground, like a wild pony. She brushed down her grass-stained trousers and looked down at her muddy boots, with the same annoyance that Kathryn had with her situation.

'Well, London is pretty dangerous and you have Lily to think of, you know that,' Kathryn stated, aware that she was sounding like some dictatorial maiden aunt.

Dawn just shot her a look which only made Kathryn try to get her point across even more.

'You can't traipse that poor child back and forth,' Kathryn stated wisely. She didn't want Lady Alison's granddaughter to be in danger. It was bad enough that Roberta was living in Throgmorton Street, in the heart of the city. Only last week a bomb had nearly hit Threadneedle Street, the next street along. That's too close for comfort now.

'I was thinking of sending Lily to Endelwise Manor for a week or two. My mother would love to have her.' Dawn shrugged, feeling defensive.

'I would prefer that to her being in London, Dawn,' Kathryn agreed, feeling relieved.

'I will help, I promise,' Dawn said, knowing Kathryn had only their interests at heart. She touched Kathryn warmly on her arm and then spun around and ran into the house.

Kathryn couldn't help but smile. Dawn normally didn't show any affection. She must mean it this time, Kathryn mused. She needed to distract Dawn from Giuseppe, one of the English speaking Italians she seemed to have become close to. Kathryn worried that she was speaking too much with him as it might well go beyond friendship, so if she could prevent it happening now, all well and good. Dawn was always down by the Nissen huts, chatting with him and his friends, and Kathryn thought it was setting a bad example. She understood, though, that Dawn needed friends, but she was still married to Sebastien.

Kathryn had nothing against most of the Italian prisoners and mostly they were a fun and amicable bunch. Occasionally, a fight would break out but most evenings they would sing and play their musical instruments outside their quarters, relaxing after a hard day's work. Kathryn had to think of ways to keep Dawn busy and helping Mr Montgomery would be a safe bet. There was painting to be done in the stables and perhaps Petra could come up with some ideas for her, she decided.

While Mr Montgomery was recuperating, Kathryn would take over some of his light duties. But for the heavy stuff, they needed more men, or perhaps women. Her duties up to now had been administrative, now the horses had gone. Mr Montgomery saw to the accounts for the farmlands and the cottages on the estate. Also he made sure the machinery, such as tractors and combine harvesters, were all in order. Kathryn had either to learn some more skills quickly or she would have to bring in some new labour. Her own money was dwindling and she had to think about her future now. If she couldn't prove her worth to stay on at Dallington Place during this time of war, she would be asked to move out and then the whole place would be taken over by prisoners. She couldn't have that. Dawn had to pull her weight. She would have supper with her tonight and express this more firmly to her.

***

Ivy Dalrymple's son, Reginald, was in the same regiment as Ernest and Sebastien. Today Ivy had decided to visit Kathryn and let her know she might have to leave her post at Bishops Cross where she had worked for twenty years. Enquiring about work in the area, she had heard that Kathryn was looking to take on new staff to cater for the prisoners of war. Ivy was fully aware of the enormous task in hand as a housekeeper at Dallington Place and especially with the challenge of it being a Prisoner of War Camp. She knew Kathryn had a small number of personal staff, with half a dozen daytime caterers cooking food for the camp. Knowing Kathryn as she did, she was aware that Kathryn would need someone around she could trust, someone efficient and reliable. Ivy prided herself on the fact that she was this very person. Their friendship had spanned over two decades, knowing each other since they were sixteen, when they both worked as maids before the Great War. As it happened, the very morning that Ivy had telephoned Kathryn to ask for an interview, she had heard the news of the imminent arrival of their boys making their way back from France, as they spoke. Kathryn could hardly contain her excitement.

Kathryn stood between the columns of the imposing doorway of Dallington Place with her hands on her hips, taking in the cool air and trying as hard as she could not to keep smiling at every person that passed by. Soldiers or laymen, she wanted to shout to them, 'My boys are on their way back!' With her heart racing, she watched Ivy cycle up the driveway, the wind in her hair and her long skirts billowing behind her. Kathryn closed her eyes for a minute as the warmth of the sun peeping through the clouds was too delicious to ignore.

'Morning, penny for them?' Dawn called out to Kathryn from the lawn. She watched the comely lady with interest as she dismounted her bicycle briskly and then bustled over to Kathryn, her pink cheeks glowing like an out of breath cherub. Ivy almost squeezed the breath out of Kathryn and Dawn, interested in who this lady was, followed them inside the house, turning to wave goodbye to Giuseppe who was smoking by the oak tree.

'Dawn, this is Ivy Dalrymple, an old friend of mine, and she has some very exciting news!' Kathryn said. She squeezed Ivy's hand as her friend proceeded to produce a letter out of her pocket, from her son.

'See, here, this is confirmation the Rifle Company are on their way back and I have had a trunk call from Reginald yesterday. They were at Dover when he called,' Ivy said, showing them the yellowing paper and sloping handwriting of her son, with the Rifle Company logo on the reverse of the envelope in bold black ink. 'Mind, I always get the jitters when I see the official documents, but you know they are safe and Reginald assured me that Ernest is on his way back too.' Ivy was excited to reveal this information to the women as fast as she could.

'And Sebastien?' asked Dawn, with pursed lips.

'Oh, yes, my dear, your Sebastien too!' Ivy replied, taking off her cardigan and placing it on the hall stand.

'Well, Kathryn, you had better change,' said Dawn, haughtily.

Kathryn had been so caught up with the good news she hadn't even been aware that she was covered in mud from the vegetable garden. The knees of her best jodhpurs were filthy, and laughing with Ivy, she showed her into the sitting room and made her excuses to change her clothes. Dawn started up the staircase as Kathryn called out to her, 'Can you possibly do the church flowers for me today, Dawn? The time has flown and I promised, but I daren't leave here, just in case the boys arrive.'

Dawn returned a smile. 'Of course,' she replied. 'Happy to be out of the way from all of the excitement.'

'Thank you, Dawn,' Kathryn said, grateful that at last she was pulling her weight. 'It shouldn't take you more than an hour,' she continued, putting her arm around her warmly as they walked up the stairs together.

'I don't mind if takes all day,' Dawn replied nonchalantly.

Chapter Four
Rounding Up the Girls, Saturday, May 1940

Kathryn was delighted to offer Ivy the position of housekeeper. It was a weight off her shoulders, to have an ally who she had known for such a long time and someone she could trust to run the house impeccably. Ivy would start tomorrow, but today there was much organising to do as the boys would be returning to Dallington Place by mid-afternoon.

Spying Petra in her motor car speeding up the driveway and then coming to an abrupt halt to speak to Dawson who was slowly raking the lawn, Kathryn seized her chance to talk to her. She, grabbed her sweater which hung crudely over the back of her study chair, Kathryn dashed out to see her.

'How did the meeting go with the Arkala?' Kathryn asked grinning, keeping her excitement to herself about the boys' return and not telling Petra the good news yet.

'Wonderfully, actually, as they really need my help, but I kept calling the Brownies the Rosebuds instead,' Petra replied, noticing how pretty Kathryn looked in her new wool suit.

'Yes, I remember the village during the Great War and they were called the Rosebuds then,' Kathryn mused, thinking on the last war. How she herself had longed to be a Rosebud when she was a little girl and her father had been ill for a long time and she and her mother had nursed him around the clock. There had been no time for frivolities such as the Rosebuds.

'Do you know, some of the girls were evacuees from Gibraltar,' Petra explained.

'My goodness, I want to hear all about it, but can I meet you in the refectory in a few minutes? We have to rearrange a few tables and chairs,' Kathryn said, heading off towards the glass building.

'We do? What for?' Petra called after her.

'I'll explain when you get here. Change, will you?' Kathryn stated, making Petra feel uncomfortably attired. Looking down at her slightly crumpled dress, she wondered what all the fuss was about. Kathryn never complained about what she usually wore. Shrugging, she headed off to find something less creased to wear. Maybe Kathryn was right, she thought, as gone were the colours of her fashionable London clothes she used to wear. Her "plumage"; Kathryn had flatteringly coined the phrase for Petra's clothes. A few months in the country with the prisoners of war and she had to admit she had become rather dowdy.

Kathryn passed Mr Montgomery at the entrance to the refectory. He was looking so much better after his fall. He showed her a list of requirements for the party. Dawson drove up and tooted the horn for Mr Montgomery to join him in the motor car for the shopping trip to the village. Mr Montgomery took the keys from Dawson and as they swapped seats, with Mr Montgomery in the driving seat, they sped down the driveway.

Kathryn waved at these two dear men who would do anything to help her. How lucky she was, she realised, and although her house was overrun with strangers, she knew she had great friends and good staff. That was something the Fitch family had taught her. "Be a loyal friend and a good employer and it will pay off." She knew Devlin would be proud of her, right now.

***

Kathryn had dashed back to the house to fetch her coat as the weather had turned and the refectory was decidedly chilly. As she walked out the front door she heard the telephone ring so rushing back to pick up the call, she was happy to hear it was Roberta, calling from the station master's office.

'Darling, I will have Mr Montgomery pick you up as soon as he returns from the village. He won't be long. He should be back any minute now. Wait a minute, I can see his motor car. I will send him to collect you!' Kathryn said excitedly, knowing Ernest and Sebastien would be here in half an hour.

Kathryn ran back to the refectory where Petra was chatting to Colonel Shaddock who was busy handing her notices to pin up on the noticeboard for the Italians. She looked resplendent in her tight navy sweater and plaid skirt, and it hadn't gone unnoticed by Colonel Shaddock.

'Colonel Shaddock, wouldn't it be better that we translate this into Italian?' she asked him.

'You know someone who could translate this for me then?' he asked, looking surprised.

'Yes, me!' Petra replied proudly.

'Fine, then the challenge is yours. Are you fluent?' he said, rather impressed that Petra would even want to bother.

'Almost,' she said, now taking back the notice from Colonel Shaddock and waving to Kathryn as she ran into the refectory. 'And Giuseppe, his English is pretty good,' Petra explained, but she didn't continue to say that Dawn had been teaching him English. She felt it wouldn't be right to gossip. Kathryn overheard the comment and bit her lip, taking off her coat and placing it on the back of the refectory door.

'Colonel Shaddock, did more chairs arrive from London?' she asked, praying that they had.

'Yes, ma'am, this morning. They are stored in the back office.'

'Well, we need to get them arranged in here for the party. Can the Italians do it, do you think?' Kathryn asked, feeling the tension of the day and the afternoon's work in front of them, making her feel hot and bothered. With her hands on her hips, she caught Petra's eye. Petra left the noticeboard and joined Kathryn and Colonel Shaddock in the conversation.

'Party, did you say? And for whom, may I ask?' Petra said, with a quizzical look on her brow.

'Oh, Petra, sorry, I haven't even had a moment to explain. The boys are on the way back and we only have less than half an hour to arrange everything in here,' Kathryn stated wearily, as she saw Dawson walking past the windows with some bags of bunting.

Petra let out a low whistle and then turned to Colonel Shaddock. 'If I knew what was going on I could at least help,' she stated, infuriated.

'Well, we have at least a hundred chairs to assemble neatly in here, by the looks of things,' he replied, rolling up his sleeves.

'Let's get to work then!' she said, following him to the back of the room.

Kathryn called Dawson into the refectory and took the bunting from him and noticed how tired he looked.

'You had better rest, Dawson, but when Mr Montgomery returns with Roberta, can you send him in, please. All hands on deck are needed!' She turned to Petra. 'We can do this, Petra. Dawn and Irene are joining us in a minute, hopefully,' Kathryn said, trusting that Dawn would have fully understood their conversation from earlier about pulling her weight.

'Phew! I'm exhausted, those Brownies have worn me out,' Petra said, momentarily shutting her eyes.

Kathryn took the chairs that had been brought out and placed them under the window. There was a box full of sandwiches that Ivy had brought with her earlier, so Kathryn set to displaying them neatly on plates, as Colonel Shaddock picked up a trestle table for her to arrange the food on.

'I'm going to have to round the men up for afternoon exercise, ma'am, but I will be back in a while,' Colonel Shaddock said as he pulled on his jacket and saluted Kathryn and Petra.

'I love it when he does that!' Petra exclaimed, making Kathryn laugh.

'You didn't tell me more about the evacuees, how many of them are there?' Kathryn asked, taking the chair that Petra had been sitting in and moving it under the window.

Petra, carrying another two chairs and placing them by the door, wiped her brow and began to tell Kathryn all about the evacuees and their plight. 'There are ten girls and of course their mothers and even some fathers, all who have been completely set adrift from Gibraltar and all that they know.

'Could they have not stayed on the Rock?' Kathryn asked her naively.

'No, the government needed to strengthen the Rock with more armed forces personnel, you know, people had to move out of their homes to house the army,' Petra continued to explain.

'I see, how sad for the local islanders,' Kathryn said sympathetically, knowing what it felt like to have her home taken over by strangers. She felt that way about the Italians overtaking her home like cuckoos.

'When is Roberta arriving?' Petra asked, regaining her strength to rearrange the chairs in line against the wall, ready for the officers' table to be put in place.

'I hope before the boys arrive,' Kathryn said joyfully, and then wistfully she thought of seeing Ernest again. Then suddenly, there was a rap on the door. Both ladies nearly jumped out of their skin. It was Ivy.

'Hello, Kathryn, it's all such good news, they are on the way but they have been delayed by an hour. I thought I would arrive early to help and let you know. I did a quick detour through the village and picked up some cakes from Jerobaums. I ran out of time to bake some myself, what with my move from Bishops Cross,' Ivy said, getting down from her bicycle.

'I cannot contain my excitement and I think I need a break,' Kathryn said, impressed with how fit Ivy was, cycling here and there, and as she caught sight of Dawn smoking a cigarette and busily talking to Giuseppe on the lawn by Bertram's bench, she decided to have a few minutes' reprieve herself before all the festivities began.

'Am I all right to leave the bicycle propped up here?' Ivy asked, suddenly aware of all these eyes on her. The Italian men were starting to mill around for inspection on the lawn. So many men in uniform, too, huddling around in groups; it made her uneasy.

'No, let's take it over to the stables, and I need a walk,' Kathryn stated, gesturing to Petra she would be back in a quarter of an hour. As they walked, Kathryn pulled her coat tightly around her. The wind had picked up; perhaps the storm was at last on its way, she mused.

'Kathryn, I dare say you have your work cut out here. Do you feel safe?' Ivy asked her, looking anxiously at the men loitering outside the Nissen huts and some older men eyeing Kathryn.

'Oh, it's fine, Ivy, really it is. Nothing terrible has happened here with them except a few fights amongst themselves. They are actually quite a nice bunch.'

'Who was the lady with you in the refectory?' Ivy asked, sure she recognised her.

'That's Petra. She's staying with us for a few months and she has managed to get a volunteer position in the village as Arkala's assistant. She is helping with the new evacuees from Gibraltar, as a matter of fact.'

'I recall meeting her before but I don't know when,' Ivy replied, always remembering a face.

'That's probably because she used to live in the village, many years ago. She is a psychoanalyst in London, but she has come here for a change of scenery and to help me here. She is a dear friend, and you know, since the beginning of the war there haven't been too many clients for her. Funny how things change from the beginning of the war. After will be another story.'

'Yes, indeed, and when will that be? I want life to go back to normal,' Ivy said sadly, feeling afraid for her son. 'But you know, I thought I recognised her.'

As they walked back to the house, Kathryn called out to Dawn, who sulkily said her goodbyes to Giuseppe and went to help Petra in the refectory.

'It's a shame we don't have the horses to distract her,' Kathryn said under her breath to Ivy. Ivy tried to stifle a giggle. Just then, Mr Montgomery pulled up to the front of the house as they approached the front door. Kathryn beamed at Roberta who was waving frantically from the motor car window.

Giving Roberta a hug and taking her luggage, she, Roberta and Ivy walked back into Dallington Place and Ivy went to make a pot of tea for everybody. Mr Montgomery carried Roberta's bag to the top of the stairs and Kathryn caught him on the way down.

'Mr Montgomery, could you do me one last favour, if you are not too weary? Could you please take the last box of cakes and bunting to the refectory, then I think we are done. That's if Dawn has done the decorations,' Kathryn said with a sly grin on her face.

'Right you are, Kathryn, then I'm having that cup of tea, after I give Giuseppe a driving lesson,' he answered.

'There will be plenty of tea down at the refectory later and, Mr Montgomery, tomorrow you must have a day's leave, doctor's orders!' Kathryn stated firmly, aware that he must not overdo it.

'I certainly will do, ma'am. Agnes has arranged a seaside trip to Bexhill-on-Sea and now I won't be letting her down. I gave her the fright with my fall.'

Kathryn smiled, searching her pockets for the spare motor car key as she gestured to Roberta to sit down in the sitting room to have the tea. Looking at the grandfather clock, she saw it was nearing four o'clock.

As she sat down next to Roberta on the red settee, she noticed how pale she was. Kathryn grabbed her hand and patted it.

***

The men were silent in the back of the lorry; weary, but looking forward to being back in the folds of Dallington Place. They sat together but were lost in their own thoughts, each not saying a word, until Ernest was brave enough to point out that perhaps now was not the best time to ask Dawn for a divorce. Sebastien put his hands up to Ernest as if to say "let's not speak".

Ernest shrugged. 'Look, it's not my business, sorry.'

Sebastien pulled a cigarette out of his pocket and offered one to Ernest, who refused and looked out at the countryside through the rear window. He was so looking forward to seeing Roberta and his mother. He had visions of what a Prisoner of War Camp would resemble. Also, he wondered would Dawn be there or in London. He hoped she was there to welcome Sebastien.

The men were suddenly jolted back to reality by a pothole in the road. Sebastien rested his head on the cold metal of the side of the lorry, making his jaw judder as they ventured over more unkempt Sussex potholes. Ernest recognised the road, as he looked up the line of a dozen or so familiar oak trees. They were back at their headquarters, only an hour's drive from home.

***

Roberta pulled her hand away nervously. Kathryn smiled back at her 'Don't fret, my darling, the boys will be here safe and sound,' she said, trying to comfort her. Kathryn could see she had lost weight, still looking as beautiful as ever, but she looked strained.

Dawson knocked at the door and brought in the tray of tea. Kathryn could hear Ivy and Irene discussing the evacuees from the hall and getting ready to leave with some more food to take down to the refectory. Kathryn gave Dawson a look, and he immediately went over to the decanter to pour a couple of glasses of brandy instead. He knew what that look of Kathryn's meant; he knew her too well. Through many years of ups and downs, he knew that look.

'Roberta there's nothing of you! Are they working you too hard in the ambulance service?' she asked her, concerned.

'No, nothing like that. It's just I've been feeling unwell of late and I miss my modelling job so badly,' she explained coyly.

'Oh my goodness, Roberta, I'm being silly,' she said, realising as soon as Roberta turned the brandy down. 'You're pregnant! Please tell me you're pregnant?' she asked, wide eyed and so excited.

'I am, but please don't tell anyone yet. I want to keep it a surprise for Ernest.'

'What a homecoming, how wonderful, Roberta!' Kathryn said, reaching for her brandy.

'I'm nervous to tell him, I don't know why,' she said shyly.

'That's natural,' nodded Kathryn, thinking she should make the two bedrooms nearest to hers into a suite and Sebastien would have to jolly well lump it in the servants' quarters with some of the officers.

Kathryn could tell she was going to burst into tears of happiness, and then tried to distract herself. 'You know the horses are gone, don't you?' she told Roberta, and then promptly burst out laughing, realising what a silly thing it was to say. They both had tears running down their cheeks when a knock at the door interrupted them. It was Petra.

'They're here, girls!' she said, trying not to notice the tears.

Kathryn took a swig of brandy and feeling rather faint, having jumped up far too quickly, reached for her cardigan and slung it over the padded shoulders of her new suit. Checking herself in the mirror over the grand fireplace, smoothing down her curls and checking her lipstick, she reached for Roberta's hand.

'Let's go and have some fun, shall we?' Kathryn said.

'Of course we must, girls!' Petra said with a wink as they slammed the front door behind them and hurried down to the refectory.

Chapter Five
The Boys Return

Sebastien watched Roberta run into Ernest's arms. Kathryn had hung back purposefully but she wanted to do the same and hug her son. Sebastien eyed Dawn from behind the back of the lorry, his cheek twitching. He was in no mood to approach her. Instead he stood for a moment watching Kathryn. He could tell she was excited to see them, waiting patiently for Roberta to let go of Ernest and then she too, would run into his arms and hold him tightly.

'You look well, both of you,' Kathryn said tearfully, as she smiled demurely at Sebastian who was now avoiding her gaze and stepping on his cigarette. After some time, he eventually sauntered over to Kathryn, not wanting to engage with Dawn.

'We have missed Dallington Place but boy look at it, it's changed, Mother,' Ernest said, holding Roberta's hand as if he would never let go.

'You are telling me! It's not my home any more,' Kathryn stated, pointing to some Italian men, working on the lawn, mending parts of a vehicle. There were tyres strewn all over the place and uniforms that had been shed in the heat. Sirens were now going off and men were running past in rows, singing.

Dawn eventually walked over to Sebastien after he and Kathryn had hugged. She half smiled and explained to him that Lily was with her grandmother in Norfolk. He looked momentarily annoyed, a darkness clouding his face, as his eyes narrowed and he furrowed his brow. Then he looked to Kathryn, and trying to jolt himself out of his black mood, asking her if there were any food and drinks to be had, endeavouring to move away from Dawn's approach for something to eat.

'Did you think we hadn't prepared anything for you?' she said, surprised by his abruptness. 'When was there never food for you here at Dallington Place, Sebastien?' she joked, trying to lift his spirits.

'Sorry, I didn't mean to snap. I'm just exhausted, that's all,' he said, placing his hand on her shoulder to placate her. Kathryn slid her arm in his and pulled him towards the refectory.

'Come on, everybody, I think we need a drink! There's a party to get to,' Petra piped up, pulling Kathryn's other arm and marching the group into the building, desperate herself.

Ernest and Roberta followed, laughing and kissing and not once did they let go of each other. As Kathryn held the door open for Ernest, she noticed he was limping slightly.

'Ernest, my darling, are you limping? Did you injure your leg?' she asked, passing him a beer, and then pouring some lemonade into a glass for Roberta.

'My knee is sore and I don't know why. I must have fallen on it on exercise a couple of times, but it's just seized up in the lorry,' he explained nonchalantly, kissing Roberta on the cheek. She was now relaxed, sipping her lemonade and leaning into the crook of his arm and just beaming. She was happy for him to be safe and to be here, and she was just going to find a private moment to tell him about the baby, once he had relaxed.

Dawson approached the two boys and shook their hands.

'Four months has it been, ma'am?' he asked her, looking for reassurance.

'Yes, Sir,' said Sebastien, patting him on the shoulder. 'So where are all the rest of the Prisoners then?' asked Sebastien, as Ivy handed him a cool beverage and he looked around the room, impressed by how lovingly it had been prepared for the party.

'They are about but mostly in the Nissen huts at this time,' explained Kathryn, wondering if Mr Montgomery had returned from Giuseppe's driving lesson.

Dawn had brought in her gramophone and set it up with a slide show of some new American dances.

'Some Italian men are allowed in today too,' quipped Petra, noticing Giuseppe walk through the door and make a beeline for the gramophone. This did not go unnoticed by Sebastien.

Some of the ladies from the village hall who were working on the church flowers for Sunday service tomorrow, were also now milling about with welcome drinks in their hands.

'Mr and Mrs Lovat are on their way,' said Dawson, chipping in merrily and looking forward to a good conversation with William.

Suddenly a cheer went up and Ernest, now sipping on some beer and then standing on a chair, called for everyone to be quiet.

'I have an announcement to make, my wife and I are expecting a baby!'

Just as he said it, Dawson put up his hand to let Kathryn know there was some kind of emergency. He could barely speak and gestured for her to look outside.

Everyone rushed to the window and then they ran outside. The large air balloon that Kathryn had seen earlier in the week was floating above Dallington Place again but it seemed perilously low, now moving slowly, eerily skimming the trees by the Nissen huts, hovering tentatively. In the basket underneath, there were six or seven people waving frantically.

'Mamma was this for us?' asked Ernest, cuddling Roberta, thinking that this contraption was some surprise gift.

'Good grief, no, who are they?' Kathryn exclaimed, shielding her eyes from the evening sun that had just made an appearance. The balloon came to rest at the back of the Nissen huts. Officers and guards rushed to the scene.

'I'll go with them,' said Ernest, now running but wincing simultaneously. For some reason his leg had cramped and he was having difficulty keeping up with the other men. Hobbling down to the field, with Sebastien now catching up with him, they stopped and stared at the passengers of this beautiful craft. All were women, wearing blue uniforms, attempting to get out of the basket. Even a small dog bounded out. Six women in RAF uniform, one with a bad scrape on her knee, walked towards the men. The balloon had come down with quite a thump, and Officer Harding and some of the guards were busily trying to tie it down, as it gently rose in the strong wind.

The Italian prisoners of war were watching with much interest, some even cheering at the women. Sebastien asked if the lady with the gashed knee was all right, and she nodded surprisingly cheerfully, taking off her spectacles with one hand and holding on to a saxophone with the other.

Then, to everyone's amusement as the rest of the party followed down the lawn, the RAF women lined up and started to play their instruments, with the little dog barking and dancing around their ankles. A tall blonde lady then played a solo on her trumpet and stepped in front of the others who played in unison at the back. Their music was catchy and all the guest at the party crowded around. Geraldine had her medical bag with her, just in case, as she, Kathryn and Mr Montgomery stood, slightly stunned, but enjoying the music.

'Mr Montgomery, who are these women?' Kathryn asked, as shocked as these women probably were, who had found themselves at the incorrect venue.

'Surely, Kathryn, they hadn't meant to land here?' stated Geraldine, thinking how amusing it all was, to have a troupe like this drop in for tea.

'It's swing music, ma'am,' Dawson said knowledgeably, with a huge grin, as he managed to pick up the barking terrier and placate it.

'Swing what?' said Kathryn bemused, and loving every minute of it.'

They all continued watching until the music began to die down. As Colonel Shaddock raised his hand for quiet, Kathryn whispered to Mr Montgomery, 'Isn't it illegal to use a civilian air balloon at this time?'

Mr Montgomery nodded. 'I think so, Kathryn, but they are in RAF uniform, if that makes any difference. I'm as surprised as anybody here.'

An army lorry was now beside the basket, and some men were dragging the deflated balloon along the ground.

'Please be careful,' shouted one of the women to the men, when she realised what was going on behind her.

Kathryn, aware things were getting out of hand, asked Mr Montgomery if he would keep the Italian men under control, and then decided to greet the players as they finished their session.

'Hello, I'm Kathryn McAlister, this is my home,' she said, realising how silly this must sound, as it was clearly an army base now. Kathryn extended her hand to the RAF ladies.

'I'm Meg,' said the trumpet player, shaking Kathryn's hand vigorously, 'and this is my sister Caroline.'

'I'm Sidney,' said the saxophonist, who had a strong American accent.

'We are the Royal Swing Players,' said the blonde, whose hair had become loose and was hanging in wild abandon down her back. She looked rather untypical of a woman in the RAF.

'I'm Maeve and this is my cousin Marianne,' the redhead said, waving her clarinet in front of her cousin's face.

'I'm Leaticia,' said the last women in the line, shyly taking Kathryn's hand, and then curtsied to her, and in Italian called the little dog over to her. 'This is Spike, he is our mascot.' The terrier was trying to jump up and lick everyone in all the excitement, his tail wagging non-stop.

Kathryn smiled at Leaticia warmly and asked her where they had come from today.

'We were going to Windsor to play for the King tonight but it doesn't look as if we will get there,' Leaticia said, as if she didn't have a care in the world.

'Well, you can leave your air balloon here with us and someone can drive you to the station if you need to be there tonight?' Kathryn said matter of factly, feeling rather privileged that these women had literally dropped in on her instead of the King of England.

'Would you like some refreshments?' Sebastien asked, gazing at Leaticia, hoping perhaps the women would like to come to their party instead.

'Meg, would you like to have something to drink and rest for a while?' Leaticia asked her, taking back Spike and kissing him on the head.

'Come on then, girls,' shouted Sidney, 'let's get this show on the road!' She smiled at Sebastien, who thought her very attractive. Dawn had now joined them as Giuseppe lurked in the shadows by the willow tree. He didn't like her around Sebastien and he chewed on the inside of his lip and spat out his cigarette in a jealous tantrum.

Sebastien put a friendly arm around Sidney as he was well aware by now of his wife's flirtation. He ignored Dawn and walked on ahead with the loud American, who chatted nineteen to the dozen about their band.

'Swing?' asked Sebastien.

'Yes. I'm from New York originally and I learnt it there. You will love it. We can play a great little number for you called *Sing Sing Sing*, everyone loves that one.'

'What are you doing here then, in a RAF band?' Sebastien asked, inquisitive to know more about this attractive American lady.

'Oh, my husband is in the Royal Band!' she explained.

'Husband?' said Sebastien. 'Lucky man.'

'Oh, I don't know about that,' flirted Sidney. 'I think I am quite the handful.'

Sidney winked at Sebastien and continued flirting with him until Dawn sauntered up. Sidney, picking up on the tension between the two, made her excuses to fetch a ginger beer. After some refreshments, the girls started up again, encouraging everyone to dance. Two girls in front of the makeshift bar stood in front of their band members, who lined up behind and started to play swing in unison. Once the two at the front played their trumpets, it made everybody in the room get up and dance.

Even Dawson danced slowly with Ivy, making her laugh and her cheeks pinken with the heat.

A few Italian men who were trusted, were allowed into the party and they mingled with the guests. One made a direct beeline for Leaticia. It was Giuseppe and it didn't go unnoticed by Dawn who pranced out of the party in protest.

Later that evening, when the guests had left, the family sat behind the house, to relax and have some privacy. A pretty twin seat and a few chairs had been carried through onto the back lawn by Mr Montgomery so they could admire the view and enjoy the evening sun setting over the Downs. It felt like old times at Dallington Place.

Dawson was happily pouring drinks, loving every moment as he felt as much a part of the family as anyone. It was a short interlude of happiness and peace and calm, right in the middle of the war, and he felt useful again, partaking in his butler duties.

William was in conversation with Sebastien as they strolled the lawn with their sherries in hand.

'So how long is your leave?' he asked him, eager to know their battalion's next move.

'A month or two, maybe less, William. To be honest, I don't want to return to France, but I have to. I could quite happily stay here and become a home guard,' Sebastien said, confiding in William.

'Well, we all have to do our bit,' William told him, but he understood how he felt. He knew, wisely, that serving your country as he had done during the First World War, makes a man out of you.

'Every man and Emperor have to do their bit!' he said, clinking sherry glasses with Sebastien.

Geraldine was walking up behind them when they said this and overheard them. 'And don't forget us women if you don't mind!' she said, hugging her husband's neck from behind, as she was feeling very happy after far too many sherries.

'Yes, my Empress, I would never forget that, and for what the women are doing now for the war effort!'

'You are a clever man, Mr Lovat,' she said, finishing the last of her sherry and going to find Kathryn, catching up with her, as she chatted with Dawson who immediately went to fetch the decanter to refill her glass again.

'I've had far too much sherry already, my dear. Why can't it be like this always?' Kathryn said wistfully.

'It reminds me of the days when we were nursing. Do you remember coming to Heilly Hospital and the fun we used to have in that tavern?' Geraldine reminisced.

'Yes, and through the gloom, we did have fun, didn't we? When we didn't think too much on…' Kathryn's words trailed away. She didn't want to mention Robert or Bertram. She wanted Geraldine to remember the happy day it was today. Geraldine was busy chatting to Dawson and she hadn't heard that last remark. Kathryn was grateful for that. Moving on, Kathryn stood next to Sebastien. She could see Dawn by the bluebells, smoking and keeping a discreet distance from Sebastien. Geraldine wandered over as Sebastien left to join Ernest and Roberta in the orangery.

'She's so unhappy without the horses, Geraldine, I don't know what to do with her,' Kathryn said, frowning.

'She will find something worthwhile to do, perhaps she will make it up with Sebastien, who knows?' Geraldine said skittishly.

'I don't think that will happen now, they dislike each other,' Kathryn said, taking a sharp intake of breath.

***

Later that night, Kathryn sat upright in bed writing a list of things to do for tomorrow. She was interrupted by a late telephone call from Pearl at Throgmorton Street wanting to talk to Petra. Petra was asleep. Kathryn didn't want to disturb her.

Pearl wanted Petra to come down to London suddenly to interview some potential guests. The government wanted some of the larger houses in central London to be used for guest houses for the Government Workers and Civil Servants. This made sense as many buildings had already been destroyed. Digs were scarce, and large family houses like Throgmorton Street were a rarity. Of course, they would pay a small rental which Pearl and Petra were thrilled about and would afford Petra to stay on at Dallington Place, but they wanted to make sure they had the right candidates for the two smaller rooms. Perhaps, suggested Pearl, they would like a bed and breakfast too. Kathryn liked this idea to increase the revenue.

'Can I have Petra call you in the morning? But you know, Pearl, I have a feeling she has a meeting with some VIPs from the evacuee department tomorrow at ten o'clock. But I will check in with her and call you back,' Kathryn explained.

Now thinking on it, she wondered whether she could stand in to interview the guests as she wanted an excuse to go to London and maybe do some shopping. She was tired and also Ernest, she remembered, had mentioned tonight he wanted to get his leg checked. She knew a consultant near the city that could do this, recommended by Dr Laraby. Perhaps she could make him an on-the-spot appointment. They could have a day together.

Her thoughts then wondered on to the 'Royal Swing Players' and she smiled to herself how much fun they had been. She hoped they had arrived in Royal Windsor on time for the dinner with the King.

Times were difficult for the Royal Family since the Duke and Duchess of Windsor had moved to the Bahamas. The reign of George VI had not been an easy transition but the people backed them. His wife Elizabeth, was a social women and Kathryn liked the idea that they asked "commoners" to the Palace to entertain them and their staff. What a boost it would be for their staff, she thought. If the royal party enjoyed the Royal Swing Players as much as they had at Dallington Place, the girl band would be a huge hit and a fantastic morale boost for the royal palace. Wondering if Dallington Place was mentioned at all at the palace tonight made Kathryn smile and she had the best sleep she had in months that night.

Chapter Six
Grounded

Pearl had called Kathryn again at eight o'clock the next morning, anxious to get an answer from Petra. Kathryn had overslept and only woke when Sebastien knocked on her bedroom door. Hearing his voice behind the door, Kathryn shot out of bed and grabbed her dressing gown.

'I will be out in a minute Sebastien, thank you!' she called, wondering if him sleeping on the same floor as her was a good idea. He seemed to be acting overfamiliar with her and took it on himself to be at her beck and call. This unnerved Kathryn and she wondered if he was up to something. She knew him well and when he was particularly kind it was because he wanted something, and usually a favour to do with Dallington Place.

Kathryn opened the door, relieved to see Sebastien heading down the stairs. As he reached the bottom stair, he looked up at her and smiled. She felt her face flush. She knew she must look a mess. She had slept deeply and she was sure her hair was wild and frizzy.

'It's Pearl on the telephone,' he shouted up, waving nonchalantly. She noticed he looked particularly smartly dressed, she thought. She wondered where he was going.

'If Petra isn't up don't worry, she must be tired. Perhaps I can interview them myself, I just know Petra is very particular,' Pearl explained to Kathryn.

'How about I come to London today?' Kathryn asked nervously. She really wanted to interview them herself and didn't want Pearl to refuse.

'That would be fabulous, could you listen in with me? I will be there too but to have your opinion would be very helpful!' Pearl said, relieved that Kathryn could help.

'Well, you are doing me a favour as I need to have a change of scene for a few days,' Kathryn said, excited to be going into London again. 'Who would I be interviewing?' Kathryn asked.

'There's a young couple, a Mr and Mrs Smithfield, and a member of Parliament for Stafford called Mr Opperly. The young couple work for the

Foreign Office. That's two bedrooms occupied, and I think that is enough. We want to keep the rest for your family. Either for you or Ernest and Roberta,' Pearl explained.

'I will double check with Petra but I think she has an important meeting with Jane Mortimer, the Arkala today. They are expecting some refugees from Sark today. I think she would be up and about by now if she were going into London. What time are the interviews?' Kathryn asked.

'Not until two o'clock,' explained Pearl, feeling the pressure to finish dusting the bedrooms.

Kathryn looked at the grandfather clock now chiming eight thirty a.m. precisely. She loved the sound of its familiar chimes which always reminded her of a day's duty about to commence. A well trusted fixture of Dallington Place, it stood and observed the centuries going by. It was never out of step thanks to a Mr Marshall, Dallington's horological expert, who took great care with it. Mr Marshall's family had been in the clock repair business for two hundred years, and Dallington's old grandfather clock never missed a beat, due to his visits twice a year.

'Right, I will catch the 10.08 from Lingfield then, so I should be with you by lunch time. In fact, Pearl, would you mind awfully to make a bed up for Ernest? I need him to come with me today.'

'Of course I will, my lovely,' Pearl replied in her West Country accent. 'I will put Ernest in the blue room and you in the yellow. I suggest the attic bedrooms should be used for the paying guests, don't you think? So, there are three bedrooms up there. Two we can use as a suite for the couple and the third smaller one for the MP, with the benefit of the balcony. He won't mind paying a little more for the view I should think,' Pearl said, knowing how stunning the views were from the top of the house and hoping Kathryn would think this a sensible plan.

'Yes, how lovely for the guest, a view of St Paul's as they breakfast on the terrace, it will be very popular,' Kathryn agreed, rather proud of the lovely Throgmorton Street house with its quaint shutters, large bay windows and an imposing black front door, right in the middle of the hustle and bustle of the city's financial district. It was a good choice Devlin had made all those years ago.

Kathryn then remembered when she had finished her conversation with Pearl, that Ivy was starting that very morning. Running back into her bathroom to fix her hair, she then threw on a pair of grey woollen trousers and a sweater and searched for her galoshes, which she found in the lower kitchen. Dawson had been tidying again, she thought, smiling to herself.

Kathryn knew where Dawn was this morning. Or so she thought. She walked down the path towards the old stables when she caught sight of Giuseppe sitting on Bertram's bench and went over to him.

'Giuseppe, have you seen Dawn please? It's urgent that I find her.'

'No, ma'am, but I think you will find her at the farm?' he replied, looking forlorn.

'The farm?' she asked 'Giuseppe, did I understand you correctly?'

'Yes, ma'am, she goes there every morning at seven.'

Kathryn gave Giuseppe a look of confusion but she didn't have time to get into it with him now.

'Guiseppe, can you drive me to the station in an hour, please? You can pick up the motor car keys from Dawson. It's about time others have responsibilities here now.'

If you see Dawn, please tell her to speak to me.'

'Yes, ma'am, I will bring the car to you at 9.45 a.m.' he said, trying his utmost to please her.

Kathryn left instructions for Dawn in a note to Dawson. Ivy put it on the hall table, on top of the visitors' book, where Kathryn had said to leave it. Dawson would be up at the main house any minute, probably tidying away everyone's footwear, and would see it immediately.

Kathryn felt cross as she sat with Ernest in the back of the Jaguar motor car. Pulling into the Lingfield station, she decided to put it to the back of her mind. Ivy Dalrymple was capable enough, she should cope without much instruction today, she hoped.

It was a dreary day in London. The skies had started to cloud over in Sussex but now it had started to rain. When they arrived at Throgmorton Street, they were late for lunch and as they climbed the many stairs to the front door, they found it slightly ajar and Pearl was in the hallway talking to a couple by the coat stand. The woman appeared much younger than the man. She was in a green uniform much like the one Kathryn had worn in the First Aid Yeomanry Service, with its knee length skirt and jacket. It took her back in time for a moment.

Kathryn and Ernest said their polite hellos, whilst placing their bags down by the hall table, and then followed Pearl into the sitting room. The gentleman was tall and bespectacled with a long fringe that he kept pushing out of his eyes with his right hand. With his left he kept pushing the spectacles further up his nose. Neither of them were sporting wedding rings, Kathryn noticed.

'And what do you do, Mr Smithfield?' Pearl asked, interested in what this tall man had to say. He immediately took off his spectacles and Kathryn noticed how green his eyes were. In fact, he reminded her of Bertram and it made her uncomfortable. There was something so familiar about him.

She looked to the woman who was now looking nervous.

'I work at the Ministry of Defence,' he said in a patronising tone. 'It is Brenda here that works at the Foreign Office.'

'I see, very good,' said Pearl, clearing her throat. Kathryn could see she didn't warm to this man either. Pearl was barely looking him in the eye and distracted herself by looking at her notes. 'I hope you don't mind me asking but how long have you been married?' she said, nervously looking up. I don't like to pry but we have to make sure we don't accommodate single people in the same bedrooms,' Pearl explained uncomfortably, now looking to Kathryn for reassurance.

'May I just interject and ask Mrs Smithfield a question?'

The woman nodded and looked to her husband.

'How long are you needing the rooms for?' Kathryn enquired, wanting to get to know Brenda a little more, and what she required.

Brenda stared at her husband, waiting for him to answer. It was almost as if she wasn't allowed to speak.

'My wife and I never discuss these matters,' Mr Noel Smithfield explained, rather dictatorially.

Mrs Smithfield excused herself to go the loo, and Pearl was at a loss to know what to say.

On paper, this couple looked the perfect house guests. Newly married, attractive, no children, good jobs and jobs to be proud of, but there was something she didn't like here. Something wasn't right.

Ernest then interrupted his mother as she was about to ask Mr Smithfield a question.

"What time did you say we needed to go to see the consultant in Harley Street?'

'Oh good grief,' Kathryn said, realising the time and picking up her handbag. She had completely forgotten their three o'clock appointment to see the consultant Dr Laraby had kindly referred them to the Harley Street practice. With the sandbagging around London to protect the streets and houses from the bombs, it would take them at least an hour to get across to Harley Street. She hadn't realised this was all going on so soon. Traffic was coming to a standstill in places.

As they said their polite goodbyes, Kathryn was sorry not to have met Mr Opperly. Shutting the front door, Kathryn was pleasantly surprised to see a taxi pull up in front of them and a distinguished gentleman was getting out. He tipped his hat at Kathryn, who asked him was he perhaps Mr Opperly.

'Indeed I am,' he said in a jovial manner.

Kathryn liked him immediately.

'May we have your taxi? I'm afraid we have to go but I hope to see you again,' she said, surprising this neatly dressed and sensible looking man.

'Did I miss my appointment?' he asked, looking confused at Ernest for an explanation.

'No, no, Pearl is at the house, she will speak to you about the necessaries.' Kathryn said, waving goodbye as she pulled the window down in the taxi.

***

'Marshfields!' Dawn shouted down the line.

'What? Speak up, I can't hear you, it's a bad line,' Kathryn said, straining to hear. The telephone in the foyer of the Café Monaco was old and there was a party of people gathering in front of the swing doors that meant it was nearly impossible for Kathryn to hear anything.

'Marshfield's, I said,' Dawn shouted getting irritable.

'Is that really necessary?' asked Kathryn, taken aback by Dawn's tone of voice.

'It was a really bad fight. Sebastien had a split lip and three other men were involved,' Dawn said, her voice wavering.'

'And Giuseppe?' Kathryn asked, concerned for the likable Italian.

'Yes, they have him too. They said he started the fight but I don't believe it.'

'Do you think Sebastien set him up?' Dawn asked, knowing that it was true.

Kathryn took a sharp intake of breath. She thought this was probably true too, as he had a glint in his eye this morning. She knew him so well. He had been up to something for sure.

'Court marshalled did you say?' Kathryn said, shouting now down the telephone.

There was a silence on the other end and then the phone went dead. Kathryn pressed the receiver a few times, but Dawn had definitely gone. Kathryn sat down on the kiosk's stool, and with her chin in her hands, thought for a moment about what to do. In fact there was nothing for her to do really, not until tomorrow anyway. She had been looking forward to a relaxing evening with Geraldine and Roberta. Now she had a headache coming on, but she wasn't going to let this spoil her time in London. It was time they all managed, and sorted out the problems at Dallington Place without her. With Ernest meeting them later as he had a meeting beforehand with a few of his old college friends, and planned to meet them at eight p.m. to dine, Kathryn headed straight for the restaurant without him.

The Gelding Club was busy and it was so strange to see people sitting at the bar, with a drink in one hand and a gasmask in the other, ready for any emergency. Some restaurants and hostelries had closed, but the Gelding Club made a stand by staying open.

Sipping her champagne in the Jockey Bar, she was handed the menu by the maître d'. Enjoying perusing the menu and having a choice of food was a great pleasure. At Dallington Place now, it was a basic and fairly inexpensive menu, to make it easier to feed the prisoners of war. Suddenly she heard laughter behind and Roberta slung her arms around Kathryn.

'I'll have one of those,' she remarked, giggling and then turning down a champagne when the maître d' immediately came rushing over to the attractive ladies.

'Is Ernest here?' Roberta asked her mother-in-law, looking around the crowded bar.

'No, he should be here at eight p.m,' Kathryn explained, giving her dear friend Geraldine a hug.

Geraldine drank her champagne as Roberta mockingly sipped her orange juice, as if it was the same.

'Widow Clicquot Champagne, just like me!' Kathryn giggled to her dear friend, now already on her second glass.

'Talking about that, is there no one for you to have a romance with at

Dallington Place?' Geraldine asked Kathryn, feeling for her and hoping she wasn't lonely. 'Roberta hates me talking about these things in front of her, but William and I are worried about you.'

'I'm fine, really I am, and I'm so happy to have my boy back and even Sebastien. And besides, when will I have time for romance? I haven't stopped working for months. This is my first break really, and I'm jolly well going to enjoy it. Anyway, we have a new army coming to save the day, but I will explain all about that later,' Kathryn stated and hiccupped.

Geraldine raised her eyebrows with an intrigued look, and then ordered another glass of champagne, just as Ernest walked through the Jockey Bar's door.

'This is fun, Mother, what made you decide to come here?' he said, looking admiringly at the plush velvet seats, corner booths and soft lighting due to the high ceiling with its glass roof.

'A friend of Nora's recommended it to me. Many politicians dine here and famous people too. I thought it would be rather exciting,' Kathryn explained, pleased with her choice of restaurant. She didn't want everyone thinking she was always a country mouse!

'So do you want the good news or the bad news?' he said, eager to tell his mother his afternoon escapades.

'What did the consultant say?' his mother asked, beginning to be concerned and searching his soft hazel eyes for his answer.

'I'm grounded, I'm afraid. They X-rayed me and apparently there's some ligament damage. It will get better but the consultant told me I needed three months to rest, so that's me out of returning to France for a while. I won't be wearing this uniform for a bit. Civvy Street for me!' he informed them glibly.

'Oh Ernest, that's not good, but at least we will have you here,' Geraldine said, putting a motherly arm around his shoulders.

'Darling boy, what will you do for work in the meantime?' his mother asked him, worried for his future.

'I'm going to work for the Privy council,' he announced, slugging back his champagne as he waited for further questions from the ladies.

Roberta raised her eyebrows and Ernest took her hand, to soothe her.

'I met an MP, a Mr George Wagstaff, this afternoon whilst waiting for a taxi. We had a drink in the Old Bear Inn an hour ago and he offered me the post. I explained how I was grounded for three moths so he offered me a part time position as a parliamentary aide,' Ernest said proudly.

'But would that mean we would live at Throgmorton Street, Ernest?' Roberta asked concerned, but excited at the same time. Her pretty blue eyes wide with interest, she looked to her mother who looked nervous about her pregnant daughter living in the middle of the Blitz.

'Well, as I said, it's only part-time and for the three months until I return to France with Sebastien. It would be up to you if you wanted to live at Throgmorton Street during the week. We could go home to Dallington Place on Thursday, or I could go into London by train every day,' he explained.

'I'm not sure London is the best option with the baby on the way, Ernest,' Geraldine interjected.

'I think we should take things day by day, don't you, Kathryn? It's not like it's forever,' Roberta said, actually thinking she would enjoy a few days in town during the week and being near Ernest while he worked. 'We could meet for lunch every day, dearest, wouldn't that be lovely?' she continued.

Ernest kissed Roberta. She was always his supporter, and although Geraldine was very concerned, they decided to put the matter to rest for the time being and enjoy their dinner.

After a wonderful meal, they left the restaurant and hailed a taxi back to Throgmorton Street. Mr Opperly had just moved in and his suitcases were still in the long hallway. The shiny black and white stone floor was littered with his belongings.

'I do apologise,' Mr Opperly kept repeating. 'I thought I would get myself organised before work tomorrow, but I seem to have forgotten how many belongings I actually own.'

Ernest offered to help and took the last remaining suitcase up to the attic bedroom.

After Geraldine and Roberta had gone upstairs to bed, Kathryn took off her coat and flopped on the settee in the morning room. After a few minutes, Pearl came in to sit with Kathryn and they shared a pot of hot chocolate together by the fire.

'Pearl, are the Smithfields moving in tomorrow?' Kathryn asked her, as she stoked the fire.

'Yes, they are moving in tomorrow afternoon but between you and I,' she said quietly, turning away from the hearth and away from the earshot of Mr Opperly, 'I honestly don't think they are married. I have asked them for a marriage certificate and I called Petra who said she would be down at the end of the next week and then she can go over paperwork with them. They didn't have a problem being able to produce the certificate for next week, so I said yes, they could move in. But you know, I don't think I have made the correct decision,' she said, feeling rather weary about it all.

'I see,' said Kathryn, going to fetch her damp rain coat to warm it, nearer the fire.

'The problem is that Mr Smithfield is a good and influential friend of Petra's, so we couldn't say no, really, but I don't think she has met Brenda and when she does, I think she will see through the situation, as I do.'

'You think she is not his wife?' Kathryn asked, her brow narrowing.

Pearl nodded and then shrugged dismissively. 'I am not sure, that's all, maybe, but something about them together, it just doesn't feel right. Then again we can only find out. Time will tell,' Pearl said, now deciding to turn in herself, and give in to the stresses of the day.

'Exactly, and you know, there are bigger things to worry about. A bomb dropped just five minutes from where we dined tonight, you know. No one is safe in London now. I can see why they are sandbagging everywhere now.'

'What time would you like your breakfast tomorrow?' Pearl asked, turning the ornate art deco lamps off.

'Early, please, Pearl, as I am catching the early morning train,' Kathryn replied, yawning repeatedly.

'Right, that's fine. I will be sorry to see you leave, you will return soon?' Pearl asked, shutting the morning room door behind them. 'Bomb blasts, you see, shutting doors is a must,' Pearl said, shaking her head. 'What's to become of us, I don't know.'

'I would love to stay another couple of days but there is a problem with the prisoners of war. I can't leave Petra to sort it out alone,' Kathryn said, looking forward to one more sleep in the comfortable bed at Throgmorton Street.

'Oh, she's great at sorting things out. Everything will be fine by the time you return,' Pearl reminded her.

'Yes, wise words and I hope this is true. She is very capable. And Ivy too! I mustn't underestimate the pair of them,' Kathryn said, wishing Pearl a very good night's sleep and rushing up the stairs to bed.

Chapter Seven
Sebastien Returns to France
August 1940

Sebastien was relieved to be going back to France. There were too many questions being asked as to why Giuseppe had been court martialled.

Dawson had had a private word with Kathryn stating that the man, although he had become too familiar with Dawn, was of good character and this was not a good enough reason to court martial him at Marshfields.

Colonel Shaddock had interviewed Sebastien, where Sebastien had said Giuseppe had become aggressive, leading to him hitting Sebastien. Whether or not this was true, Kathryn and Dawson had no idea, but it was clear Sebastien was extracting his revenge here. The men in charge were only doing their jobs and, of course, the prisoner would always be found guilty if a British soldier had reason to believe this to be true. Kathryn and Dawson knew Sebastien's character and worried that this rather charming Italian man would fall foul of the law, through his rival's jealousy. Sebastien could well ruin this man's life with his antics and manipulation of the situation.

Sebastien could feel the heat. He knew he was in the wrong and wanted to extricate himself from the situation. He felt Dawn was always bringing trouble to his door and he needed to get away.

Rising early, so as not to see Kathryn, he left a note for her in the drawing room. Penning it quickly, he placed it on her bureau. It read:

'As the lilies grow
I have to leave.
May this time be it a small reprieve.'

With love, Sebastien.
PS I have left you a package downstairs in the kitchen. I hope it protects you from harm.

***

Having arrived back at lunchtime yesterday, Kathryn had gone into her bedroom to find a young soldier up there, coming out of her en-suite bathroom. What he was doing in her bedroom, she didn't know, but his excuse was that he had become lost in the house and had used her bathroom.

Kathryn had checked her jewellery was still in its box on the vanity table. Nothing appeared to be amiss but he startled her. This was the first time she had felt alone and vulnerable in her own quarters.

Colonel Shaddock had spoken to him and found his explanation plausible but Kathryn had a feeling of unease and demanded a lock on her bedroom door.

A young man of not more than eighteen, Kathryn felt she wouldn't want him to be in serious trouble but she felt that perhaps he was an opportunist. There were enough men going to Marshfields so that she didn't want any more of this, especially on her conscience, as the thought of Robert Alton Weaves came to mind. She shivered at the thought. She wouldn't want a mother or sister to go through what Geraldine had in the First World War, with Robert's unjust execution.

Sebastien, feeling protective over Kathryn, had brought her a present. He hoped this would help and was grateful that he hadn't got himself in serious trouble too.

He always knew when it was the right time to leave a situation. He knew his timing was impeccable.

Making his way to the Lingfield station with a young officer on light farm duties, collecting produce in his lorry, Sebastien was dropped off. The station was unusually quiet and taking out a light and rummaging in his deep pockets for his cigarettes, he realised he had left them with Ernest. He kicked the ground in frustration. He was going to miss Ernest and especially Kathryn.

***

Picking up the note and reading it, Kathryn felt sad that Sebastien had not said goodbye. But her mood lightened when looking out of the bay window, she saw lilies. Tiny shoots, but they were there. She had to make sure. She could see Ivy cycling up the driveway and Kathryn opened the window and waved vigorously. Grabbing her coat, she rushed out to meet Ivy and look at the lily shoots. Crouching down, as Ivy approached, she counted the lilies. Exactly eight of them! Only eight but at least it was a beginning.

'Morning, Ivy!' Kathryn called, as Ivy cycled past to place her bicycle in the stables for safekeeping.

'Morning, Kathryn, how are you?' Ivy said, as she stopped for a quick chat before her duties of the day.

'I'm fine, thank you, but Sebastien left without a goodbye, which is sad. But look here, the lilies have gained ground and I think these may just take,' explained Kathryn, now thinking on what Sebastien had left for her. He was always the joker so she presumed perhaps it was a bunch of flowers. But no flowers could compare to these, she thought.

'How lovely,' Ivy answered. 'Dawn mentioned she had seen some near Maples Wood, you know near the farm? Oh, and before I forget, I bought you some newspapers,' she said, showing Kathryn the headlines. Ivy wiped her brow, as the rain had cleared the overcast day of yesterday and the sun was just peeping through the clouds. It was going to be a hot day.

'Thank you, Ivy, you know Dawn didn't mention the buds to me. Do you know why she goes to the farm so regularly?' Kathryn asked.

'She didn't tell you? She told me she's teaching some of the evacuees to horse ride.'

'Really? She never mentioned it to me,' Kathryn said, puzzled at Dawn's lack of communication with her. 'I didn't know they still had horses there,' she added, under her breath.

Ivy shrugged and said she would be back in a few minutes to bring Kathryn a cup of tea.

Kathryn walked over to Bertram's bench and sat down to wait for her. She was happy that Ivy had come in today. Ernest and Roberta were busy in London and what with Sebastien leaving without saying a proper goodbye, she was feeling a little deserted. Geraldine had left this morning, back to Bexhill-on-Sea, with Dawson driving her so he could visit his sister there. Even Mr Montgomery was on sick leave with a bad cold and Petra was still in London.

Dawn had gone to fetch Lily from Norfolk two days ago and she hadn't returned yet. Kathryn suspected it was to avoid having to say goodbye to Sebastien. Dawn had said she would be back yesterday in case he was leaving soon, so he could see Lily once more before he left. But of course

Dawn was playing her usual games and hadn't followed through with his request to see Lily. No wonder he left in a mood, Kathryn thought. She began to feel a little sorry for him and then she reminded herself the trouble he had caused for Giuseppe, and shook off all her feelings of empathy towards him.

Army uniforms ruled today, she thought, as she watched the men being paraded up and down on the front lawn or where the front lawn used to be. Now it was worn turf with no flower beds. She didn't expect the new orange lily buds to survive this.

Lorries were arriving with deliveries and an army truck arrived from Marshfields. She didn't even notice Giuseppe getting out of the back of the truck as she sipped her tea nonchalantly. Normally she would have asked what was going on but today she didn't want to get involved. She was fed up with all these prisoners around.

Her chin was resting on her open palm, her elbow resting on her thigh, lost in thought when Ivy came to join her with a cup of tea and Kathryn, pleased for the company, sat with her on the bench as they enjoyed the sunshine together.

'Do you fancy a piece of one of those jam sponges that Dawson bought yesterday?' Ivy asked, getting up to fetch some quickly.

'Unless Sebastien has eaten it all,' Kathryn said with a jovial wink.

She put down the newspaper and followed Ivy into the house. She had had enough of watching the men potentially ruin her new lilies and wanted to sit in the kitchen instead. The officers scuttled past her at the bottom of the staircase. She didn't even say good morning to them as they politely tipped their caps. She just nodded back so as not to appear too disrespectful.

As she started down the back staircase, Ivy was coming up them rather fast.

'Kathryn, there's a box by the sink and it appears to be moving. It gave me quite a fright. There's something in it, you better take a look!' Ivy said, her face flushed.

'What the devil is it?' Kathryn said, missing the last step after hearing scratching and sniffing noises coming from the box. She ripped open the box and there staring at her was a tiny puppy – a white, fluffy dog with big ears and a slightly pointy nose.

'Oh, my goodness, where did Sebastien get him from?' Kathryn said, amazed and shocked. 'But I love him already.'

Ivy began to laugh. 'Looks like a lump of porridge to me,' she observed as Kathryn lifted him out of the box.'

'That's it, let's call him Porridge. He is divine,' Kathryn giggled, kissing him on top of his little head. He licked her face in response.

'Sebastien said he left something to protect me, this must be it. I have never owned a dog before, but I have always wanted one. I loved the large dogs that Lord and Lady Fitch had but he is so cute,'

'Do you think he came from the farm, Kathryn?' asked Ivy, now sitting down to make a list of the food supplies needing to be ordered for the prisoners.

'It's possible, maybe we should ask Dawn. She would know if she's at the farm every day. I will telephone her. I need to confirm if she is returning tomorrow with Lily anyway, and we need to make up the beds,' Kathryn decided.

'We need to find Porridge a bed, and he must be thirsty. Goodness knows how long he has been in that box,' Ivy said, placing her pen down and looking for a bowl to use for his water dish.

Kathryn clung onto the puppy, she didn't want to let it go.

'Maybe I should take it for a walk, or perhaps I should take him to the vet, Ivy? I know there is a Mr Sommers who visits the farm regularly. I will call Mrs Matthews and see what she says.'

'That's a good idea,' Ivy, said placing a dish of water down on the kitchen floor.

***

August 15th 1940. Memories of the Gateway to the bay of the Somme.

This time Sebastien had been transferred to the British Expeditionary force. Sleepy and taking his turn to rest his face against the window pane as the lorry juddered forth, he shut his eyes and memories came flooding back.

Memories of the gateway to the bay of the Somme.

Occupied now, those German tanks stand.
Our boys in boats by Dunkirk did land.
Innocence and full of verve,

None of this will ever swerve,
My thoughts that look back to Abbeville,
The gateway to the bay of the Somme.

The turn of the road,
That brings us the poppies,
Picked in good deed.
Where Ernest and I stood,
Uniform amongst uniform
And where as a boy, I sat with Bertram
On the brow of the hill
In Mesves-sur-loire.

The aeroplanes that soared above us.
How Bertram wanted to be up there.
And in my mind's eye,
As my arm rests on the distant window sill,
I spy only distant memories in my head.
Maybe one day I will be back
To the gateway of the bay of the Somme.

The burnt-out churches,
The bicycles that lie abandoned on the
Dusty highway,
Marigolds and sunflowers cut down
And lie by the side of the hedge,
My mother turning and smiling,
Beguiling,
As she in the still moments, amongst
The picked lavender, hangs out the washing,
Clean and untainted.
The sun behind her glints
In that frozen memory,
In contrast to the people
Running for their lives.
Husbands and wives and their cries.
My thoughts roam back to Abbeville.
The gateway to the bay of the Somme.

Sebastien was travelling to Paris and from there he would make his way to South Western France and meet with a Pastor, who was doing some great work for the Resistance.

Sebastien knew Paris well, since travelling there many times in the past with Bertram. He was slightly apprehensive as he had been given a few names to contact in the Bastille arrondissement. This Bastille area was particularly fraught at the moment, with the Germans having cancelled Bastille day celebrations on the 14th July. The Parisians were very angry.

The lady that he was to meet was a friend of Jean Moulin the founder of the Resistance and he knew he had to impress her. He would be honoured to meet her.

Her name was Elizabeth Chapiro and she had helped rescue dozens of Jewish children from occupied Paris to the hidden areas in the countryside. But first he was to meet two contacts who would test his mettle, to see if he would be given permission to allow this meeting with Elizabeth to take place. This was what Sebastien was worried about. What if they were some kind of heavies? Some people talked about being tested before being allowed into the inner sanctum of the Resistance. This underground movement. How would they test him? he wondered.

***

'Will Ernest and Roberta be returning tonight?' asked Dawson, rather missing the cheery, young man about the house.

It was Friday, the last Friday in August. It had been hot, all week, and the Prisoners of War had become restless and noisy. Kathryn shut the sitting room window, to block out the loud singing and shouting coming from the Nissen huts.

'Well, I think Dawson, the plan was for he and Roberta to come back tonight but he hasn't telephoned. He does like his Saturdays and Sundays here.'

'Should I tell Ivy that perhaps it's just you and Dawn then?' he replied, looking a little agitated.

'Let me see. I don't like it when he doesn't let me know, I worry about them with the bombings now in London,' Kathryn said, now sighing and kissing little Porridge on the top of his head.

'Have you seen Dawn?' Kathryn asked, thinking perhaps she would take Porridge for a walk down to the farm, if the weather didn't turn. 'Let's wait an hour, Dawson, then I will telephone him instead. He should call by five o'clock, I'm sure of it.

Putting Porridge's lead on, she got ready to leave for the farm. She had been down to the farmhouse last week and nobody was home. Even Milly, the farmer's wife, was out. A farm hand working with the cows in the next field explained that there had been an emergency and they hadn't been back all afternoon. Kathryn had returned none the wiser about where Porridge had come from; this time she was determined to speak to someone.

Paperwork had kept her busy all week and now today was the only day she had had all to herself without worrying over finances, balancing the books and the government schemes for the prisoners of war. Kathryn looked up at the grandfather clock as she entered the hall with Porridge to check the correct time. Geraldine was arriving in an hour for a Saturday lunch meeting and she was going to stay until tomorrow afternoon so Kathryn was happy with that, except she was impatient to hear if Ernest and Roberta were returning tonight. It wasn't like them to keep her hanging like this.

Just as she was putting on her light coat, the telephone rang from the study. She ran for it, letting Porridge go, with his lead dragging behind his little body. Determined not to miss the call from Ernest, she reached quickly over the large dark desk and grabbed the receiver.

'Hello! Is that you, Ernest?' she answered, anxious to hear his voice.

But there was silence. Now her heart was beating fast.

'Come on Ernest, ring back!' she demanded and almost as she said this to herself, Porridge entered the room and sat, cocking his head to one side when the telephone rang again.

'Ernest?' she said loudly.

'Mamma, you sound upset, are you all right?' he asked, hearing Kathryn's breathless tone.

'Did you just telephone a minute ago? The line went down, was it you?' she asked, relieved she was talking to her son.

'No, it wasn't us, we were ringing to say we are getting the five o'clock train. Roberta has some light ambulance duties to attend to, then we will board the five o'clock train and be with you by dinner time,' he explained.

Calling out to Porridge who was heading for the hall again, she picked up his lead and walked towards the door. She needed to clear her head and she and Porridge set off for the farm. Kathryn didn't want to keep worrying about Sebastien too. She had a headache coming on, and so she walked briskly as Porridge happily sniffed the grass as they went across the fields behind Dallington Place.

Kathryn normally knew where Sebastien was stationed in France, which had been in the news headlines quite a bit lately and his regiment was regularly mentioned too. She knew Ivy's son was safe as she had received a letter last week, but there had been no news of Sebastien. Kathryn was beginning to be concerned for his safety. She missed his mischievous smile and thought about how he would poke his head around a door at any given moment and give her a fright.

'Are you talking about me?' he would say and everyone would roll their eyes.

'Not everything revolves around you!' Dawn would snap with annoyance.

She had reached the stile and let Porridge run on ahead. She couldn't get the mystery telephone call out of her head. Only last week the same thing had happened, with crackling down the line, and a distant, fussy voice could be heard. She didn't know if it was a male or female voice.

Porridge was gambolling around the bottom of the stile, so she scooped him up and carried him over it. She saw the farmhouse in the distance and could feel the rain in the air, and hurried her step. She hoped Mrs Matthews was in, as an uneasy feeling took hold of her. Perhaps a storm was coming, she thought, as she rapped on the large black door.

Mrs Matthews answered the door, and two children stood behind her.

'Good afternoon, Mrs Matthews, Milly, I was wondering if I could have a word?' Kathryn asked, smiling at the children whose faces had lit up at the sight of Porridge.

'Yes, of course, come in,' she said. 'Excuse us, we have all been washing our hair.'

The two children, rather thin, with little elfin features jumped and skipped behind Mrs Matthews.

'May we stroke him? He used to be ours,' said the young boy.

'He was yours?' asked Kathryn, her brow wrinkling with worry.

'Oh, don't mind the twins, there were three pups but the twins claimed all three as their own!' laughed Milly.

'Their mother is in the stables with Ralph right now. The mother of this little one came over from Sark with them. It was a surprise when she gave birth.' Milly explained, patting Porridge on the head.

'I said to the twins they could keep their mother, Kia, but I didn't know about the rest,' Milly said, chuckling again. All too beautiful to give away, really!' she explained. 'But Sebastien did persuade me to give this little fella away. I thought perhaps it would be a present for his wife. He said he wanted him to be a present and so of course I couldn't say no, not to Sebastien anyway.'

'Yes of course,' Kathryn said wryly, looking down at the sweet children.

Kathryn realised the twins were the new evacuees from Sark that Petra had been talking about.

'Well, I have called this one Porridge,' said Kathryn, smiling at the two children. 'Mrs Matthews, I hope Sebastien didn't intrude on your privacy buying this puppy from you?' she asked, knowing no one could refuse the charming Sebastien!

'No, not at all. He came here three weeks ago, looking for Dawn actually. He saw the pup and he wanted to buy it before he left for France. He mentioned he wanted to buy it as a present, so I said yes. I thought it was for Dawn. She has been helping me so much of late that I couldn't refuse.'

'I thought as much,' Kathryn said, thinking on why he had been looking for Dawn there. She knew he wasn't one to seek his wife out. Maybe he had come to ask her for a divorce, she realised.

'No love lost there, though, I dare say, they didn't stop bickering that day I saw them in the stables.' Milly continued.

'Well, I suppose that is their business,' Kathryn said wisely, not wanting to talk out of turn, or behind someone's back, when she wasn't aware of what they had argued about.

'Listen, I don't like to gossip but I presumed he had been having an affair,' Milly said in hushed tones, as the children were now at the other end of the room playing with Porridge. 'I thought perhaps the dog was an apology gift,' she whispered, conspiratorially.

'Oh, I don't think so, I would have known, he'd only been back a month before he left and he certainly was busy helping myself and Ernest with the duties at Dallington Place,' Kathryn explained, finding herself defending Sebastien and she didn't know why, as she knew him to be a tricky character.

'Well, all I know was that she shouted at him and I had to usher the children in from the front garden, Mrs McAlister. And I heard him say he was in love with someone else and he wanted a divorce,' Milly continued.

'I'm sorry about that but surely not, Milly,' I am sure there must have been a misunderstanding. I haven't seen him with anybody,' Kathryn said, not wanting to further the gossip.

'Well I'm just repeating what I heard. I felt rather sorry for Dawn and she has been giving the children riding lessons, very kindly of her. Milly said, now boiling some water on the stove.

'Yes, I'm pleased that she's been able to do that, she misses the horses so,' continued Kathryn now wanting to leave and not listen to Milly ramble on.

'I must be going, but it's been lovely to meet the twins. Maybe they would like to pop over and see Porridge sometime?' Kathryn asked.

The children overheard this and put up their hands in excitement.

'Can we, Milly, please let us?' they asked, their faces beaming.

Kathryn smiled at the youngsters and told Milly she expects them soon, if they wish.

Leaving the path to cut across the field, Kathryn clutched Porridge tightly as she walked fast due to the fact that Geraldine had probably arrived already.

Just as she walked through the front lawn, she could see Geraldine getting out of the motor car. Giuseppe was driving and he helped her with her overnight bag. Placing Porridge in the long grass, she ran behind him, excited to see her dear friend.

Hugging her friend, Kathryn chatted animatedly about the Sark evacuees and introduced her to Porridge, who was now sleeping in his basket.

At dinner, Dawn was in a bad mood. She knew that she had been forbidden by Sebastien to fraternise with the Italian prisoners and he had threatened her with divorce and scandal if she continued the flirtation. She was afraid she would lose custody of Lily if she did this, so she complied for the time being. It didn't stop her pouting though and she was short tempered with everyone. Roberta tried to cheer her up but she flounced off to bed once the pudding had been placed on the table. Kathryn was pleased Lily was back from Norfolk and she sat next to her, telling her all about Porridge and his adventures. She let Porridge go to sleep on her lap throughout supper which he seemed to love, especially as he was exhausted from his trip to the farm.

'Tell me about your work at the House of Lords, Ernest,' Geraldine asked, also eager to hear about Roberta's work with the light ambulance service.

'Well I'm helping out at the Privy Council. Starting off with some administration work with Herbert Stanley Morrison of the London County Council,' he explained, pouring his wife a glass of water.

'Roberta, do you think working for the ambulance service could be too much for you, now you are expecting?' Geraldine asked, concerned for her daughter during the air raids.

'Mother I will be fine, I can't sit at home and wait for Ernest all day,' she declared. After all, she had always been independent up until the war began with her modelling which she missed terribly.

Yawning, Ernest suggested an early night and Geraldine agreed as they had a meeting with Colonel Shaddock tomorrow about some new developments with the prisoners.

As the grandfather clock struck eleven, Kathryn carried a sleeping Lily upstairs to her bed. She thought it was so lovely having children here again, and she hoped the evacuees would visit soon. All the military men in the house had retired for the night, and Dallington Place was all hers for now. Ivy had left two hours previously and she sat sipping Horlicks she had heated up herself on the stove, and with her hands cupping her chin, she savoured the peace and hoped it would reign for a little while.

Kathryn had fallen into a deep sleep when suddenly the sky lit up and there was a noise like thunder and then an eerie whirling sound. She woke up with a start, jumped out of bed and rushed to look out of the window. There behind the Nissen huts was an enormous fire, flames licking the roofs of some of the huts, and the orange and black flames were now reaching up thirty feet in the air. Was a Nissen hut on fire? she thought. She could hear officers and men running down the front lawn to the fire. Should she call the Fire Brigade? she wondered.

Kathryn grabbed her dressing gown and ran down the stairs, making sure she held on to the banister, as she went into the study. She had no time to switch on the lamps. Grabbing the receiver frantically and looking to the window, she dialled the local police and fire service.

'They have already been called,' Sergeant McCloud said from the doorway. 'Seems you have got yourself a Hawker Hurricane on fire down there. Stay put, madam, there's not much else you can do,' he instructed.

Everyone else in the house came running down the stairs, all at once.

'Is everyone accounted for? Please no one go out,' Kathryn said, looking to Ernest and Roberta, Geraldine, Petra and Dawn. 'I hope Dawson will be safe!' she worried, watching her son run down the stairs to them.

'What is it, Mamma? asked Ernest, now rushing to the window to the right of the front door.

'It's a Hawker Hurricane aeroplane, it's gone down in the field next to the Nissen huts,' Kathryn told him, biting her lip and smoothing down her hair nervously.

Chapter Eight
Hawker Hurricane

'I hope the men are all right. My goodness the aeroplane could have landed on top of them!' Kathryn said, switching on the gas lamp on the side bureau. 'Where's Porridge? Has anyone seen Porridge, he was on my bed and ran down the stairs with me,' she exclaimed, hoping he hadn't dashed out.

'He has probably gone down to the kitchen for some warm milk, don't fret we will find him, Mother!' Ernest said, running down to the kitchen.

Just then there was loud knocking on the front door. Kathryn let Colonel Shaddock in, his face pouring with sweat and dirt.

'Ma'am,' he said, 'I'm afraid we have one casualty but one man is alive. There was a pilot and co-pilot. I'm going to round the Italians up into the refectory, I hope you will sit tight here! Now we don't want mutiny and anarchy, so please lock the doors and let's hope for order!'

'I'll check the kitchen door,' said Petra, running down the stairs. Kathryn followed, hoping Porridge was in his basket.

'Let's close all the windows!' said Geraldine, now rushing into the sitting room, as sirens could be heard from the fire engines rushing up the driveway.

'Poor men,' said Geraldine, her eyes watering with pity for them.

The home guard were rapping on the kitchen door and Petra looked through the small window above the sink to check who it was. Two men of the home guard stood there patiently. The older man carrying a small, white poodle.

Petra unlatched the door in a hurry.

'This yours, ma'am?' he said to Petra.

'Oh thank goodness,' Kathryn said, taking the small, white, mischievous bundle from Petra, and thanking the man, who had rather a wide moustache and grey whiskers, and tucking the wriggling rascal, firmly under her arm.

'Would you like to come in?' Kathryn asked them. She thought they looked exhausted.

'Thank you ma'am, you don't have any brandy, do you? This young fellow here found the dead pilot in the field. I think he is in shock,'

The young home guard couldn't have been much older than twenty years old.

'Yes, do come in, both of you and then we will lock the door behind you,' Kathryn said reassuringly.

'There're a lot of men out there, ma'am. How many people do you have in the house with you, are they all accounted for?' the home guard continued.

'Yes, yes, we are all fine, thank you. Come in and sit down,' Kathryn answered.

'I'm Petra and this is the lady of the house as you probably know Kathryn McAlister,' Petra said proudly, stepping to let Kathryn stand in front of her.

Kathryn stepped forward towards the men and offered her hand for them to shake.

'To be honest ma'am I didn't, it's our first week on duty. All a bit new to us,' he explained, looking directly at Petra and then looking Kathryn squarely in the eye.

'I'm Ted and this is Tommy my grandson!' the older man said, introducing his grandson proudly, rubbing his cold hands together and taking Kathryn's hand to shake. 'We are not from Dallington Village but from Burwash. This isn't our usual patch. It's all hands on deck here tonight though.'

Dawn rushed down to the kitchen to look for Petra and Kathryn, when she stopped in the doorway suddenly seeing the men. Tommy gawped at Dawn like she was a screen goddess at the picture house. His mouth, fell open. She noticed and pulled her silk dressing gown around her, rather self-consciously. It was not like Dawn at all, who was normally so provocative. Sebastien's threatening words had frightened her and she didn't want to be accused of anything!'

Kathryn put Porridge down into his basket whilst Dawn picked up a pack of cigarettes that were on the sideboard and lit one. Tommy stared at her with great admiration.

'So who were the pilots?' asked Dawn rather calmly, then inhaling and searching for an ashtray.

'Well, we will not know for sure but we think they had taken off from

RAF Brize Norton airbase bound for France. The one chap that is alive though is curiously a Sikh.'

'A Sikh?' asked Dawn, now looking to Kathryn.

'He's refusing to go to hospital,' said Tommy

'And he was unconscious but they brought him round, thank goodness, but he was shouting that he mustn't go to hospital,' explained Ted.

'Maybe a religious thing,' said Petra chipping in now pouring some brandy into some glasses for the men.

'Could be,' said Ted. 'He has a turban, maybe he doesn't want it to be cut off. He has scratches and bruises on his face but otherwise unharmed, we think.'

'Would you like another drop?' Kathryn asked the shaken and tired men.

'I'm a retired nurse and Kathryn nursed with me in the First World War, do you perhaps we should check on him? Perhaps if he is all right he could sleep here?' Geraldine enquired.

'I don't know about that, I could ask for you, but do you want that, madam? I mean the bother of it!' said Ted, looking at Kathryn intently and getting out a notebook from his green jacket.

'It will be no trouble,' said Kathryn, understanding with Geraldine perhaps the pilot needed a woman to communicate his plight if it was a religious reason for his refusal to go to hospital. She remembered the Sikhs in the First World War and their refusal to enter a hospital then. She knew they were very proud and private.

'You stay here Grandad and I will ask to see if it's safe for the lady to accompany me into the ambulance,' Tommy replied.

'The men should be in the refectory by now,' said Kathryn, wondering if anybody else was hurt by the Nissen huts.

'I will go up and get dressed. I will be down in a tic!' Geraldine said, grabbing a piece of toast.

'I will come with you Geraldine,' said Dawn, stubbing out her cigarette.

'You will do no such thing,' Kathryn ordered her, knowing Dawn's reasons for wanting to go outside. She knew she was going to seek out Giuseppe and this was not safe in the middle of the night with the fire blazing.

'You can stay here and look after Roberta please. Ernest you can come with me,' as her son came in and joined the men with a brandy.

Kathryn looked sternly at Dawn, who went to the cupboard for a glass, her bottom lip pouting in defiance.

'It's a beautiful house you have here ma'am,' said Ted, enjoying his brandy.

'Well as you can see, it's not as it used to be, but I have always loved it,' Kathryn said, opening the back door for them.

'Been here long?' he asked her as she started up the stairs.

'Nearly all my life,' she answered back, with a little wry smile.

'Ah yes, always the lady,' he said, smiling back at her. If only he knew, she thought.

Petra locked the back door behind them and took Porridge upstairs.

'Be careful with him,' Geraldine ordered the officers, who were having to carry the stretcher into the house, and struggling with it. 'I would love to call Dr Laraby, but I don't think he should be involved until it's quieter outside.' They could still hear the prisoners of war milling about. There had been a fight amongst a large group of men. Someone had been playing a banjo which had been stolen a few weeks back. Now there was a fight going on about the ownership of it.

A window in the refectory had been broken. If it wasn't enough there was an aeroplane in the fields that was still on fire, smouldering, and ten extra emergency motor vehicles outside. Now we have a pilot in the house and nobody knows his name.

'Did he have a flight plan?' Kathryn asked Captain Witherall. 'His name would be in the book,' she added knowledgably.

Captain Witherall from a nearby barracks just shrugged. He had no idea.

'Only time will tell what's left of the Hawker Hurricane,' he started to explain. 'It will have to be left for a couple of days to smoulder before anyone can investigate. That's if there is anything much left of the cockpit. I don't know how the fellow survived ma'am. The tree cushioned his fall. Maybe he jumped out before it crashed,' he deduced.

'Ah the willow tree! I suppose,' Kathryn said, thinking how lucky the aeroplane came down where it did. It made her shudder to think if it had crashed into Dallington Place.

Dawn peered at the poor pilot who had now been placed at the foot of the staircase on the stretcher. He was asleep but Dawn looked at his exotic face and thought he was the most handsome man she had ever seen. His aquiline nose, full lips and high cheekbones. A black beard and black eyebrows and a cut above his right eye just marring his beauty. His large turban was now covered in dirt and soot.

Dawn felt sorry for him. He looked like a thoroughbred stallion who had lost a race from exhaustion. His eyes were shut but his thick, soft eyelashes covered them with a look of vulnerability.

The next day when some experts from the RAF recovery team had cordoned off the crash site, the men could go back to their huts. Most of them had not slept at all and there had been more fighting among them. They were all grounded until the next day and told to stay in their huts until further notice.

Kathryn and Geraldine visited the crash site with Mr Montgomery. The Rolls-Royce engine splayed out on the grass. Some men from the military were inspecting it and taking samples of the surrounding grass. An army-green propeller lay in a ditch a few yards away, the distinctive red, white and blue markings on its tail.

'How sad,' remarked Geraldine.

'Do we know who the pilot was that was killed?' Kathryn asked Mr Montgomery, looking over to the huts to check if the men were all enclosed. They could hear singing and shouting.

'I think it was a young man, local I think, but on a training mission. Apparently he was supposed to go over to France and fly straight back but had engine problems and was diverted to land in Kent. But obviously he lost power. The home guard said they saw the aeroplane approach steeply from the right and then too low over the fields,' he continued. 'They must have been bravely trying to avoid Dallington village.'

'We were so lucky it didn't hit the house, it's a lucky house our Dallington Place!' Kathryn said, feeling relieved for her family but then sorry for the pilots.

Just then, Colonel Shaddock walked up to them briskly.

'Ma'am, I was wondering if I could have a word,' he asked her.

'Yes, Colonel, of course, would you like to meet me at the house? We can talk over a pot of tea. I really need to sit down. This has been quite the shock,' Kathryn said, walking back with Geraldine up the steep bank and onto the front lawns of Dallington Place.

Pouring the tea, as Ivy added some biscuits and cake onto the tray, passing Colonel Shaddock a gingerbread slice, she asked him what he had to tell her.

'It's a couple of things, ma'am. Firstly, I want you to know, I had a telephone call yesterday, from the War Commission, and they want to house more men here. With your permission, ma'am, they asked if you would agree on a new building being built in the grounds here to house them. They fear the huts may not withstand the extremes of temperatures, especially when winter comes. Also more men can be housed here. Their rowdy behaviour is gradually getting worse in such enclosed quarters.'

'Really? Is it necessary? Can they not build elsewhere? They surely must have other large houses in the area, where they could extend?' Kathryn said, feeling anxious and looking to Geraldine who was trying not to interfere and sitting on the other side of the room by the fire.

'Perhaps, Colonel Shaddock, may we just digest this and Kathryn will meet you in a few hours, in the orangery, to discuss this further?' Geraldine interrupted, noticing her friend was close to tears.

'How about four o'clock in the orangery, Colonel Shaddock? But do finish your tea. I think I need to go and rest,' Kathryn said, wanting to get away from all this news of overwhelming responsibility and discussions. 'Geraldine, I don't know if I can take another year of this war! "Winter", he said, as if it was just another day, another season. How long do you think this war will go on for?'

Geraldine was pensive. She had no idea either and she was worried for her daughter and Ernest living in London. But she didn't mention her worries to Kathryn as she felt she had enough worries on her plate. She just held up her hands as if to say, I have no idea.

***

Kathryn poured the tea again, this time in the orangery, as Colonel Shaddock took off his cap, his perspiring face glinted in the afternoon sun. The orangery, although small, had a sense of grandeur but yet it was peaceful. Thank goodness Sebastien had encouraged her to go ahead with plans to build it after Dallington race course was complete. It was her refuge and a place where she had fallen asleep many evenings after a long stroll. Now, with Porridge at her feet and Geraldine by her side, she felt calmer to talk to Colonel Shaddock in a civilised manner.

'I suppose whatever I say is not going to make the slightest difference,' Kathryn said, defeated, looking to the Colonel for some useful suggestions.

'Well, it's not as daunting as it sounds, as it may be to your advantage to build at this time. You see here, I had some plans drawn up and I thought in keeping with the period of the house, you could have a pool house built with accommodation on the top and behind. The government are paying for this and after the war you will have your pool house all to yourself, without any cost to you. The accommodation behind can be less structural and can be torn down after the war, but you will still have a lovely pool house remaining with its guest house on top,' Colonel Shaddock explained, feeling rather smug about the designs.

'That sounds intriguing and I dare say appealing,' Geraldine said, peering at some of the designs, now spread out on the table, as Kathryn cupped her chin in her hands, in deep concentration.

'You are right, Colonel Shaddock, and from a business point of view, if we get the races up and running after the war, some of the overseas jockeys could stay there. They had to stay in the village or at the farm before,' Kathryn interjected, feeling more encouraged by this situation.

There was a knock on the glass door and Kathryn could see a couple of officers who had been waiting patiently for Colonel Shaddock, peer in through the glass to capture his attention.

'Excuse me a minute,' he said, standing up politely excusing himself to the ladies.

'He is ever so charming, don't you think Kathryn, is he married?' Geraldine whispered.

Kathryn laughed. 'Well, all the good ones are, aren't they?'

Colonel Shaddock quickly walked back to the ladies.

'I'm sorry about that, but I have some information on the Indian pilot. We have discover who he is. His name is Rani Singh-Hithop. Apparently he is from Brighton. His mother is British and his father is from Assam originally.'

'How interesting,' said Kathryn. 'Is he feeling better?'

'Yes, thanks to you ladies, and he wants to meet you both. After a couple of days rest he will be fit to go home to Brighton. After he is questioned about the crash, of course.'

'He won't be in any trouble, will he?' Geraldine asked, concerned.

'No, definitely not, he and the other pilot were superb at their jobs and it seems it was engine failure, not pilot error. Very sad for the other chap, of course,' Colonel Shaddock replied solemnly, sitting back in his chair and sipping his tea in contemplation. 'Just procedure that's all, I expect.'

'So Colonel, when will the building work commence?' asked Kathryn, now mirroring his relaxed posture.

'As soon as possible ma'am, this is the time to build before the Winter. We can at least proceed with the less complicated buildings at the back, which will only take three months. Then they can house another sixty men.'

'Sixty? Colonel Shaddock, that seems a lot,' she replied.

'Well, we have to do what the Government wants us to do. If we make it easy for them, they will negotiate with us.'

'I can see that,' said Kathryn nodding, knowing how lucky she was to keep hold of her house and not to be forced to move out.

'Ma'am before I go, there is another idea I have. Obviously, the Government are funding this project which in the long term will benefit you. But they feel, to make it justify the money that they are funding on this build, which comes out of the kitty as it were, they said they wanted a monument to the soldiers here in the grounds.

'Here?' Geraldine said, surprised.

'But we have one at the front of the house here in the fountain. Kathryn interjected.

'The horse and rider, Colonel, surely not another one?' Geraldine asked.

'The Fitch family built that after the Boar War.' Kathryn nodded in agreement with Geraldine.

'They are keen to have some sort of monument to the fallen soldiers from the last war and this. I think it will be fitting, especially as we have lost a pilot here too,' he said, trying to reason with them.

'You are so right, Colonel, we must do this. It is a very good idea,' Kathryn said, agreeing after thinking on this.

'And may I be so bold as to suggest a monument design,' Colonel Shaddock said, clearing his throat.

'Yes, of course, what did you have in mind?' Kathryn said, feeling overwhelmed. New buildings… monuments… There wouldn't be any grass left at all, she worried.

Colonel Shaddock sat forward as if to whisper conspiratorially to the ladies. 'Have you ever heard of the monument called the Chattri on the hill?' he asked.

'Oh yes, I have heard of it. It's in Patcham, is it not, near Brighton?' Geraldine ventured, joining in the conspiracy.

'Exactly and it's a very attractive monument, a pagoda in fact and a memorial to all the First World War Indian Sikh soldiers who fought for the British and died for us too. Seeing young Rani here gave me the idea. I think a stone Pagoda rather like that one to remember all our fallen men. The foreign that are here and the pilots too, the RAF,' the colonel explained.

'What an excellent idea!' said Geraldine, really liking this clever man.

'Now we have to keep these men busy, there have been too many fights lately. I have done my inquiries and lots of these men have qualifications to build. Some were ship builders in their native home of Naples, and some were stone masons too. It seems we have our task force already. Some have told me they would like to garden so we need to perhaps have another larger plot of land, perhaps at the back of the woodland? We are going to have to be more self-sufficient,' he explained, making notes in his pad that he just pulled out of his pocket and set it down on the marble table in front of them.

'That wood is precious though, Colonel Shaddock,' Kathryn stated, feeling rather cross.

'What with the bluebells and the wildflowers,' Geraldine agreed.

'They will be destroyed, Colonel, and our lilies will not be able to grow again,' Kathryn said, deflated, leaning back in her chair, with her hands firmly under her chin.

'Yes, they are not taking any more, Colonel, with all the men stamping over the seeds.' Geraldine waded in, doing her best to support Kathryn.

Kathryn's eyes watered with nostalgia. 'There were some small buds showing a few weeks back but they didn't take,' Kathryn said sadly, reaching for her handkerchief.

'Please, ma'am don't be sad. I'm sure they will grow again one day,' he reassured her, uncomfortably.

Kathryn nodded back politely at the kind soldier.

'Colonel Shaddock, as we are all going to be working together on this project, maybe we should be on first name basis. Mr Montgomery calls me Kathryn, so I don't see why you should not,' Kathryn said, warming to this nice man. She was grateful to this man who was only doing his job, and rather well, she thought.

'Well in that case ladies, you can call me Colin. We will be all in this together and by the looks of things for quite some time!'

Kathryn closed her eyes for a moment to envisage all these new ideas. Geraldine squeezed her hand to comfort her, thinking what a great, but exciting task ahead they had!

***

Rani Singh sat up in bed and smiled at all these women fussing over him. He was used to his mother and sisters fussing over him at home but this was something new. Dr Laraby had given him the all clear to go home and he was leaving Dallington Place tomorrow.

'Here is your breakfast, Rani Singh,' Dawn would say, and Kathryn thought it a miracle she would get up at seven in the morning for anybody unless it was four-legged. Dawn fussed and cooed over him and brought his breakfast on a tray. His tea and bread that he had asked for was neatly placed on the tray by Ivy. Ivy, as surprised as Kathryn at Dawn's insistence to wait on the man, asked if she would rather if it was she, that took up the tray.

'Oh no thank you,' Dawn answered politely, dressed sweetly and demurely in a light cream, cashmere sweater with delicate pearls around her neck.

'I think Dawn has a crush on Rani, what do you think?' Ivy said to Kathryn, discretely, on the morning that he was leaving.

Rani's family had sent a car for him and it surprised them all when a beautiful Rolls-Royce Silver Shadow pulled up and a very exotic older lady got out slowly and majestically, followed by Jorie.

Geraldine stared in disbelief. How did Jorie know Sangeeta, Rani's mother? she wondered. The exotic lady was wearing a sari in purple and gold and in her ears, huge hoop earrings and strings of brightly coloured necklaces around her neck. But she didn't resemble Rani at all. She was as fair haired as Jorie.

'Mother!' Rani said, as he waited on the steps of Dallington Place for her to approach him. She kissed him on both cheeks, and then stood back.

'Where is Mrs McAlister, please?' she asked Rani.

'I am she,' said Kathryn, walking forward. She now wished she had put on a smarter dress. Her sundress and simple hat felt very unsophisticated to meet this exotic lady.

'Thank you so much for what you have done for my son, I will never forget it,' she said sincerely.

'We did nothing, I can assure you. If you please, you are all very welcome to return here at any time. I'm sorry you find us in unusual circumstances,' said Kathryn, aware that Dallington Place was not the magnificent place it once was.

'We all have to make sacrifices,' Sangeeta agreed, nodding to Jorie.

'How are you, Jorie? How do you know Sangeeta?' Kathryn asked, smiling as Sangeeta and Rani were getting into the back of the Rolls-Royce.

'Our husbands know each other and when Sangeeta mentioned she was coming here to pick up Rani, I said I would visit you and find out about Sebastien.'

Kathryn waved to the Singhs and Dawn ran alongside the motor car waving goodbye to Rani and they drove off slowly and in a stately fashion.

'I know Sandra well. But tell me did I miss Sebastien again?' Jorie asked tentatively.

'I'm afraid you did, but do you not want to see your grandchild? She is with us full-time now. You are very welcome to stay,' said Kathryn, wanting to know more about this woman before she disappeared again.

'That would be kind, Kathryn,' she said, almost as if she had expected her to ask. 'I would like that very much.'

Chapter Nine
Land Girls and Lumber Jills
22nd October 1940

After a late night, listening to the radio to Churchill's speech to France, Kathryn had lain in this morning. She heard the grandfather clock strike ten and she rushed to get ready for her lunch meeting she had planned with Jorie in the village. Petra was going to join them later. Since Jorie had stayed over the night after Rani Singh had left, the two women found they had rather a lot in common. They had both made a pact for the time being not to discuss Bertram and found when his name was kept out of the conversation, they actually enjoyed each other's company.

They both had an interest in architecture and Jorie had recommended a designer for the building at the back of Dallington Place. Her husband Giles used to have a large construction company and there were always architects on hand before the war. Jorie had found a chap called Mr Longfellow, who she felt was the best.

Mr Longfellow designed many smart buildings in Brighton and was indeed busy designing air raid shelters for London. Kathryn was looking forward to meeting Jorie today with some ideas of her own. The government had come up with a basic design but neither of the women approved it. It wasn't in keeping with Dallington Place's grandeur. She felt as she was the one that would be living here after the war, she should have more of a say. At least she was going to try.

She ran up the main staircase passing Officer Harding on the way.

'Morning, ma'am, we have Government Officials doing an inspection tomorrow, and they are bringing the plans with them for the new buildings.'

'Yes, good morning, Officer. Yes, I do know, and I will be there,' she said, feeling a little anxious.

'I think we should meet in the orangery at four after their inspection, I'm bringing my own plans too,' she continued, clearing her throat.

Officer Harding looked rather surprised but pleased. 'Good, good, it's helpful we are all taking an interest,' he stated, before he tipped his cap and walked on to his duty in the refectory.

'Helpful.' Kathryn thought, straightening her blouse and putting on some red lipstick at the hall mirror and then searching for her blue jacket. She was going to be more than helpful. She was going to remind them that this was her house, even though all these cuckoos had landed. One day she was going to claim it back.

More determined than ever not to let those officials have their way, she marched down to the stables where her Jaguar motor car was. She knew she couldn't really afford the petrol today, for such a lavish car but she was going to make allowances. She didn't want Giuseppe driving her today. Right at this moment, she didn't want anything to do with the army. At least for the afternoon. She was relieved though for poor Giuseppe who had been let go, and brought back from Marshfield's only yesterday a free man, but she wanted time alone.

She also wanted to impress Jorie who would probably arrive in some very smart motor car. Jorie had suggested they meet at a hotel on the outskirts of the village. It was called Heatherley's, a small boutique hotel owned by a Scottish couple. It had only been open three months before the war had begun and so business wasn't as good as it should have been. Jorie liked to see herself as one supporting a good cause and bolster local businesses if she could.

'The food is excellent, their chef is fabulous, such a charming couple, I can't tell you,' Jorie exclaimed, in her attractive Texan accent.

The Heatherley's were a young couple who had lived in Edinburgh and both husband and wife had met at culinary school there. They had decided to come down south to live with Hugh Heatherley's parents who agreed to convert their home into a seven-bedroomed small hotel.

Kathryn was surprised that Jorie hadn't arrived yet. She was fifteen minutes late and Kathryn sat at a corner table feeling rather self-conscious as she perused the menu. An elderly gentleman was eyeing her from his table in the centre of the room and then the door opened and a couple walked in laughing and catching Kathryn's eye yet again. She hoped she wouldn't have to wait long. She needed to get back to Dallington Place to make sure everything was as it should be for the inspection tomorrow.

The waitress came over to her to take her order.

'I think I will meet my colleague first thank you,' Kathryn said now feeling a mild irritation with Jorie for being so unpunctual. Just then Petra walked in and Kathryn was so grateful to see her.

'Where's Jorie?' Petra asked, as she flounced in looking rather exhausted, as if she had run there.

'I have no idea,' Kathryn said flummoxed, until the young waitress came over to the table this time with a note.

'Kathryn McAlister?' the young girl said shyly.

'Yes?' Kathryn answered, taking the note from the girl who was uncertain who to give it to. It was just a couple of sentences that obviously the receptionist had scribbled down quickly:

Sorry. Will be delayed, I will be there at 2.30. Carry on without me, I'll be as quick as I can. Bad news but on my way,

From Jorie

'Well I'm going to order something. I can't sit here all day,' Kathryn said to the waitress, after thanking her.

Petra took the menu quickly after seeing Kathryn's usually unflappable face cloud over with irritation.

'The pea soup please followed by the chicken breast and a cup of tea for me,' Kathryn said to the waitress, who was having trouble finding a pen.

'I will have the salmon please. I presume it is fresh?' asked Petra, noting they had fishing rights for the lake to the back of the hotel.

'So Petra, I have some plans here for the new buildings and I was hoping Jorie had brought hers for us to see,' said Kathryn, now reaching in her bag to pull out her drawings.

The young waitress brought Kathryn's tea and she took a sip and winced.

'That's awful!' she said, offering for Petra to try. Petra knew not to argue about tea, with Kathryn. She knew her to be a tea connoisseur.

'No thank you. I'm going to have something stronger, a brandy perhaps.' Petra said, waving at the waitress to order her drink. She had been helping with the Brownies all morning and was tired out.

'You know Kathryn, I had an idea, especially after meeting Mr and Mrs Heatherley the other day. You know we discussed clearing the woodland where the Pagoda Memorial is going to be placed? Well, we need an army of women to do that. The men are not going to have the time to do it as some of their schedule is to be confined to barracks. We need a land army of women, you know, to rival the men's. Talking to Talia Heatherley, she mentioned that her sister was joining a new Army Corps called the Women's Timber Corps. It started in Scotland and is now being introduced to other parts of the country.'

'That's interesting,' Kathryn said, giving up on her tea and splashing some of the contents onto the saucer. 'Tell me more!'

'Well,' continued Petra, 'they are known as the Lumber Jills and only just recently formed, but why don't we have our own women's army here at Dallington Place?'

'I was thinking more along the lines of the land girls who already work at the farm. Just expanding on that,' Kathryn answered, but intrigued by this news of the wonderfully named Lumber Jills.

'But we need women that really know what they are doing without supervision. I must say these ladies are training to do a marvellous job!' said Petra, proud to be a woman.

Just at that moment Jorie entered the dining room, her face flushed, looking rather strained.

"I have some news,' she interrupted them, 'but I do want you to look at some plans first. I don't want us to stop on this. But I do need to talk to you Kathryn, in private, after,' Jorie said, leaning into Kathryn rather conspiratorially, putting Petra's nose out of joint.

'Everything all right, I hope?' said Kathryn, now feeling anxious.

'I think so, but let's talk about business first.

The waitress brought their meals and Jorie just ordered a glass of wine. Kathryn was concerned that something was seriously wrong but dismissed it for the moment. There was business to be done and plans had to be sorted out for tomorrow's meeting with the Government Officers.

'Look here, I need you to decide on the design of the Pagoda like the one at Chattri. Can you visit it tomorrow with me? Bring Dawn. I have already spoken to Sangeeta and Rani. Rani rides well. He and Dawn can ride up there together. It's absolutely beautiful. You do ride don't you Kathryn?' Jorie said, very enthused by her own idea.

'Badly but I can manage, but I have to be back by four o'clock for the meeting. Will we have enough time?' answered Kathryn.

'How about we start out early, a dawn ride, say six a.m.? It's beautiful across the Downs at that time in the morning. The mist is about to clear then and on a good day you can see right across to Brighton and back over to here. It's magnificent and enthralling.' Jorie stated knowledgably.

'I'm most jealous,' said Petra, who wouldn't go near a horse if you paid her.

'But the thought of riding on a hill on a horse would unnerve me!' Kathryn said, laughing. But I will give it a go.'

'So Rani rides?' Kathryn asked Jorie.

'Apparently very well. Rani said he and his father would ride every morning by the banks of the Brahmaputra in Assam, a most beautiful river to oversee the tea plantations and the tea workers. They would then continue to ride past the tea gardens and the Brahmaputra flood plains,' Jorie explained enthusiastically.

'Well, Dawn will be pleased. Yes, let's do it, I'm intrigued by this monument.'

'So can you meet me in Patcham, say about five thirty a.m.? There are some riding stables at the entrance to the ride up to Chattri. It's called Fairmount Drive,' explained Jorie, jotting down directions on a piece of paper for Kathryn.

'Yes, I will drive myself. Petra would you like to come?' asked Kathryn, excited by the thought of discovering something new, she wanted to share it. She felt buoyant that they were sorting out their plans for the monument.

'No, I can't. I have a meeting in the morning, and I also may have to go back to London. Pearl rang this morning and she's worried about the tenants. You know the Smithfields?' explained Petra. 'Sorry, I meant to mention it to you at breakfast, but I was in a rush this morning.'

'I hope everything is fine with them?' Kathryn asked, now concerned for Pearl.

'Yes, everything is under control but she wants my advice on some paperwork for the house, so I had better make a trip up to London. Something about Mrs Smithfield's passport too. We had better clear this up, best sooner than later, so there are no misunderstandings,' Petra said, getting her purse out of her bag.

'Yes, I see, that's fine then. At least no one has run off with the silver! I never know what is round the corner!' Kathryn said laughing with Jorie, her pretty blue eyes sparkling with happiness to be having some fun with her friend.

Jorie's face suddenly fell and Kathryn saw her sad expression.

'What is it, Jorie?' Kathryn said aghast looking at Jorie's pale face. 'I know there is something really troubling you.'

Petra excused herself to go to the ladies, saying she would meet them outside by the motor cars. She knew when to make herself scarce.

Kathryn, I'm sorry I should have told you sooner but…'

'What is it?' Jorie you are frightening me!' Kathryn said aghast, looking at Jorie's pale face.

'It's Sebastien, he…' she said, taking a sip of water.

'For goodness' sake Jorie, tell me is he… dead?' Kathryn asked, her throat closing tightly and her voice dull.

'No… well, yes, well, we don't know. It's strange but I had a telephone call. Giles answered it at first and they gave us a little information that some of the rifle fusiliers and some of the lorry drivers were killed near Cambrai.'

'But why didn't I receive a telephone call? Why was I not informed of this?' Kathryn said startled, her breathing quickening with shock and anger. She held on to her chair tightly, her palms sweating as she gripped the leather.

'I don't know, maybe he had me down as next of kin,' said Jorie, now feeling she had spoken out of turn.

'Is it definite or are they just speculating?' Kathryn wondered, trying to calm herself.

'Giles got some information after, by calling his friend James Smothers at the War Office. It's official that many lost their lives but of course it hasn't been confirmed who it is. Sebastien is… missing,' Jorie said, reaching for Kathryn's hand across the table.

'How am I going to tell Ernest? Oh my goodness. I really don't feel well.'

'It's the shock, maybe Petra can drive you home,' Jorie said now paying the bill quickly and helping Kathryn to her feet.

Kathryn had paled so much that Petra looked worried for her. She was smoking and leaning on the Jaguar door, looking at some of the plans that Jorie had brought with her. She put them down immediately when she saw Kathryn, quickly stubbing out her cigarette.

'Petra, can you drive Kathryn home please?' Jorie asked, giving Petra the rest of the plans and placing them on the back seat as she helped Kathryn into the motor car.

'Whatever is the matter, Kathryn?' Petra asked, taking the motor car keys from Jorie.

'It's Sebastien. He is missing, presumed dead!' exclaimed Kathryn, now bursting into tears.

Petra started the engine, and wound down the window to speak to Jorie. 'Jorie, we will call you about tomorrow,' she called, putting on her driving gloves.

'Yes, yes and if I have any more information about Sebastien, I will let you know,' she replied, feeling rather unsteady on her feet herself.

'I wasn't even informed,' said Kathryn, now sniffling into her handkerchief.'

'Kathryn, I don't want to speak out of turn but we don't know everything yet. Maybe, just maybe he is alive?' Petra said, thinking they shouldn't jump to conclusions.'

'But Giles, Jorie says is a practical man and presumes he probably is dead,' Kathryn said, resigning herself that Sebastien had probably gone.

'Well, I would want the facts, and between you and I Kathryn we both know Sebastien is a wily chap. Is it possible he may have been captured?'

Kathryn couldn't answer, her thoughts were racing. She felt she had been kicked in the stomach. Her thoughts were of Dawn and Lily, and whether she should tell Dawn yet? Would she care? she wondered. Getting out of the car slowly, holding on to Petra's arm, Kathryn realised Dawn would not actually care about Sebastien's fate. Resigned to the bad news, Kathryn went for a lie down, she had work to do. She had cleaning to organise for the inspection tomorrow.

'Thank goodness, Petra, we have my Ernest here,' Kathryn said squeezing Petra's arm in solidarity

'That's my girl, best foot forward, we need to keep strong and carry on,' Petra said in a motherly tone.

'Thank you, Petra, what would I do without you?' Kathryn said, now bucking up. But she couldn't help mulling over in her mind, what would she tell Dawn?

After a rest, Katheryn felt brighter and as the rain had stopped, she decided to look for Dawn down at the farm. Pulling on her galoshes in the porch, she was disappointed to see the rain start again. She stood under the porch contemplating what to do next. She was just about to go inside, when she caught sight of Mr Manslake cycling up towards the front of the house. Dismounting, he made a quick dive for cover under the porch as the rain came down in torrents. The type of rain that makes the river burst its banks.

'I have a letter for you, Mrs McAlister,' he said, dipping into his post bag.

Passing it on to her, her heart lifted. It was Sebastien's handwriting.

Smiling and wanting to give Mr Manslake a huge hug, she offered him a cup of tea and some shelter from the rain.

'I'm sure Ivy is making some scones this afternoon, would you like some?'

'Oh, thank you very much, shall I come in?'

'Yes, yes of course you must. Take your boots off and come down to the back kitchen,' Kathryn said almost skittishly.

Mr Manslake did as he was told and followed Kathryn down the back stairs but then he noticed Kathryn had been crying.

'Everything all right, ma'am?' Ivy asked her, concerned, as she gave Mr Manslake a pitiful look.

'Yes, I think so. Look it's a letter from Sebastien. I was worried about him you see.'

'Well there you are then, a nice letter from him!' Ivy said smiling and now buttering the scones. It reminded Kathryn of years ago when she and Mrs Potts were in the large kitchen during the First World War, when she was awaiting news of Bertram. Mr Manslake's eyes lit up when he saw the tasty scones that Ivy was buttering.

'There we go, Mr Manslake, that will keep hunger at bay!' she said, thinking he was the thinnest man she had ever seen. All that cycling perhaps, she thought.'

Kathryn opened the letter slowly, unable to eat anything but sip her tea. Mr Manslake didn't dare ask anything and chewed on his scones quietly, and checking on his pocket watch as if he wanted the ground to swallow him up.

It read:

30th August 1940

Dearest Kathryn,

I am sorry I didn't say goodbye to you or anybody. Unlike me I know but I didn't want any trouble. Dawn had infuriated me and I had to go back to France as quickly as I could. Once here, I regretted my actions, but I hope you like the pup and that he has settled in happily keeping everyone on their toes! Like me!

Please don't be angry with me if he ruins the furniture! I hope he keeps you safe.

I don't know why I wanted to leave you and Ernest so quickly.

Sometimes I'm hot headed and now I wish I was back in the fold of Dallington Place.

I don't feel safe. We are here at Vichy for a few days and then we are moving on.

It's decidedly hot and we are having to sleep in the lorries for now. We are here protecting the locals but we have not enough manpower and the Nazis are coming. There's a tremendous uprising here, and the Nazis are gathering the Jews and sending them to camps. But we are all in danger. I am lucky I am French and can speak the language.

We think now the best plan is to get some of the children away, especially any Jewish children and see if we can hide them in local farms. This is risky, especially for the farmers who will be executed on the spot if found out.

We are working alongside the Resistance, who are incredible. There is one lady called Anne-Marie who has walked all the way from Paris with three Jewish children. Their parents were picked up one day on the streets of Paris by the Nazis and have disappeared. My job is to protect her and the children but I am afraid I cannot do such a good job. I hope so.

I want to be back in England, I miss you and everybody so much. Think of me when you can.

Yours, Sebastien.

Kathryn went upstairs to lie down. She felt so lost again, and was surprised how numb she felt. She wanted to sleep but she decided to ring Jorie instead and tell her about the letter.

'Please let's go to the Chattri tomorrow Kathryn. The fresh air will prevent us from folding in on ourselves. The horses always give me strength, please Kathryn?' begged Jorie.

'I will try,' said Kathryn. 'May I make the decision later?'

'Yes of course but I just have to let the stables know in time, please call me later,' Jorie said, hopeful that she would come.

Kathryn agreed and thought it was wise to keep the appointment, but how was she going to tell Dawn about Sebastien. She just didn't know.

***

'They rode on horses to Chattri. Where many can come and whisper their name.'

It was five o'clock in the morning. The stillness reminded her of when she was a maid at Dallington Place, all those years ago. She smiled to herself. Then she felt guilty for smiling. Although Dallington Place was overrun with military, it was still hers. How lucky she was, she thought. Then she immediately felt guilty for smiling. She also felt guilty for not telling Dawn either about Sebastien. Yet.

Pulling on her jodhpurs, a warm sweater and a silk neck tie, she then went to find Dawn who was already downstairs making herself some breakfast.

'Do you want me to drive Kathryn or shall I?' she asked sleepily, but looking radiant as usual.

'You can if you like,' said Kathryn, wondering if Ivy wouldn't mind walking Lily to school. 'Perhaps, Ivy, you could get a lift with Colonel Shaddock?' Kathryn said as Ivy came down the stairs holding Lily's hand, knowing how much Lily loved the ride to school in the military lorries.

'She was looking for you, Dawn,' Ivy said, smiling at the two glamorous women who looked very smart in their riding attire.

'Mamma, may I go with you?' she asked now, becoming quite a good little horse women herself.

'Not today sweetheart. Kathryn and I need to meet some people today in Patcham and you have school. It's important business, but next time you can come with us, I promise,' said Dawn, taking her red lipstick from Lily and applying it in the small, round kitchen mirror.

Kathryn could see the little girl pout as she watched her beautiful mother in the mirror.

'Next time, my darling, we will ride together to Chattri,' Kathryn assured her.

Lily beamed a huge smile at Kathryn and repeated the name Chattri... Chattri, Chattri, Chattri,' she giggled.

'Yes,' repeated Dawn to her daughter, It's quite a steep ride.'

'I've heard the views are very beautiful from the monument,' said Ivy, thinking on what a lovely day they would have.

'I've made some bully beef sandwiches for you,' Ivy said fetching a container from the cupboard.

'I have heard the monument is very atmospheric,' said Kathryn looking very much to the day ahead. She hadn't ridden for such a long time; it would be lovely to see such views from up high.

'My husband told me all about it, a few years ago,' Ivy remarked. 'He was working on some farmland in Patcham. He had to make a delivery near to the site and a farmer showed him the monument.' she explained, passing Kathryn the wrapped sandwiches.

'When was it built?' asked Kathryn, placing the sandwiches into a bag.

'Around 1920 but it has fallen into disrepair. It's a shame. They bought the marble for it from Sicily. Funny now, that we are going to have our Italians build our monument here.' Ivy said, now looking out of the window.

'That's incredible!' said Kathryn, now excited to see it.

'It was designed by an Indian architect and proposed by Sir John Otter, who managed the build! I will never forget that name as my husband used to love painting the otters down at Pitham Farm lakes, nearby.'

'Do you remember the picnics we used to have there, Kathryn, before we became staff to the big houses? Your mother was such good company!' she said, looking misty eyed. 'Those were the days, with my John, and before we worked all hours!'

'I do remember and then how our lives changed when the First World War came,' Kathryn said, sighing. 'And now another war!'

'It's good you take time out to do something different, like the old times!' Ivy said, reassuringly.

'Do you mind accompanying Lily to school for me?' Dawn asked, kissing her daughter on her head as Ivy plaited her hair.

'Actually, I wouldn't mind a walk, would you Lily, instead of riding on the dusty lorry?' said Ivy, realising the sun was rising and casting a glow over the party and the beautiful Dallington Place. It was going to be a fine day.

Lily nodded her head and ran off to play with her dolls' house. The she peeked her head around the door, just like Sebastien does, and said, 'I like to walk,' and with that she ran off with Porridge to the playroom.

***

As they approached Standean Lane, Kathryn looked for a parking space near the stables, and then drew up by a water fountain. Dawn could see Rani chatting with Jorie. He looked magnificently handsome, with a red turban wrapped tightly around his head, and she noticed his facial injuries had healed. She thought him very beautiful and blushed as she chose her horse.

Jorie looked amazing in a green, tweed riding jacket which fitted tightly at the waist and her pretty hair in a net. Kathryn wished she had worn a net, she knew her hair would become frizzy. Why didn't she think of that! Jorie had already chosen their horses.

'I have a map!' shrieked Jorie, as she kissed Kathryn on the cheek. Bringing over her horse to Rani, Dawn smiled sweetly at him. He helped her saddle her bray and as their hands brushed underneath the horse's chest, she felt herself blush profusely.

'How are you Rani?' Kathryn asked him, pleased to see the young man looking so well and recovered from his flying ordeal.

'Much better thank you Mrs McAlister, thanks to you and your family!'

'Please call me Kathryn,' she said, smiling as she stroked her horse.

Dawn mounted her horse and led the way. Kathryn put the few sandwiches in a small, leather pouch which she had around her waist, she mounted and they set off.

'We should come to a stile here in a minute, which we can swing open and let the horses through,' Jorie shouted back to Kathryn, who was at the back. Dawn was behind Jorie, and Rani followed the ladies through the stile. It was a crystal clear day and as they climbed the small hill, at first Kathryn was a little nervous. Her horse was obviously the smallest and calmest but she was never really a confident rider. Rani turned around a few times to reassure her, knowing she was nervous.

Jorie had asked him to keep an eye on her. As they all slipped through the stile, they all stopped to take a look at the view. It was stunning, with views of all of surrounding Patcham and the valley overlooking the South Downs, over to Brighton and Hove.

They dismounted and passed the water bottle around as it was getting hotter and Rani was starting to perspire. Dawn passed the bottle back to Rani.

'Where did you learn to ride, Rani?' she asked, admiring this handsome man and his caring nature as he watched over Kathryn's horse.

'In Assam, when I was small living with my grandparents. They lived on a tea plantation in the west, near the city of Guwahati. That's why my father works for the British East India Company and he had met my mother in England,' he said, proudly. 'I moved with them to Sussex when I was nine years old. But I was already a good horseman by then!'

Dawn smiled, knowingly.

'And I know you were brought up in Texas, Jorie told me,' he said, smugly.

Dawn was rather chuffed he had found out about her and gave him a pearly white smile.

'Jorie says you are the best horse women she has ever seen but you are wilful!' he said, chuckling, his face lighting up.

'She did, did she!' Dawn said loudly. But she could not be annoyed for she found his sense of humour very attractive, the way he boyishly teased her and then looked away as if he knew he had teased her enough.

'Do you know Chattri means umbrella in Hindi, Punjabi and Urdu, Dawn?' he asked her.

'No, I don't know much about the monument really, it was just a surprise visit.'

Placing the water bottle back into his sleeveless cream jacket, he explained.

'The Chattri was dedicated to soldiers who had died in the First World War, and it was a cremation place for Hindu and Sikh Soldiers.

'It's sad in a way,' Dawn said, listening to his every word.

'Not really, I find it rather romantic, rather mystical,' he said.

'Like your name, Dawn!' he exclaimed and then jumped back on his horse.

Dawn blushed. She was not normally shy around men but with Rani she was.

They all followed Rani, this time with Dawn watching over Kathryn.

Following the bridle path for another twenty minutes, they slowly climbed the hill. They passed a farmer and his sheepdog and they all stopped for a minute.

'Look up there, there it is!' Rani exclaimed, as he took out his binoculars to check the monument.

Kathryn looked and seeing this majestic and rather, what came to her mind, a lonely looking memorial. On a summer's day like today, it gleamed over the South Downs but she could imagine it could look isolated on a gloomy day.

As they approached it, they jumped off their horses, tethered them to a tree and walked up the small hill to the Chattri.

Kathryn traced her hand over the marble inscription but some of the letters were missing and the marble was dirty.

'This needs repairing,' she said to Jorie.

Rani shrugged. 'I like it like this. As if the weathered and beaten monument expressed the suffering the Indian soldiers endured during the War,'

As Rani spoke, he painted a picture of what their lives would have been like.

They sat down by the Chattri. Rani read out the names of the fallen who had been local men and they all sat in reverence for a few minutes. Rani then took out a notebook and pencil and started to sketch the Chattri. He was looking forward to helping Kathryn design the monument at Dallington Place. He sat silently working out the scale, so he could put it down on the paper as accurately as he could.

Kathryn passed the sandwiches around and they munched on them quietly, while taking in the view.

'You draw well Rani,' said Jorie, getting up and looking over his shoulder.

Dawn wondered if he was hot in his turban but she thought he would be used to it.

'What are these bullet holes?' Kathryn asked surprised, as she traced her hand again along the marble.

'I don't know Kathryn,' Jorie said, 'we will have to ask when we get back.'

As they left the Chattri, Dawn turned to Rani. 'Does it make you proud to be a British Sikh?' she asked always proud to be a British American.

Rani just smiled and then changed the subject.

'Do you like Assam tea, Dawn?' he asked, as their horses nuzzled each other's neck, as they set off together in front of the others.

'Never tried it!' she said.

'Well, I will bring some for you, next time I see you' he said confidently.

Dawn followed his horse out through the stile not replying.

***

Kathryn didn't want to be late. The meeting was in a few hours but she wanted to be prepared. Seeing Colonel Shaddock on the driveway as they pulled up outside the refectory, she lowered her window and called to him.

'May I meet with you? I have the design for the Chattri!' she called out to him, hoping he would like Rani's design.

'Did you enjoy your ride, Kathryn?' he asked, opening her door for her.'

'It was a marvellous morning, as I'd never seen such beautiful views towards Brighton before. It was quite the trek but worth it. The Chattri is really atmospheric. Can we meet in fifteen minutes?' she asked, eager to get on with building designs before the government officials arrived.

'Yes, I will be on lunch duty until two, so let's get this sorted. I will be here,' he replied, looking forward to what she had to show him.

Kathryn ran upstairs to wash and change. She thought she would walk down to the lower woods with Colonel Shaddock and show him exactly where she thought the monument should be placed. She didn't have long, so kept her jodhpurs on, changed her blouse and brushed her unruly hair. Running down the stairs, she noticed he was in her study.

'Sorry, just looking for a pen,' he remarked, embarrassed to have been caught out without proper work materials.

'There are some in the pot on the right,' she said, turning off the side lamp on the desk. Dawn must have left it on, she thought, after she and Dawn had driven back from Patcham this morning, Kathryn had let her know about Sebastien. Dawn had become very withdrawn and once they were back to Dallington Place, she had insisted that she write him a letter. She wanted to write to the war office too.

She had telephoned Sir Nicholas who had kindly made inquiries for her. Kathryn was impressed that she had been determined to help find him. He was Lily's father after all. Maybe she did love him, Kathryn thought.

But just then as she had passed her on the way down to the kitchen, she took Kathryn aside and she could see the old Dawn returning.

'I don't love him any more Kathryn, but I know you and Ernest do.'

It had taken Kathryn aback. She seemed almost heartless, yet she wanted to protect her and Ernest from any more heartache. All Kathryn could do was to squeeze her arm in an affectionate manner. Whatever will become of Sebastien, it was clear he didn't have a wife to come home to.

Kathryn and Colonel Shaddock decided to walk down to the far woods to mark the exact spot where the memorial would be. The government officials were running late so they took their time and chatted.

'Do you have children, Colonel Shaddock?' she asked him, not expecting an answer particularly.

'Call me Colin,' he said, rather boldly. 'Yes, I have two and I'm married.'

Just then a rook flew out of its nest amongst the cedar trees and it made them laugh as it almost flew into them, probably protecting its own nest. They were all protecting their own nests right now.

Colonel Shaddock turned to Kathryn, caught hold of her arm, and then bent down to kiss her. Kathryn was caught by surprise and didn't kiss him back.

'Colonel Shaddock!' she exclaimed and then looked as if she had been stung not kissed.

'I will meet you in the orangery,' she said, extremely ruffled.

Kathryn didn't look behind her and almost ran to the orangery, where she could see some official men drinking tea and Ivy leaving with a tray.

'Thank you, Ivy. I didn't know they had arrived already!' she said, flustered

'You can manage with all these men Kathryn?' she asked, thinking these men rather stern.

'Ivy, can you ask Petra if she could listen in, please? I don't want to be… alone.'

'Yes dear, are you all right?' Ivy asked, concerned Kathryn appeared flustered.

'I'm fine, I just want Petra's advice on the building work. Can she bring Jorie's plans? I couldn't see them in the study. I hope I haven't mislaid them with the worry over Sebastien,' she said, biting the inside of her cheek with nervousness.

'Don't worry, I will send her right over,' she said, giving Kathryn a sympathetic look.

Petra came along just as Kathryn had sat down. Looking up, she was relieved to see Petra carrying her plans. Colonel Shaddock came in carrying Rani's designs that Kathryn had given him earlier. He didn't meet her eye. He wasn't sure what had come over him earlier.

A rather large man, George St. John, introduced himself to Colonel Shaddock and then introduced the younger, slimmer man, a Mr Longfellow.

'Mr Longfellow is an excellent architect and has carefully designed excellent drawings of the memorial,' he said rather smugly, as he introduced Mr Longfellow to the ladies.

Mr Longfellow opened his briefcase and laid out some sketches on the wrought iron table, next to the smaller table with the tea tray.

Kathryn and Petra peered at his designs simultaneously. It was smaller than Rani's design of the monument and much less majestic. Both Kathryn and Petra were less than impressed.

'We thought perhaps we would model the building on the Chattri design,' Kathryn ventured to say.

'Ah yes, the Chattri, yes, but madam, we were perhaps thinking of something a little more modern,' he said, twiddling his moustache and his beady eyes fixing on the sponge cake Ivy had brought with the tea.

'Would you like a slice, Mr Longfellow?' Kathryn asked, hoping this would make him more affable.

'Well, we are rather fixed on this design that Mr Singh designed. I do rather think it is super,' Petra said, now joining in to support Kathryn.

'Please let us show it to you,' Kathryn suggested, smiling her best smile she could muster, even with her stomach full of butterflies.

Mr St. John peered at Rani's design imperiously and to their surprise he didn't look displeased. Nodding as he surveyed it, as if to say he rather liked it.

'Well, we need to get down to showing you the Government Building where the Prisoners of War would sleep and a recreation room which Mr Longfellow designed too.'

Kathryn peered at the design and rather liked it.

'What do you think Petra?' she asked her friend, hoping she would agree with her.

'It's in keeping with Dallington Place, with the two large colonnades.' Petra replied, liking it too and checking her coat pockets for her lunettes so she could take a closer look.

'I do agree,' Kathryn said, relieved at least she liked this building.

'We thought perhaps we could call it *Churchill's Rest*,' Mr Longfellow piped in excitedly.

Kathryn wrinkled up her nose. She understood why he wanted to name it after the Prime Minister but she was thinking ahead. She didn't want to be particularly reminded about the war after it had ended and she had an idea for the building once the war was finally over, eventually.

'Well if we keep some of the woods behind, why don't we call it Tree Top House?' she said defiantly. She was beginning to feel pushed about and she was going to put her foot down.

'More sponge cake, Mr St. John?' Petra asked him quickly, with a twinkle in her eye.

Colonel Shaddock kept his opinions to himself. He didn't feel he wanted to upset Kathryn, and after the meeting came to a close, he walked quickly behind the women and the government officials.

Kathryn shook both men's hands and waved them off on the driveway, letting out a slow whistle when they had gone.

When Kathryn turned around, she saw Colonel Shaddock heading back into the house and she hung back.

'Colonel Shaddock seems rather withdrawn and he didn't say much during the meeting, unusual for him,' Petra muttered to Kathryn over her shoulder.

'That's probably because he made a pass at me in the woods!' she said, now beginning to feel the whole thing was farcical. Both women had smiles on their faces and started to giggle. She felt perhaps they were hysterical but she didn't care, she hadn't laughed in ages.

Chapter Ten
The Legend of Hades

'The legend of Hades was upon us.
Dark skies appeared, the enemy has landed!
For God's sake hold your ground.'

Kathryn woke feeling forlorn. Her light mood had disappeared.

Not only had she been worrying about Sebastien and what she could possibly do to trace him but she felt let down by Colonel Shaddock. He had told her he was married and she had felt comfortable enough to walk through the lower woods with him and then for him to make a pass at her, she felt betrayed. If she didn't feel safe with him who else could she trust? Then she sat upright in bed, her hand clutching her cheek. Perhaps she had led him on, giving him the wrong signals. With her grief for Sebastien, she must have appeared more vulnerable than usual, and he, being the kind and gentle soul, and perhaps with loneliness, he had made a pass at her without thinking. Who was she to judge? Feeling guilty, Kathryn had not done anything to relieve his discomfort. She must make things right with him she decided.

Rushing downstairs to have a quick breakfast, she found Ivy was making toast. A daily newspaper was placed on the side of the table and the headlines rung out.

"Bus in Trafalgar Square blown up."

Ivy had already read it but hoped perhaps Kathryn wouldn't read the paper today. It was too depressing for words.

'My, you look smart!' she said, thinking how pretty Kathryn looked in her jodhpurs, sweater and a neat little blue neck scarf.

'Are you going riding again, Kathryn?'

'Ivy, I look tired!' Kathryn exclaimed, 'but yes, I enjoyed it so much yesterday I thought I would go to the farm and see if I could have a riding lesson. Perhaps, Dawn will help me today as it was nice to see her look so happy again,' Kathryn stated.

'Well, the fresh air will do you good then!' she said wisely. Placing the washing basket on the kitchen table.

First though, she had to find Colonel Shaddock, she didn't want to appear too familiar. She thought she wouldn't call him by his Christian name.

He was out near the lower woods doing drills and physical training with the men. In fifteen minutes he would be on his way to breakfast duty. She would take the opportunity to wait by Bertram's bench and catch him on his way back.

Rushing and taking her toast with her, she sat as the morning mist cleared over the downs. She could hear the familiar morning call of the deer and stags which she loved.

Porridge had followed her out and his ears pinned back at the sound of the mating call. He sat at Kathryn's feet obediently for once. She could see Lily at the front door and then the little girl waved and dashed back inside. There was no school for Lily as it was a Wednesday so Kathryn wondered perhaps they could go riding together at the farm.

Knowing Dawn was probably having breakfast in her room with Lily, she thought she would pop back up after she had spoken to Colonel Shaddock. Dawn's bedroom looked over the forecourt and seeing a shadowy figure in the window, she waved up at her. Dawn had looked so happy yesterday, while they were riding to the Chattri, as if both their thoughts were of better times, in the good old days, not wondering if Sebastien was alive. Kathryn rested her chin with her hand. Lily was waving from the upper window in front of her. Opening her eyes, she saw Colonel Shaddock approaching across the lawn. She braced herself for the confrontation. Standing up, she nervously brushed the crumbs of her toast from her trousers and took a deep breath. Porridge started to yelp, so she smiled meekly at Colonel Shaddock as he came closer.

'Morning Kathryn,' he said, his cheeks blushing a bright puce.

Kathryn was just about to speak when she heard a buzzing noise from above. Looking up she could see an aircraft coming in low over Dallington Place, and then another.

'What the!' Colonel Shaddock exclaimed.

'Get down,' he commanded, grabbing Kathryn and pulling her behind the bench.

First, something hit the house and then the refectory. Kathryn could hear the ground shake beneath her. Screams and shattered glass followed.

'Bombers!' shouted the Colonel to the back of the lawn.

'Oh no!' Kathryn gasped.

'Lily!' she cried. Porridge was under her, struggling to get away and she put her weight on him to stop him wriggling.

'A morning raid,' said Colonel Shaddock, 'bloody Luftwaffe bombers!' His hands were holding Kathryn by her wrists tightly, his palms sweaty.

They heard two hits, and then nothing. The aeroplanes had gone as quickly as they had arrived.

"Don't move! he ordered Kathryn, 'they may come round again.'

After what seemed ages, they could hear people running towards them. She hoped not many were in the refectory. Then she thought of Dawson. He was always the first to take his breakfast!

Colonel Shaddock loosened his grip on Kathryn and as they got to their feet, realising the aeroplanes were not circling, they both ran to the house. Kathryn holding Porridge tightly as his little ears flew back, his eyes startled and his little body shaking

'Oh, my God, Dawn and Lily!' Kathryn said gasping, her heart pounding as she could see Officer Harding coming out of the refectory in shock and then slumping down on the grass. A large cut was visible above his right eye and his hand was covered in blood.

'I will see to him, Kathryn, you check the house!' Colonel Shaddock shouted, nearly knocking down a dazed and shocked soldier as he ran towards the refectory.

Kathryn stormed through the open door and with relief she could see both Dawn and Lily running down the main staircase towards her. She then caught a glimpse of Ivy who had gone extremely pale and was holding on to the doorframe.

'Thank goodness you're not hurt.' Kathryn exclaimed, hugging Lily to her and Porridge who was wriggling furiously.

Was there anybody else in the house?' she asked Ivy who was still shaking. Putting Porridge down as he was about to fall from her grip, he ran off in the direction of the sitting room and started to bark at the doorway.

Kathryn followed him in and to her amazement, there was a huge hole in the middle of the floor. Looking up she could see a gaping hole in the ceiling, something having just missed the chandelier, which was still swing precariously above her. Kathryn picked up Porridge.

'Out quickly,' she shouted, sweat beginning to shine on her forehead.

'I think it may be unexploded bomb,' she added, feeling sick and then making a grab for Ivy. She ushered them quickly out of the house and ran over to Bertram's bench. Kathryn looked around for someone to help them.

'You have to clear the area,' Kathryn shouted to an officer who was helping an injured soldier walk across the driveway. 'I think there's an unexploded bomb, it's fallen through the middle of the house!' she called as the officer immediately waved at Colonel Shaddock to come and help. Colonel Shaddock left the soldier sitting on the bench.

'Is there anybody else left in the refectory, Colonel Shaddock?' Kathryn asked, repeating the message about her fear of the bomb exploding.

'Dawson is there, go and see for yourself, he won't move,' he replied, his stricken face as shocked as hers.

'Is he hurt?' she asked, her fears beginning to show.

'No, Kathryn, he is eating toast and refuses to move!' he answered her forlornly.

Sighing with relief, she passed Porridge to Dawn and ran towards the refectory

There he was still at the table which was covered with splinters of glass but he sat silently munching on his toast. Kathryn hugged him.

'Come on, Dawson, we have to leave and clear the area, there's a bomb in the house,' she said calmly, helping him back to his feet.

He stared blankly at her for a minute, then a large smile spread across his face as if he finally recognised her.

'I thought you had been hurt,' she said, relief flooding her in waves. 'Come on, we have to move quickly and get out of here,' she instructed, hoping the room didn't fall down around their ears.

Clutching his toast, they made their way back to the ladies, Dawson making an almost comical figure with his breakfast still in his hands.

Dawn was now by the willow tree shielding her eyes from the bright morning sun, to see if she could catch sight of Guiseppe by the Nissen huts.

Earlier, the Italians had all been confined to barracks by Officer Shaddock and most hadn't been allowed to take their breakfast as yet, due to a fight that had broken out during the night. Normally they would have been in the refectory by now and there would have been more casualties if that had been the case.

'Ivy, you were so lucky not to have been in the lower kitchen when the bomb came through the roof, you could have been killed. The kitchen must be in pieces!' Kathryn exclaimed.

'I know, I'm trembling at the thought,' she said, her eyes wide open with shock.

'You know, Kathryn, I was, but just as I was about to make some fresh bread, the telephone rang from the study and I ran to answer it. You see, Sir Nicholas had rung earlier and said he would ring back to speak to you. So I rushed for it, you see. I didn't want to miss his call, lovely man he is. But it wasn't Sir Nicholas, there was no one on the line… just crackles, as if someone was there but couldn't speak. Then the line went dead and there was an explosion! Looks like whoever it was, was my guardian angel,' she said, wiping tears from her eyes with her large blue handkerchief.

'I had a call like that the other day,' Kathryn said, taking Ivy's hand and patting it. They sat silently for a minute, wondering who this guardian angel could be.

'Ma'am, best you get yourself out of here for now, down to the farm perhaps?' the officer interrupted.

'I'm not going anywhere, thank you. That's my home and I'm not leaving,' she staring back.

'Kathryn, we should go down to the farm but please be careful,' Ivy said, knowing full well, Kathryn wouldn't leave her beloved Dallington Place.

'Well, all right, ma'am, but please keep away from the house and the refectory and let the men do their job. I have called the bomb disposal unit.' The officer relented.

'I will wait here. I presume I am far enough away officer?' she asked, just to make sure.

'I would say so ma'am, just be cautious. And please, not the orangery because of the glass windows, they could shatter if the bomb goes off!'

Kathryn nodded and plonked herself down solemnly on the bench as the ladies walked towards the farm. Dawn was carrying Porridge, who was desperate to run around as Lily skipped alongside her. She could see Officer Shaddock now charging back through the tree-lined path towards her, sweat pouring from his brow. She wanted to avoid him but she knew she had to talk to him, and thank him for protecting her. He approached her in a business-like manner. They were both awkward with each other.

'Kathryn, the bomb disposal unit may not be able to get here yet. It could take days, so you will have to move out I'm afraid to say and not only that, the damage will need to be repaired! It will be dangerous for you to live in, at least for the foreseeable future." he said, not looking her in the eye and authoritatively took hold of her arm. Kathryn was about to protest when he fixed her gaze.

'This is imperative for your safety, and an order. You have young people in your care and we are also going to have to temporarily move the Prisoners of War who aren't working on the new building to move out. There's only room for a few here while the refectory is out of order!' he exclaimed, looking stressed.

'I, for one, will have to move in with them in the Nissen huts. The others can either go to Marshfield's or Tranbridge House in Dorking, at least for the foreseeable future. It's going to take months to rebuild and the government are not going to part with their money easily, it will be a slow business,'

Sighing, Kathryn reached for a tissue in her pocket. Her eyes were watering. She was determined not to cry.

In a gentler tone he asked, 'Do you have anywhere else to go?'

'Yes, London, Throgmorton Street,' she answered, as if she had resigned to her fate for the time being.

PART TWO
Throgmorton Street

Chapter 11
Moving to Throgmorton Street
November 1940

Hugging Dawn and kissing Lily, Kathryn watched the train pull away on its way to Norfolk, back in the safety of the arms of the Fitches at Endelwise Manor.

'Just a few months my darlings,' Kathryn said, holding back her sobs.

Petra was in the driving seat today and with all their worldly goods they could fit into the back of Kathryn's Jaguar, they set off for London.

'I hope they look after the house,' Kathryn said, knowing it would probably be a different house to come back to in a few months.

'Let's keep positive Kathryn, at least we are alive,' Petra said cheerily.

'Let's hope Sebastien is,' she said, going very quiet.

Petra said nothing. She feared the worst but didn't say anything to Kathryn.

Kathryn watched the hedgerows go by, with their leaves with snowy white tips where the frost had settled, which were now dispersing. She felt sleepy. She had been up early helping Dawson to pack to go to his sister's in Bexhill. The stoical man had not wanted to leave either and asked to go to Willow Tree Cottage. But Kathryn was worried if he stayed there, he may be vulnerable especially due to the bitter winter that was firmly on its way. So off he had left this morning, on the bus to Bexhill-on-Sea for the time being.

'I'm coming back ma'am, you know I am,' he said sweetly.

'Of course, Dawson. Dallington Place is always your home,' she said in a reassuring manner to the old man. She didn't want him to think he wasn't welcome. In fact she wasn't feeling very welcome in her own home either. But she didn't want to appear as nervous as him so she put on a brave and reassuring face.

'Do you remember the Winter of 1929, Petra?' Kathryn asked, remembering how snowed in they were that Christmas. She pulled her cardigan around her shoulders, reminiscing how cold it was.

'Well I was in London but I do remember, even the snow settled on the steps of Throgmorton Street,' Petra reminisced.

'Devlin was ill, and I remember being snowed in for days!' Kathryn continued. 'Mr Evan was a dear and did his best to get out to the village for us to collect Devlin's medicine's. But it was quite a trek and it took all morning. I don't think Dawson could cope alone in the cottage if we had another Winter like that.'

'If we do have snow like that this year, the Italians are going to feel it in the Nissen huts,' Petra stated. Kathryn nodded in agreement.

'Any emergencies will be taken up with war duties too and, yes, Dawson will be better off by the sea with his sister,' Kathryn had decided, knowing she had to be cruel to be kind.

Parking in the back street behind Throgmorton Street, the motor car came to a sudden jolt as if it had had enough of the cobbles.

'I think we did well without too many hold ups on the road, considering the weather!' said Petra.

Apart from a security check as they motored down the mall past Buckingham Palace, they had not had to stop once.

'Wait here Kathryn,' Petra said, yawning. 'I will get the keys from Pearl for the garage,'

Kathryn sat waiting, looking up at the rear of Throgmorton Street with its large bay windows with security locks and the little balcony on the top floor, which had a little table and chairs neatly placed so Mr Opperly could have a bird's eye view of St. Paul's Cathedral. How fortunate she mused, Devlin had the foresight to buy in London, even if the purchase had been for a complicated reason at the time. How she enjoyed Petra's friendship now too. He had always looked after her, even now. She smiled to herself as Petra ran towards her shaking the keys and almost tripping on the cobbles.

Once they had installed all their belongings, Pearl greeted them in the dining room where Mr and Mrs Smithfield were taking their lunch.

Kathryn didn't want to disturb them but Mr Smithfield stood up and introduced himself and his wife once again. His wife was subdued, nodded a hello and went back to her meal. Mr Smithfield then realised it was Kathryn, the lady of the house and made his apologies.

'Sorry, Mrs McAlister, I realise now you are one of the ladies of this fine establishment.'

Kathryn smiled back at him. 'I hope you are enjoying living here Mr Smithfield,' she said, giving him one of her most charming smiles.

'Very much, thank you, and the food is incredible!' he said, now sitting down to finish his meal.

Kathryn chose a corner table so she could talk to Petra privately. Sitting down opposite her, Petra whispered, 'Doesn't Mrs Smithfield look unhappy? I wonder what's going on there?'

Pearl came over to them and took their order for lunch.

'Pearl, what time do Ernest and Roberta usually return from work?'

'About five o'clock. I normally get them a light supper and then they go out again,' she said, with a wink. 'Those two have such a fun time together!'

'I can't wait to see Ernest and by the way how is our Mr Opperly? Is he enjoying his stay here?' Kathryn asked.

'Loving it, I should say,' confirmed Pearl. 'He just adores his suite of rooms with his balcony. He tells me two pigeons join him for coffee sitting on the iron railings in the morning, cooing at him. They fly off after about fifteen minutes in the direction of St. Paul's. He calls them Cardinal and Pope!' she says, laughing.

Seeing the Smithfields leave their table, she turned to Kathryn and whispered, 'As for those two, I just don't trust them. A different kettle of fish and there's something fishy going on! I don't believe they're married for one bit. He is always disappearing and leaving her here alone. She never goes out without him, mind!' Pearl said, with a defiant nod.

'From Friday to Monday she stays mostly in her room, just coming down for meals. She says she's doing research up there but I hear her crying. I knocked on the door but she doesn't answer,' Pearl continued gathering up some plates.

'How awful. Still I suppose it's none of our business,' said Petra, now intrigued.

'Maybe I should have a word with her Pearl, what do you think?' Petra asked, disliking the idea of anyone suffering in silence in her home.

'Up to you, you are the psychoanalyst!' she said, now going over to their table and clearing their plates.

As the ladies got up to leave their table, Pearl came back from the kitchen.

'Oh, Petra, I forgot to give you this letter that arrived yesterday, from the foreign office. I asked Mr Opperly if he could kindly help look into Sebastien's whereabouts for you. I suppose this is your answer!'

'You did that for Petra? Or should I say us,' Kathryn said, feeling overwhelmed with gratitude.

'Well with all these officials living at Dallington Place and Throgmorton Street, we would be foolhardy not to try. Plus Jorie put in a good word for us, her husband is quite in the know.'

Petra hesitated for a moment and then opened the letter with Kathryn peering over her shoulder.

It read:

Dear Miss Turoc,

Thank you for your enquiry about Sebastien Comte-Wright. I am sure you are aware that Mrs Giles Blomberg contacted us as well, to give us permission to search for him.

As you had feared, he had left his regiment in September and is or has been working for the Resistance. A group called 'le Favre Liberte'.

There are many small groups calling themselves different names but this one works in and out of Paris. They travel to Vichy or surrounding villages in the south west in the countryside. They are, as far as we know, smuggling Jewish children out of Paris.

As Mr Sebastien Comte-Wright is French by birth, we do not have the power to court-martial him and bring him home, although, he could have a tough time trying to get back into Britain. He would be seen by some as a traitor for deserting his regiment.

We understand though, he is married to a woman who has ancestral ties to England. Her family being British aristocracy.

This would help his case in order for him to return to England after the war.

According to our records, there were the last sightings of Mr Comte-Wright in Paris on the 29th October, so we believe he is still alive. He is travelling under the pseudonym of Sebastien Le Reynald but I understand these people change their names at the drop of a hat. It would probably be impossible for you to find him completely. They disappear into a dark net and if they do appear again, they vanish as quickly as they came.

I hope this information helps you and gives you some hope that he is still alive but I advise you not to look into this further.

Yours faithfully,

Colonel Peter Seward OBE

'So he is alive?' Kathryn said, wanting to cry with relief.

'Looks as if but what made him do such a foolhardy thing and leave his regiment?' Petra asked.

'Maybe he met someone in the Resistance and thought it a worthy cause,' Kathryn said, knowing what he was doing was highly dangerous but for a worthwhile cause.

'He is brave, I will give him that!' said Petra.

'I think you should inform Dawn. After all, she is his wife.'

'Yes, I will. Maybe, we should send the letter on to Endelwise Manor. But I do want Ernest to see it first, see what he thinks of all this,' Kathryn said, firmly, relieved she could tell Dawn good news, this time.

Petra went to see if she could contact any clients that may want appointments, now she was in London. She was sorry she had had to let go of so many of her clients while she had been working for the Brownies and the evacuees at Dallington Place.

'I will have to reclaim my study,' she said, knowing that Mr Opperly was using it to read and relax there of an evening.

'He's a very good chess player. He and Mr Smithfield play on a Tuesday night by the fire,' remarked Pearl.

'He often states Mr Smithfield cheats. Well, that doesn't surprise me,' she said, enjoying her usual titbit of gossip. 'But there's always a nice atmosphere, and Ernest sits over in the corner reading his political books,' Kathryn smiled back, imagining the life her son was now leading. 'And what does Roberta do whilst this is going on?' Kathryn asked, amused.

'She's occasionally still working with the Ambulance Service on some evenings, even until ten o'clock at night.'

'Don't you think it's unsuitable now she's pregnant Pearl?' Kathryn said, knowing she shouldn't interfere, but she worried for her safety. But Roberta was as headstrong as Geraldine, so there was no telling her what to do. Pearl just shrugged.

'She's a big girl, she knows what she is doing. I'm going to take

Porridge out for a walk and see if I can get any ideas on what I'm going to do in London for the next four months!' Kathryn said, needing some air. It had started to rain and Kathryn picked up Porridge and stuck him under her arm.

'Sorry Porridge, it looks as if it isn't going to be a long walk today!' she said to the little mite, who seemed scared of the London traffic as once she put him down, he wanted to return to the house, pulling on his lead and refusing to walk any further. She doubled back after only a few minutes, giving up and going back to the house to finish unpacking.

Kathryn put her few belongings away in the large oak cupboard and her one pair of trousers swung lonely from the hanger. The only ones she had managed to take with her. She hadn't managed to return to the house due to the bomb but Milly at the farm had lent her a few warm sweaters and a pair of beige slacks that she hoped would fit her. Her make-up bag was luckily already in her handbag but she really needed to buy a few more clothes. She decided a shopping trip was on the cards and she would go today. Counting the clothing coupons that Pearl saved, twenty in all, she would be able to buy a dress and some shoes with that.

Wondering if Nora was in town, Kathryn decided to telephone her. Nora was often in London visiting her "fancy man".

'How lovely to hear from you, Kathryn, I will be in Harrods at four o'clock for tea with some of our committee ladies, I hope you can join us!' she shrieked joyfully down the telephone.

Kathryn agreed but then thought better of it after catching herself in the mirror and seeing the state of her hair. She thought perhaps she could get her hair done! She hoped to get a quick appointment before meeting Nora. Hoping Chez Victor could fit her in as it was nearly two o'clock, she asked Pearl to call ahead for her and secure an appointment.

Running out of the house as fast as she could to hail a taxi, she wished she had been wearing something smarter. Looking out through the steamed up windows of the taxi, she noticed the bomb damage only two streets away from Throgmorton Street. Feeling guilty for worrying about her appearance when people had lost their homes she thought on the news this morning that Coventry were trying to rebuild since they were bombed greatly a couple of months ago. Coventry Cathedral had been hit too and now it was London that was suffering.

Kathryn watched anxiously as a red bus had been immobilized on the side of the street near Tottenham Court Road. It had Bovril written on it in large letters on a bill board on the front, just above where the driver sits. The glass had gone and she looked away. Jumping out of the taxi, clutching her gas mask, all so new to her that she nearly left it by the coat stand. She made her way to Knightsbridge's Brompton Road. By the time she had reached Harrods, the atmosphere was so depressing she longed to go back to Sussex. After listening about the Coventry bombing last night on the radio, Kathryn wondered when the sirens could possibly go off here. The bomb at Dallington Place had probably shaken her and taken its toll on her, her nerves felt raw but she stoically brushed these feelings aside but she did have an uneasy feeling today.

Unfortunately, Victor was too busy for her to have her hair cut but had time to quickly set her hair for her. It would have to do she thought. Placing her black hat on, that Pearl had lent her, her hair curled around the edges, rather unfashionably but at least it was clean and shiny. She had time to peruse the Harrods food hall before meeting Nora.

Food was scarce now, and this was very apparent here. The usual hustle and bustle of the food hall was now taken over by a quiet hum of a select few, shopping for certain foods they couldn't purchase in their local shops. Certain foods were not available any more and only the very well off could shop here. She was just chatting to a charming man at the cheese counter, when suddenly an air raid siren sounded. Disoriented for a moment, a kindly gentleman behind the counter directed Kathryn to Knightsbridge tube station.

'I'm afraid ma'am you are going to have to leave Harrods and go down into the Knightsbridge tube for shelter. I have to make sure my customers leave safely,' he instructed her.

Panic took hold of her usual calm demeanour. She had meant to meet Nora on her way out of the food hall and now she had no means of contacting her.

Streams of shoppers were now in a line, trying to get out of the store. She wondered if Nora was one of them. Luckily for her she was on the ground floor, but what if Nora had been in the clothes department on the top floor. There wasn't much she could do and took her place in the line as people pushed and shoved. A woman in front of her with many shopping bags, stumbled forward, dropped her grocery bag, and apples started to spill out on to the floor. Kathryn bent down to pick a couple up and as she stood up, the women in front had moved along the queue. As Kathryn craned her neck to see if she could see Nora, she caught sight of a large gentleman opening the doors for a lady. He then walked through the doors himself. There must have been six or seven people in front of her, obscuring her view but he did look familiar. In fact she could have sworn it was Alexander. Then someone pushed her and she looked around and the man now had disappeared through the doors.

Some people had chosen to go through the revolving doors but this too was a disadvantage, because if people were not pushing the doors fast enough, people were getting agitated and shouting. This wasn't helping anybody.

'Hurry up!' customers were shouting, and a fight broke out to the left of her. Just then, she heard someone call her name. She looked ahead and she could see a man waving at her from outside. Then her view was blocked again by a tall man who had pushed in front and by the time she and this tall man had reached the doors, the person that was waving at her had disappeared.

She stood on the pavement outside and then they were being directed straight down to the tube station. People were starting to run so she went with the crowd and down the steps of Knightsbridge tube station. She had no time to look around her to see if it really had been Alexander. By the time they had reached the nearest platform, it was crowded and people were sitting on the ground. Then, suddenly, Kathryn caught sight of Nora and a gentleman. They were huddled together on a seat. Kathryn waved and made her way through the crowds towards her.

'Nora, I'm so relieved to see you, you must have got out before me,' Kathryn said, kissing her on her cheek.

'Kathryn, my dear, thank goodness you got out. Mr Burbridge led me down the fire escape himself and then Mr Rogers here, took me outside. I was quite unsteady on my feet!'

'Do you mean the owner of Harrods?' Kathryn said, wide eyed that the owner of Harrods had selflessly led Nora to safety.

'Oh yes, quite the gentleman. Mr Rogers here, works in the clothing department, he made sure I got here unscathed.'

Kathryn noticed they had now let go of each other's hands and were now pretending to sit like strangers. The handsome man, of not more than thirty years old, didn't say anything to Kathryn but tipped his hat at her.

'Did you see the aeroplanes Kathryn, those damn Heinkel bombers!' Nora said, wanting to cry. She reached into her handbag to find her handkerchief.

'No, I just ran, but the strangest thing happened as I was queuing to get out,' she started to explain.

Nora interrupted. 'You had to queue? How undignified and now look at us down here like rats! And carrying these God-awful gas masks everywhere we go.'

'Yes, but I think I saw Alexander, Alexander Pillard!' Kathryn exclaimed, trying to get Nora to listen.

'Your Alexander, American Alexander?' she said.

'Yes, you know maybe I was mistaken. It was all such a blur and people were shouting and pushing. Maybe I dreamt it.'

'Probably dear, it's the shock of all this,' she said, patting Kathryn's hand that was still holding the apple.'

Kathryn just nodded in response. She must have been dreaming. What would Alexander Pillard be doing in Harrods, London? Unless it was for work, she supposed it was possible. Had he changed that much she wondered? The man she had seen looked a lot older to when she had seen him last. His hair seemed to have receded and he didn't have a moustache. But she rarely forgot a face, and she was normally right. It did sound like Alexander. It had been at least two years since she had last seen him. Biting into the apple, she dismissed it. It probably wasn't him. He would be in New York with Pearl. Honestly, she decided she must have had a moment of madness with all these bombs. They had affected her nerves.

Two hours later, after saying goodbye to Nora, she found herself on the Knightsbridge street, alone. She was late back to Throgmorton Street and she thought perhaps Petra would be worried about her. She could see a fire in the distance, probably where a bomb had hit some building. Fire engines were now tearing along the street. Motor cars were abandoned, bicycles too. It was almost like a ghost town. People were emerging from their hiding places, with stricken looks on their faces. There wasn't a taxi in sight. She wanted to get back to Throgmorton Street as fast as she could but how, she wondered? Giving up on the thought of a taxi to get her home, she decided to see if Riley's restaurant was still open. She could use their telephone and have a stiff drink to relax while she ordered a car.

Feeling more steady on her feet, she ran across the almost deserted Old Brompton Road towards Trevor Square. A shifty looking man tipped his hat at her and she ran faster hoping that the restaurant would still be open. When she pushed the revolving door it didn't move. There was a light on inside but to no avail, when she pushed the door again, it just didn't budge. Feeling defeated, she turned around but just as she did so, she bumped into the maître d' who was leaving the restaurant by the side entrance.

'I beg your pardon, madam,' he said, and then he realised who it was.

'Madam McAlister so good to see you, how are you?' hoping he hadn't knocked her too severely.

Kathryn recognised his friendly face. 'I'm very well thank you but rather shaken by the air raid,' she said, imploring him for sympathy.

'Madam I was locking up for the day, but would you like to come in and sit down? I can get you something to drink?' he asked, seeing how shaken and pale she was now.

'Thank you, that would be most kind, I really need to use the telephone, is that possible? I need to telephone my son. You see, I am supposed to be home by now, my son will be worrying about me.'

'Of course, do come in, but if you don't mind using the staff entrance,' the maître d' said feeling a little embarrassed to ask such a grand lady to use the staff entrance.

'No, of course not," Kathryn said with a wry smile. The maître d' had no idea that Kathryn was once staff and was in service at Dallington Place herself all those years ago.

Once inside the restaurant he fetched her a glass of champagne. Downing the reviving liquid, she asked him if she could now use the telephone.

'By all means, madam, as long as the lines are working, would you like me to order some transport for you? It may take a while to arrive,' he stated, relieved there was a signal as he tapped on the receiver a couple of times. Kathryn nodded at him, thankful for his kindness. She always remembered him to be a charming and courteous man.

Did you see Mr Pillard today, Mrs McAlister? Had you meant to meet him here? It was so nice to see him back in London again!' he said, not seeing her surprised expression as he topped up her champagne glass.

'Mr Pillard did you say?' Kathryn asked, knowing she had heard him correctly. So it was him after all, her mind hadn't been playing tricks on her. At least that was a relief.

'No, I missed him unfortunately,' she said, answering the maître d'. What a coincidence to have seen him but she wondered if it was a good thing she hadn't managed to catch up with him in Harrods but it was a shame not to have at least exchanged pleasantries. She wasn't one to hold a grudge, especially in wartime.

'Well, ma'am, it was the first time we had seen him in a long time.'

Getting up to use the telephone to call Ernest, she put him out of her mind for now.

'Ernest, whatever is the matter?' Kathryn said, knowing something wasn't right by the strained tone of his voice.

'Mamma, we can't find Roberta. She went out in search of Porridge who ran off and we haven't seen her for an hour. There's been a bomb in Threadneedle Street and we just can't find her,' he said again.

'I'm coming home,' Kathryn stated firmly.

Chapter Twelve
Homecoming

Arriving home to Throgmorton Street, Kathryn fumbled in her handbag for her keys as she walked up the steep steps to the front door, just as Pearl was opening it. Kathryn could see Pearl had been crying.

'Oh, my goodness, Pearl,' Kathryn said, dropping her handbag to the floor and hugging her.

'Ernest has gone out to look for her, but she hasn't been seen for two hours now Kathryn, I'm fearing the worst,' she cried into her handkerchief.

Kathryn felt sick. Not only had Roberta been missing, Ernest was gone too.

'Where was he heading for, do you know?' Kathryn asked her, trying to calm so she could think clearly. An ambulance drove at speed with its siren's blasting, passing the house and it made Kathryn even more nervous.

'No, I'm not sure, he just grabbed his coat and mumbled something about Threadneedle Street and left in a hurry. I tried to stop him so he could wait for you but he wouldn't listen,' she said, now burying her head in her hands.

'Well, I don't blame him, he loves her, that's why he didn't wait. Where's Petra?' Kathryn asked, trying to keep her nerves from fraying.

'She's on the telephone, and to make matters worse, Porridge arrived back half an hour ago, just wandered up the stairs. Causing all this chaos,' Pearl said, sniffing.

Kathryn walked into the kitchen and there was Porridge in his basket fast asleep, without a care in the world. Petra came in and flung her arms around Kathryn. She wasn't usually the warm type but she was clearly distressed.

'I'm sorry Kathryn, I tried to stop him going until you arrived back but he wasn't having it.'

'I know, Pearl told me, don't worry, it is not your fault, he's as stubborn as me!' Kathryn said stoically.

'Shall we wait or go to try to find him?' Petra asked, now at a loss as what to do.

'I think we should go together, maybe he is searching the hospitals.'

'Shall we try there then, the London or St Thomas's?' Kathryn suggested.

They ran upstairs to fetch their coats. Changing into her heavy woollen jacket and, after changing her shoes, she was at the top of the stairs just as Brenda Smithfield was leaving her bedroom. She looked as if she were on her way out too, dressed for rain and carrying a large umbrella.

'Mrs Smithfield, there has been a lot of bomb damage in Threadneedle Street, is it wise to go out? I'm going out to look for my son and daughter-in-law, they are both missing.'

'I will help you,' she said calmly, 'you need a torch and take some drinking water with you.'

Kathryn, taken aback by this women's kindness and forethought, thanked her and agreed to meet outside in a few minutes. Standing in front of the hall mirror, she pulled on a woollen hat to protect her from the rain and as she tucked her curls underneath it, she could see Petra race down the stairs towards her, wearing her smart raincoat. It was becoming dark and chilly outside and Kathryn shivered, feeling cold and nervous.

'Brenda's coming with us!' Kathryn said as Petra hurried to the door. Petra raised her eyebrows as Brenda walked towards them. As they were about to leave, Pearl called out to Mrs Smithfield.

'Your husband is on the telephone Mrs Smithfield.'

Brenda waved her hand as if to dismiss the fact that her husband was calling her. She had something much more important to do.

'Could you please tell him that I have gone out? Thank you so very much.'

Pearl nodded and shut the front door, still sniffling into her handkerchief.

The ladies made their way down to Threadneedle Street and passed the "Worshipful Company of Merchant Taylors". They could see the extent of the damage to the building.

'Maybe we should ask someone if they have seen Roberta who had been with a small white dog?' Brenda said sensibly.

Looking to the ambulance crew who were taking people on stretchers into a dozen ambulances parked at the end of the street, the ladies made their way over to them.

'What's the damage here?' Petra asked a man bandaging a young boy, who had a nasty leg injury.

'The main hall has gone and the staircase, luckily most people got out,' he said, pointing back to the damaged building.

Kathryn spoke first, 'We are looking for a tall, young lady with a dog. Have you perhaps attended someone of that description?' she asked the man in uniform.

'Or seen someone?' Petra asked, stepping in front of Kathryn, aware she was too emotionally involved in this.

'Red hair and the dog was small with white fur?' Brenda interjected.

Kathryn looked imploringly up to the man who shook his head. But the young boy grimaced through his pain and said, 'Yes, I saw a red-headed lady but not a dog. She was leaving the building when I fell. She fell and injured her head. The ambulance has taken her.

'Where? Where did they take her? Which hospital?' Kathryn asked, at her wits' end.

'Wait… was she wearing a blue dress?' asked Petra, wanting to be sure it was Roberta.

The boy nodded. 'Yes, pretty and she was a very tall lady.'

'That's got to be her,' said Petra excitedly.

Brenda went over to the men who were shutting the doors of an ambulance.

'Which hospital are they taking the survivors to, please?' she asked

'Paternoster Square,' he replied

'Oh god, no!' Kathryn murmured on overhearing what he had told Brenda.

'You haven't seen a young man, blond hair, hazel eyes, looking for his wife?' she added.

'Yes, an hour ago a gentleman asked us about a young lady, his wife sounds like the same lady to me,' he replied helpfully, now jumping into the front seat of the ambulance.'

'That must have been Ernest,' Kathryn said, relieved.

'We sent him to the London, didn't we, George,' the ambulance driver confirmed as his colleague nodded in agreement. 'Bad cut on her forehead though but she was conscious, best you hurry to the London hospital,' George called through the open window as the engine started.

Kathryn clung on to Petra feeling rather faint. 'Let's take the bus, I know which one,' said Brenda, 'my brother lives in Whitechapel.'

An hour later, they were at the London Hospital.

'I'm looking for a Roberta Comte-Wright please. I think she was brought here by ambulance a couple of hours ago. Maybe about five o'clock after the air strike in the city. Kathryn asked a comely looking matron.

'Let me look for you on the list,' she replied, putting on her glasses and flicking through a mass of paperwork on the reception desk. We have had quite a day. As she scanned the names, Kathryn's heart was in her mouth, willing her to hurry up. The matron clearly couldn't find her name.

Kathryn willed her to find it, biting her nails and watching Petra's face for any sign of positive news. Just as Kathryn thought she may pass out, with the thoughts of what she would tell Geraldine, she suddenly saw Ernest walking fast towards her.

'Oh, my goodness, Ernest,' she shrieked, as she hugged her son tightly.' She could tell he was exhausted by the way he held himself and she begged him to tell her any bad news as quickly as he could.

'Tell me she is fine, Ernest, quickly,' Kathryn said, her face paling as she searched his eyes for clues to what had befallen Roberta.

'Mamma, don't worry, she's fine, fine, more than fine!' he said holding her tightly.

'Oh, thank goodness, Ernest. If something had happened to her… well, what could I have told Geraldine,' she said with tears rolling down her face.

'She's got a nasty cut on her forehead but they have stitched it. It's stopped bleeding, but they are taking extra care as she's pregnant.'

'I know, the baby… is the baby, all right?' Kathryn asked her heart beating fast again.

'Yes,' said Ernest, 'more than all right.' His large toothy grin, the same as Sebastien's, lighting up his handsome face.

'The doctor found two heartbeats!'

***

Keeping Roberta in the hospital overnight to check on the babies, the women couldn't contain their excitement for her to come home the next day. Geraldine and William were on their way to Throgmorton Street by train. Pearl had made a grand lunch in celebration for Roberta's safe return and was setting the table for nine people. Mr and Mrs Smithfield were joining them. Kathryn and Petra were so thankful to Brenda for giving them support. Stood in the sitting room waiting for Ernest and Roberta, they clinked their sherry glasses together as little Porridge danced around their heels. Pearl had to fetch an extra bottle from the cellar as they finished the first so quickly.

Mr Smithfield had been about to leave for Surrey, but had dutifully agreed to partake in the celebration before he left on his way. But he wasn't his usual pompous self. He looked as if he couldn't wait to get away. He wasn't speaking to Brenda either. She didn't seem bothered by this though and she was more animated than usual. She was relaxed and laughing, with Petra in the corner of the room. Discussing the red curtains Petra wanted to change. Brenda was trying to persuade Petra to keep them.

'Blue or yellow? Kathryn what do you think?' called out Petra, who was tipsy by now and pulling the curtains along and draping them over herself as if the material was a luxury couture.

'Blue definitely, my favourite colour!' Kathryn called back as she sat chatting with Geraldine on the comfortable Chesterfield by the fire.

Just then the door burst open and it was Ernest... looking happier than Kathryn had ever seen him. Geraldine ran over to see her daughter who was looking in the mirror by the hall table.

'Mamma!' she cried and hugged her mother tightly.

'Look at my scar mamma.'

'Never mind that, it will heal, Geraldine said, ignoring the large gash on her daughter's head. Thank goodness you are alive and the babies...'

'Mamma I'm having twins, can you believe it?'

Porridge started to bark from the kitchen, and Roberta's eyes lit up.

'They found Porridge?' she asked, now so happy.

'He's in disgrace, Kathryn's put him in the kitchen for safe keeping.

'Oh Mamma, let him out, I can't wait to see him.'

The little dog lapped up the excitement as he wandered in and out of the table legs under everyone's feet.

***

Later that evening as everyone had gone to bed, Kathryn and Ernest stayed up talking by the sitting room fire.

She had passed him the letter from Officer Seaward and Ernest mused on what to do with it.

'I will call Dawn in the morning for you if you like. You look about as done in as I feel,' he said, helpfully.

'Thank you my dear. I can't face any more drama's this week, if you would be so kind to do that. I would be most grateful,' she said kissing him on the cheek and getting up to draw the curtains.

'I think I will go to bed it's been quite the day!' she said, coming back to hug her son. 'Blue, or should the curtains stay the same?' she asked him.

'Definitely blue, Mamma!' he smiled.

Kathryn blew her son a kiss, turned out the side lamp and retired to bed. Ernest stayed sitting, sipping his brandy. He yawned and kicked off his shoes as Porridge lay by them. His snout touching the sharp, brown brogues as he slept soundly.

Ernest re-read Officer Seawards letter again and his mind ticked over.

'What had become of Sebastien?' he worried.

***

'This is Rani Singh speaking. Dawn is out in the paddock,' he said, firmly. 'The Fitches are not at home.'

For a minute Ernest thought he had telephoned the incorrect number. Normally, Lady Fitch would answer. Now there was a stranger's voice on the other end of the line. Then he registered who Rani Singh was. It was the name of the young pilot that had crashed in the fields of Dallington Place.

'Oh it's you Rani. Could you please ask Dawn to telephone me back as I have some information about Sebastien's whereabouts? He normally would have kept this information quiet to a stranger but for some reason, he didn't follow his normal way of doing things. After yesterday he seemed to have changed his view on keeping things so much to himself. The war was on and time was of the essence.

'Can I help?' Rani asked.

Ernest did feel uncomfortable to discuss Sebastien with him but the man's voice was so gentle and reassuring, he found himself discussing Sebastien's plight with him more easily as the conversation went on. They chatted about Sebastien's dilemma and the fact they had both been wounded in the war fairly recently and discussed how they were recovering.

They actually found they had a lot in common and were speaking for about an hour, when Rani interrupted him and explained that Dawn had entered the room.

'I would like to discuss this with you further, and meet up in London, will you meet me?' Rani asked.

1st December The Gelding Club.

The men had made plans to meet at the Gelding Club. The club had come to resemble an officers' mess. All uniforms were acceptable. Ernest and Rani had decided to go for lunch and, were drinking brandies by the fire in the day room.

'What's the plan then?' Ernest asked Rani.

'Well, it would all depend when you can leave. As soon as possible would be preferable,' he said, question marking some dates in his notepad.

'I can ask for some leave nearer Christmas time, say in two weeks? We'll try to find Sebastien and hopefully make it back in time for Christmas,' replied Ernest, looking rather pensive.

'That could be a possibility,' Rani said, writing some notes and then swigging his brandy back in one go.

'It's best we don't discuss this with too many people,' he added apprehensively.

'I will let my mother know, for emergencies sake but I don't want Roberta to worry,' Ernest said, not quite sure how he was not going to let his wife know he would be going away and placing himself in a dangerous position out in France.

'It's a tricky spot to be in, you sure you want to? We have to make plans and we don't want to hesitate,' Rani urged.

'So Rani what makes you so keen to save Sebastien?' Ernest asked, trying to relax back into his comfortable chair. He knew the reason and had a knowing smile on his lips.

'In my country, we pay back the kindnesses, such as the good service your family has bestowed upon me and of course, Dawn. She may be married to Sebastien, but she is with me now,' he said, showing his white teeth and a glint in his eye, reaching out to clink glasses with Ernest and acknowledging a club member that had entered the room, he cleared his throat. Talking about Dawn did make him nervous but he knew Ernest would understand.

It's not that Ernest and Kathryn didn't know this but it was almost too straightforward. The man was clearly going to save the husband of his lover so he could ask the man's permission to be with her. Sipping his brandy, Ernest wondered if this sat well with him and he found it did. It was almost endearing in an unconventional way. He liked this man's convictions and his confidence in them.

Kathryn hadn't returned to Dallington Place for weeks. This time she was pleasantly surprised at the progress of the repair of her beloved home and now she was relieved the refectory was under repair at long last.

'It should be completed by March we hope,' said Colonel Shaddock still rather shy around her.

'And Tree Top House?' she asked, eager to go and see the new build take place. She was glad to have worn her warm woollen coat and trilby hat this morning for her journey to Dallington Place by train this morning. It was as cold in Sussex this morning as Dallington Place was unrecognisably stark.

The snow had started to fall gently and a blanket of white, crispness enveloped the ground, as their boots crunched on the short spiky grass. But right now, it didn't feel like home and Kathryn could return to Throgmorton Street before the light faded.

'That's almost complete,' Colonel Shaddock said, proudly as they made their way past the clipped back willow tree and along the path to the Nissen huts. The men were resting this afternoon, due to the cold, but Kathryn was relieved she didn't have to see them milling about. Right now, she didn't want to be civil to any of these cuckoos who inhabited her home and she was the one who had had to move out.

Looking up to the magnificent building that was almost complete, its roof scraping the tree tops and being positioned perfectly so far from the view of Dallington Place, it was hidden mysteriously and discreetly, Kathryn sighed with a peaceful conviction. At least this wasn't a building that she would have to fight against. Although she had ceased resistance to the build, she was relieved that she liked it and would be an extra bonus to the estate.

A "Nafnah" Rani had called it in Urdu. An extra dividend he had said wisely. He was right and she would telephone Sangeeta to tell her so.

'The monument will not be started until the new year. Government officials have yet to agree on the design,' Colonel Shaddock explained.

'Well, that's a bore,' said Kathryn now feeling the cold and wanting to go back into the warm. Walking back to Dallington Place, where men were still working on the roof and two officers were standing on guard at the door, they hurried inside. Kathryn nodded a hello as the men saluted her. Walking back into her study, leaving the door open, Colonel Shaddock offered her a sip of whisky from his hip flask. Kathryn shook her head.

'I will have a pot of tea at the station, thank you,' she said, now looking forward to making her way back to London. Ivy, who was caretaking the place while they were away in London, was on shopping duties in the village and her beloved Dallington Place felt lonely to Kathryn without her friends milling around. She thought she would never feel this way, but a change was as good as a rest and it would feel like the old Dallington Place when she returned in a few months' time. Much of the furniture had been covered in dust sheets so they had nowhere to sit.

The Colonel spread the sketches of the new Chattri onto the dusty mahogany desk.

'This design feels too similar to the actual Chattri at Patcham, don't you agree? We need to tweak it a little. Make it softer,' he said.

'We have to think of a name too, Colonel Shaddock,' Kathryn said, acknowledging the design needed a less harsh line.

'A different angle here would soften it, don't you think?' he asked her as she peered over his sketch.'

'Keep it simple, Colonel Shaddock, I think that's the key and so the same should go for the name, something to honour the Chattri,' she said

'Yes, always best to keep things simple,' he said, not looking Kathryn in the eye. Peering at the design again, she had a thought.

'Perhaps the top half of the stone carving could be shaped like a boat. You know, as if we are all in the same boat so to speak. All of us, no matter where we come from,'

Colonel Shaddock looked at her with an amused expression. 'Well, if you can draw it, I'm sure they will have a look,' he said, smiling.

'But I can't draw but I will try. Here pass me the pencil. This is not my forte or finest hour but I will give it a go,' she said, laughing.

Their rapport seemed to have broken the ice between them.

'Would you like me to drive you to the station, before the snow settles?' he asked her as she finished her attempt to sketch the monument. Looking out to the front lawn and seeing the grass covered in glistening powder, she agreed and placed her trilby hat back on, she felt her job was done for the day

Walking through the front door of Throgmorton Street, Kathryn could see Roberta pacing up and down in the sitting room, as she slung her heavy coat on the back of the hall chair.

'Kathryn, Ernest hasn't come back from work and I had a call from his office to say he has had some emergency assignment to work abroad. I'm worried sick, tell me, he will be all right? I didn't know they could do this,' she said, her face etched with worry.

Kathryn sat down at the hall table and sighed. She was annoyed Ernest's employers had told his wife over the telephone.

'Come, let's go downstairs and have some tea. I need to talk to you about something,' Kathryn said, placing her arm around Roberta and leading her to the kitchen.

Pearl put the kettle on and as she prepared Kathryn some toast, she suddenly remembered that Giles, Jorie's husband had called.

'Thank you, Pearl, I will call him back later,' Kathryn said, passing Roberta a china cup.

'I will leave you two to it. I have some accounts to catch up on. Oh, and also before I forget, Mr Smithfield hasn't paid his bill for two months now. In fact, I haven't seen him for quite a few days. But don't worry,' she said with a wink, 'we can discuss this later,' Pearl said, taking off her apron and shutting the door on the two women behind her, reading Kathryn's mind to have the kitchen alone with Roberta.

***

The Parisian station was crawling with Nazis. 'I will do the talking, you just keep your head down, all right?' Ernest said, knowing that he and Rani would not go unnoticed.

'Luckily my French is good, you will pass as "my man". Just try not to talk.' Ernest had instructed him earlier in the carriage.

How Rani's mouth twitched in annoyance. He didn't like this idea at all. It had been his idea to fly them into Paris but Giles had disagreed with him. He didn't like to keep quiet at the best of times, but there was nothing he could do. If they suspected they could speak English it would be all over for them. They had had special papers drawn up for their new identities.

Rani was Aarush Gupta and Ernest was Ernst Faucon. Ernest posing as a newly trained doctor starting a post in the countryside. Rani was a medical student, specializing in foreign medicines.

Giles had suspected that Sebastien had been persuaded to work for the British Ops, a group of men and women who work for causes such as the 'Maquis', a French resistance group. Getting him safely back through England would be easy and he wouldn't have any problems with the authorities if Sebastien was working for the British Ops but getting him out without the correct papers could be a challenge.

Giles had suggested they should contact him as soon as they find Sebastien, so they could be brought back by aeroplane on stand-by for them.

'Unterlagen?' a young German officer said to Ernest.

He repeated the question loudly and Ernest fumbled in his coat for his identity papers. Ernest spoke in French to Rani who passed his papers to the officer who cast his eyes downward and scanned the papers. The German officer then gazed up at them and stared at Rani. He looked as if he was going to say something but then passed the papers back without a word. He nodded and pointed to the exit of the station.

They had to find their way back inside the station and to somehow get back to the end of the platform without being recognised again, to catch the train to a commune in the Haute-Loire department, a village called Chambon-sur-Lignon. Sebastien had been seen here helping Jews make new lives, hiding out with them in the monastery and farms. Taking children from Paris whose parents had been sent away to camps, or just separating them to keep them safe. Ernest thought perhaps there had been a lot more planning and secrecy in this than Giles was letting on. It sounded to Ernest that Sebastien had been handpicked for the job, as he was a French national. Giles had suggested that they stay in the countryside for, no more than two weeks, and if they were unable to locate Sebastien in this time, they would have to return without him for their own safety. There would be nothing much they could do after that. Giles had promised them an aeroplane home on the 22nd December from the air base, Laon-Couvron, to reach there by dawn and Squadron Leader Richard Davidson would meet them at 0400 hours. A much more dangerous journey would then ensue to get out of occupied France. Not only would they would be severely interrogated. It was imperative they were on this aeroplane, to avoid the ports.

The men ran back through the arches to the back of the station. They could see their train about to pull out of the station. Luckily for them, someone had left a train door open to a carriage at the back and they sprinted for it. Rani caught his toe on the step and lunged forward pushing Ernest into the train but Rani then fell awkwardly on to his side. Ernest turned around, pulled him up quickly and slammed the door shut. Rani winced with pain. His ribs throbbed as he tried to recover to find themselves a seat amongst the locals returning home. Rani sat next to a young woman with a dog in a large wicker basket, who was staring at him with much interest. Rani closed his eyes to recover from his fall and collect his thoughts.

Ernest was boxed in nearest to a window seat. An old man reading a newspaper shuffled up so he could sit down next to him, then he spread his newspaper over Ernest's knees. He wouldn't normally have minded but it was humid and uncomfortable. But if this made him resemble a local man then this was an opportunity to look less conspicuous.

Ernest knew the less they communicated together the better and when a German officer walked through the train, he eyed Rani suspiciously. To Ernest's surprise, he didn't question him and they saw no other soldiers on board for the rest of the journey.

Hours later, it must have been at least five hours, there were two loud whistles and the train pulled into a station.

Ernest got up to get out and the old man cried, 'Non, non.'

Then Ernest realised no one was getting off at this stop – German soldiers were getting on. Rani stared wide eyed. They were going to have to get off the train and quickly. Rani got up first followed by Ernest. They walked quickly down two carriages. They could almost feel the hot breath of the German soldiers on their necks. Just as the train pulled out of the station, they jumped. Ernest landing heavily on his right foot and wincing, he followed Rani down the deserted platform and they ran towards greenery in front of them and to freedom. After squeezing through a small break in the foliage behind the station sign of Saint Agrève, they stopped to catch their breath by an oak tree and sheltered under its branches, a shadow casting over them, keeping them cool from the heat. Ernest passed Rani his water bottle. he closed his eyes.

'That was close,' he said, now sitting down against the tree and rubbing his ankle. 'We have to make it to the monastery by dark,' Ernest instructed, spreading out his map over the crisp and dried grass.

'We can walk behind hedgerows, and out of the sight of main roads. By my calculations, four maybe five hours walk.'

Rani just nodded. The less energy he expelled the better. His ribs hurt him even when he talked. He was concerned he may have fractured some of them. He sat down next to Ernest and closed his eyes again.

The bright winter sun was bearing down on the countryside now as they walked by the thorn bushes and winter holly berries, and taking in the scent of the mulberry and eucalyptus trees, they slowed their pace a little. But it was mid-day and they had to keep moving.

Watching a tiny bird for a moment as it hopped in front of them about furtively looking for worms to take back to its nest, Ernest looked at Rani. He didn't want him to collapse in pain, so they stopped for a few minutes for a bit of their roll and butter which they shared.

'Right let's get going again!' instructed Ernest, who was aware that Rani may fall asleep if they tarried too long here. He patted Rani on the shoulder who dutifully slung his backpack over his shoulder, grimacing in pain as he did so.

***

'You say the man that knows Sebastien's whereabouts, is Paster Jerome?' Ernest asked an old gentleman, who was leaning against his bicycle outside the post office.

'Pastor Jerome, Monastere!' the old man explained, pointing to the road. 'There!' He pointed to a building at the end, near the turn of the road.

***

One week later.

The men had been staying at the Monastery of Chambon-sur-Lignon. Rani had kept hidden most of the time, in the cellars by the pastors. Ernest though could move about easily, mingling with the locals and masquerading as a French farm labourer.

Pastor Jerome explained to them that Sebastien would return with the children and then disappear again. Pastor Jerome wouldn't say any more, maybe he didn't want Ernest to know of Sebastien's movements. He would walk in and then walk out as quickly as he had arrived. But it was good to know he was alive and perhaps they would manage to catch up with him.

Ernest knew they would have to wait it out now. People didn't like it, information was hard to come by. The less people revealed the safer they were. Lives and livelihoods would be in danger if they revealed too much information. It was well known in the village that Pastor Jerome was helping with the Maquis to get French Jewish children from Paris, safely installed in the village without suspicion. Talk that Sebastien would turn up like a ghost and then disappear again, likening him to an apparition, an angel, and taking the children to the mushroom fields where they were safe from a possible raid from the Nazis. He would then walk them back to the Monastery after and then disappear again. A phantom figure. His timing always impeccable. Ernest knew this to be Sebastien. He had always appeared to him this way – in doorways, fortuitous moments, listening and planning.

He had probably picked up this skill from their father, Bertram. How he would suddenly appear at the door of the dining room whilst having breakfast. Nobody knew how long he had been standing there, listening to private conversations at Dallington Place.

They had four days now to find him, then it would be too late and they would have to leave and return home without him. At that moment, there was no sign of finding him in the immediate future and Ernest had to come to terms with the fact it was a fifty-fifty chance of them catching up with him. They may have to return to Dallington Place without him[1].

---

[1] During the First World War, Manta Singh and George Henderson fought alongside each other in Neauve Chapelle. Manta Singh saved George's life. Manta Singh sadly lost his life. The families a hundred years on are still friends.

Chapter Thirteen
The Ghost of Abbeville

The Ghost of Abbeville.

Click down on this earth beyond,
Your rifle lays in the mud.
Catch a light,
A ciggie bright
To keep the cold at bay.

Click down,
I see you frown.
You know we won't make morning.
All seeing face,
Crack in disgrace,
Your loyalty has me again.

Click down,
There on the road home
I without you.
I am afraid of the turn in the road.
I am alone, and without you I will be scorned,
I came back without you.

Click down.
Am I alive?
My fingers burn brightly in the mist.

Click down I hear you say.
I am one soldier listed,
perished at Abbeville.

23rd December 1940

The German soldiers had been back and forth raiding various establishments and farms in the local area today. Ernest and Rani had been hiding in the cellars of the monastery. Two bunk beds fixed to the wall and one light blanket was their only comfort. Pastor Jerome had a signal for them, two raps on the door and they knew to keep hidden. This morning, they heard him. They sat still and heard footsteps down to the cellars, their hearts beating fast.

Two, three men perhaps? thought Ernest.

Then all went quiet. Ernest put his fingers to his lips to warn Rani. He tip-toed to the bolted door. There was no one there, he thought. He unbolted the heavy door and opened it just ajar, to let a little light in to see if it was safe. From the far end of the room, he could see a Nazi uniform. He shut the door fast, bolting it too noisily. Then there were footsteps and the door started to rattle furiously.

'Damn,' he whispered to Rani.

Rani sat upright on his bed, but couldn't move. Just then, shots rang out and Ernest could hear fast running footsteps, and shouts. He held his breath and opened the door, just as Rani put up his hand to say stop.

The German soldier had gone. They walked up the stone stairwell, it's uneven paving making them slow down as their hearts raced. There was no one. Ernest sidled up against the stone walls and made his way to the large windows, cowering behind the curtains. He could see a German truck and a soldier with a strong hold on Pastor Jerome as they shoved him in the back with other prisoners.

Ernest beckoned for Rani to join him once the truck had gone.

'We have to make it to the mushroom fields, he whispered.'

'Yes, the children,' Rani whispered. 'We have to warn the children, that's where they are taking Pastor Jerome. They are using him as bait.'

Outside the monastery, there were no vehicles. A young man in a stable across the courtyard was sitting shoeing a horse, as if nothing had happened, carrying on his business as if none of this had taken place a few minutes ago. Maybe he was in shock or maybe turned a blind eye for his own safety's sake. Maybe this was something that happened frequently.

There was no sign of soldiers so the men made their way up the road, until they reached a fork in the road and then they turned left and into a field. It started to snow lightly, and the men began to shiver as Ernest beckoned Rani to keep up and run alongside him. The ground was wet and the snow became heavy, giving them a cloak of invisibility. As they made their way to the field in front of the woods that Pastor Jerome had shown where the children go to keep away from the raids.

Just then, as they reached the field, they could see a figure half running towards them out of the woods. The man was limping and then he stopped and a trail of blood encircled in the snow around him, he leant forward and then collapsed a few feet away from them.

'It's Sebastien!' Ernest cried.

***

'What makes our grass grow?'
Blood and soil,
Blood and soil,
My fellow Tommie boy,
I will keep you safe.'

***

'I am not going to make it, Ernest!' Sebastien whispered, as his stretcher was placed in the back of the Hawker Hurricane.

'Keep talking to me Sebastien,' Ernest said, with tears in his eyes.'

'You will make it, you have to get home to Lily and Dawn, and Kathryn.

'Kathryn,' he whispered.

'Keep talking to me, Sebastien,' Ernest said, holding his blood-soaked hand.

Ernest looked into Rani's eyes. He could see there was not much hope by the look in his friend's eyes. Ernest moved to the other side of the aeroplane. and he was sitting quietly now, as if in prayer. The aeroplane was noisy but he wanted to keep talking to Sebastien. Ernest kept repeating a poem Bertram had written about soldiers on the battlefield.

'Come on Tommie boy, you will be fine, just hold on!' Ernest would say, and then he would repeat the poem again.

'I want to tell you about the ghost of Abbeville,' said Sebastien, quietly.

'Tell me when we get home, it won't be long,' said Ernest, biting his lip.

'I'm afraid of the turn in the road,' said Sebastien. And then he promptly closed his eyes in defeat. Ernest prayed he would hold on.

***

24th December 1940

'Ernest are you all right?' Kathryn screeched down the telephone line in panic.

'We are at the Military hospital, in Gravesend. We are fine. Sebastien's a bit bashed in, but he will live,' Ernest said, buoyantly.

Kathryn put the receiver on her lap for a second, tears rolled down her face.

'They are safe, they are safe,' she repeated to Petra and Roberta.

'Ernest, can you get here for Christmas day?' Kathryn asked, desperate to see him.

'I will try to make it in the morning, if I can get a train Mamma. Sebastien sends his love to everyone!'

Kathryn rung her hands together in relief and then put her head in her hands and wept. Little Porridge was wagging his tail and then he settled at her feet. Wiping away the tears she picked up the receiver again and rang Lady Fitch in Norfolk.

'Kathryn my dear, what good news and Rani is he safe?' she asked, after coolly mentioning Sebastien.

'He is fine, fine, I'm so proud of them both,' Kathryn said, listening to Lady Fitch's relief that both men hadn't been hurt in rescuing Sebastien.

After placing down the receiver and hugging Roberta, she couldn't quite understand Lady Fitch's cool demeanour towards Sebastien. She knew him to be difficult and wayward at times but he was still Sebastien and he was dear to her. Maybe she thought there was something Lady Fitch wasn't telling her. Something she knew about Sebastien's character that she hadn't noticed.

Dismissing the dark thoughts, she went to fetch a warm coat and continue her Christmas day plans. There was shopping to do.

***

Sunday January 1941

Petra had volunteered as an air raid warden and one of her main duties was to enforce blackout regulations. Sometimes this would keep her out all night and today when she was returning home, she saw a figure of a man on the steps of Throgmorton Street. As she sat chatting to her friend Nadine in her new motor car which was parked across the street from the house, she wound down the window to take a closer look.

'That surely can't be Sebastien, can it?' she mumbled to Nadine, as this thin man in a light sports coat and crutches limped slowly up the stairs. But his hair was unmistakable. They knew it was him and he was home. Ernest and Roberta heard the doorbell and they looked at each other. They knew he was home. Meanwhile, Kathryn was upstairs fussing with her hair and trying to tame her curls at her vanity table. She was meeting Nora for an early breakfast and she was running late. She stopped abruptly when she heard the bell and put down her hairbrush. Peering over the mirror, she looked out onto the street. She could see him on the steps. She gave up on her hair and grabbed her coat and ran for the door. She bumped straight into Brenda who was red-eyed and tired.

'So sorry, Brenda,' she called out without stopping.

'Careful!' she called out to Kathryn, as she tripped slightly on the stair carpet and clung onto the banisters, as she took off down them to get to the door first before anyone else did. Pearl was still in her curlers and hung back by the kitchen doorway to watch.

"Sebastien!' Kathryn exclaimed, throwing her arms around him.

'Easy!' he said, his American accent still as strong as always.

Kathryn found she had kissed him on his cheek and for a minute forgot herself. Pearl raised an eyebrow then caught Sebastien's eye. He smiled and in returning his smile, she went into the kitchen to make a pot of tea and to unclip her hair. Kathryn linked arms with him and led him into the kitchen, followed by Ernest and Roberta. Porridge was jumping up at Sebastien and Kathryn was pushing him away from Sebastien's injured leg.

'We thought the worst Sebastien,' Kathryn said, excusing herself to telephone Nora and hopefully catch her before she left Harrods. She rang the reception and they passed the message to her that Kathryn would be a half hour late.

'I didn't think I was going to make it either,' he told her as she came back into the kitchen.

Kathryn went over to him and squeezed his hand. 'See you made it back home,' she said reassuringly.

'I remember seeing Ernest and Rani coming towards me and then I collapsed. I didn't remember anything else, except Ernest's voice. In my dreams he was telling me this story of a soldier from Abbeville that walked back home with his friend. They were returning from war. But when they got nearer to their destination, the soldier found he was disappearing into the mist and fog and his human form was fading as they made a turn in the road. He realised he wasn't alive but he had made it home, just to die on home soil.'

'Oh, don't Sebastien, you are giving me the shivers,' said Roberta, giving him a sisterly hug. Sebastien winked at her. 'Just a silly story, how is the baby then?' he asked her, mesmerised by how swollen her belly was.

'Babies!' exclaimed Roberta, now looking at Ernest proudly. 'I have a hero husband!'

Sebastien's face darkened as Kathryn passed him a cup of tea.

'Why was Rani with you Ernest? I never got an answer from you in the hospital.'

The room went quiet, and Sebastien put two and two together.

'Oh, I see... Dawn. He was feeling guilty, am I right? And where is my Lily, and that silly woman!' Sebastien said, not looking so happy and relaxed now.

'They are at Endelwise Manor,' Ernest said, uncomfortably.

'And Rani, I suppose he is with Dawn?'

Ernest didn't reply and Sebastien chewed on the inside of his lip. He looked worn, older to Kathryn, but maybe wiser she thought. Getting up to feed Porridge, turning her back on Sebastien for a moment, she felt a sudden surge of love for him. Not the usual friendly love that they had enjoyed. Their friendly banter and her telling him off for being irresponsible, but a different feeling. A passionate one and she couldn't look at him. She wondered where this emotion was coming from and pouring out some dog food for Porridge, she felt her face go red as she knew he was watching her.

'I'm off to get some sleep,' Petra announced, taking her tea and some biscuits up to bed.

'Let's finish our chess game Ernest,' Roberta said, sensing that Kathryn would like some time alone with Sebastien. She kissed him on his cheek in a sisterly manner and hugged him again. 'I'm so pleased you are home.'

'Thanks sis!' Sebastien said, in his usual jovial manner.

'And Kathryn, do I get kisses from you?' he said, in the flirtatious way he always joked with her. Roberta heard this and turned to look at them both at the door.

But this time Kathryn didn't laugh back or tell him off. She sat down again and tears fell down her cheek. Waiting to speak to him privately, she watched for Roberta to leave the room.

'I was so worried about you Sebastien, I was surprised at myself how worried I was. I didn't want to lose you.'

Sebastien swallowed some tea and put the teacup down noisily, almost as if he dismissed what Kathryn had said.

'Well, I'm here now, and by the way, when are we all going back to Dallington Place? I can't abide London like this. Not sticking around for the air raids,' he stated, as if he was bored with London already.

'A couple of weeks I hope. Your refectory is nearly finished,' she announced, proudly.

'Long were the days when it was Sebastien's!' he said, smiling.

'Yes, you are right, long were the days!' she answered, cheering up and sipping her now cold tea. 'What have I missed?' Petra beamed at the door.

Sebastien beamed broadly, 'Nothing for your ears,' he said cheekily.

Chapter Fourteen
Return to Dallington Place
February 1941

'Don't stand on ceremony Kathryn you are making me nervous!' said Petra, not caring if her overalls didn't make her look feminine.

Kathryn had done her hair and had changed into a pretty dress. One that made her waist look tiny. She wanted to look young and she knew why.

'Sebastien seems excited there's new young females arriving,' said Petra, hearing the news that he and Dawn were divorcing.

'Do you think so?' Kathryn said, slightly frowning. I think he would have more on his mind,' she said, busying herself putting a letter in an envelope.

'I do think you are rather in love with him Kathryn, it's obvious to everyone!' said Petra with a smile.

'Oh Petra, don't be so ridiculous, he's nearly twelve years younger than me and he's nothing but trouble. Besides, he's Sebastien, if you know what I mean,' dismissing Petra's comments as nonsense.

'Yes, but don't you love trouble?'

'No I do not, and please stop saying this, Sebastien will hear you,'

'Kathryn don't be dim, the man has been in love with you for years, it's so obvious.

'What?' Kathryn said, aghast at what she had just said.

Just then they heard a lorry park up in front of the house.

'See you are overdressed!' said Petra, laughing at the sight of six girls dressed in rather unflattering overalls. Some Italian Prisoners of War had stopped working on the repairs to a lorry and were watching the girls with interest. Kathryn checked her reflection in the new hall mirror and went out to greet them.

Shutting the door behind her, she saw Sebastien walking from the Nissen huts towards the house.

'Good morning girls,' Kathryn said, as she greeted each one as they jumped down from the open truck. They each introduced themselves, carrying their small bags.

May, Elizabeth, Corinne, Jacqueline, Judith and Constance were all wearing the same beige shirt, green pullover, jodhpurs, beret and tie.

'Come in and have some tea and I can show you your rooms,' Kathryn said, shaking their hands one by one, introducing herself.

They followed Kathryn down to the small kitchen where she introduced them to Ivy. They were quite subdued and Kathryn was surprised by how quiet they were. Corinne was the first to speak to her. 'This is the most beautiful house I think I have ever been in,' Kathryn just smiled, knowing how daunting the house was at first. Even without some of the palatial furniture it used to have.

'Well, we have had so much bomb damage but most of it is repaired by now,' she explained.

'A rare occurrence, I might add,' said Ivy, not wanting to frighten the girls.

'Have you lived here all your life?' Elizabeth asked, taking a teacup from Ivy.

'Nearly!' said Kathryn, nodding at Ivy who laughed.

'I came here when I was sixteen and stayed really.'

'But you own the house?' asked Jacqueline who was desperate to know how she came to own such a beautiful manor house. Constance nudged her in the ribs for being so forward.

'I'm sixteen,' said Corinne.

'Well, you must be feeling rather overwhelmed today. I remember my first day here like it was yesterday. I couldn't believe I was actually going to be living here when I arrived,' said Kathryn reassuringly.

'Did you marry young then?' asked Elizabeth again and everyone giggled.

'I will tell you my story another time,' Kathryn smiled, taking her to do list from the kitchen drawer.

'Kathryn always looks young,' said a familiar voice in the doorway. Sebastien was standing, hands on hips and in full flirtation mode. His grin was infectious and he winked at Ivy. The girls smiled back at this handsome stranger

'This is Sebastien Comte-Wright,' Kathryn said, with slight irritation.

The girls unisoned a "hello" at the same time and thought him very attractive. When he turned, his limp was noticeable and he disappeared again.

'Sebastien's been injured so he will be around helping me,' Kathryn explained.

'Is he American?' asked Constance as if his reputation preceded him.

'Well French actually, but he lived in America and you will meet Dawn too, she's from Texas.

'Texas, America?' asked Jacqueline.

'Yes and that's another story. Now I need all of you to listen as I have some errands to run this afternoon, so I need you to heed some warning as you are in a Prisoner of War camp and it's imperative for your safety to listen.

Then Kathryn saw one of the girls, May, crying at the back of the room.

'Oh no, nothing to be afraid of. It's fun here. But you must not talk to Italians alone. They are a friendly, social bunch mostly but, like you, they are away from home and we must keep you safe. Can I suggest you go everywhere in twos, so if you could pair up that would be helpful,' Kathryn continued.

Ivy put her arm around May.

'Well, you all know my name is Kathryn McAlister and I am lady of the house, so any problems you run them by me. You will all share a bedroom in the attic, they are all lovely,' she added.

'My cousin works in Scotland and she has to sleep in a hut,' explained Constance.

Kathryn smiled. She knew the girls were lucky to be sleeping in such a lovely home, but she was also aware of homesickness. She wanted them to be as happy as possible.

'This is Porridge, my dog,' Kathryn said, as Porridge trotted in. May bent down to stroke him.

'I think today you can just settle in, so no work and lunch of cold meats will be in the dining room at twelve.'

'There are also officers living at the house and my son Ernest and daughter-in-law Roberta. And of course my friend Petra. Sebastien is living in a cottage on the estate and Dawson too, who used to be my butler. He is living next to the refectory. You will all have met him earlier.

'Your butler?' asked Corinne wide eyed.

'Well, he is semi-retired but he lives here,'

'We don't have butlers where I come from,' said Judith.

'And where is that?' Kathryn asked, genuinely interested.

'Birmingham, most of us are, and Corinne's from Manchester.

Just then, Petra came in looking for a cup of tea. She waved at the girls and smiled. 'I'm Petra.'

'Oh yes, if anybody has any personal problems don't hesitate to ask Petra, she is very understanding. She looks after some evacuees in the village and is one of the local Arkalas.' Kathryn explained as they all stared at Petra with interest.

'Someone said there are horses here?' piped up Elizabeth.

'Well, we used to have them here before the war, but not now. If anyone wants to ride on their afternoon off you can book in at the local farm.'

'Or I can teach you,' said Sebastien, at the door again.

'Thank you, Sebastien and would you like a cup of tea?' Kathryn asked him, even more annoyed by him. She shot him an imperious look.

'Kathryn, I need to talk to you about some of the building work,' he said, walking over to her and placing his hand on her shoulder. It took her by surprise. Kathryn swung around to get him a tea cup and shoved it in his hand.

'Right girls, Petra will show you to your rooms and come down say in half an hour for lunch,' she said, now ignoring Sebastien for a moment.

The girls trooped off upstairs after Petra. Kathryn looked Sebastien sternly in the eye. Ivy was answering the telephone and it was just them in the kitchen.

'Do you have to be so familiar with me, in front of the girls? I swear you do it on purpose.'

'You look very pretty today; you always do when you wear a dress.'

Thank you Sebastien,' Kathryn said again, putting her list down and blushing, she had to admit she was flattered by his attentions.

'What's wrong with the building work today?' Kathryn asked, thinking he was making an excuse to talk to her.

'No, actually don't go mad but Officer Harding suggested we get rid of the willow tree to make way for another Nissen hut for supplies.'

'What? You have to be kidding me? Sebastien, under no illusion is that tree going to be touched,' she scolded him.

'I think Officer Harding thought the lumber girls were going to chop down all the trees,' he said.

'Ridiculous!' Kathryn almost spat, angry now. 'They are going to work on the outer wood where Tree Tops is, not the willow tree or the lawn. Have they all gone mad?'

'Let's go down to the officers. They are in the orangery having a meeting,' he suggested, sitting down for a minute, his leg making him wince.

Ivy walked in, waving a message and then noticed Kathryn's red face. 'Could you call Jorie please?' she asked before scuttling out knowing she had caught Kathryn in an angry moment with Sebastien.

'Yes, thank you, Ivy. The girls will be down in half an hour. Come on, Sebastien, let's sort this mess out,' Kathryn said, determined to sort out this debacle.

Sebastien got up and kissed Ivy on the cheek. She batted him off with a tea towel.

***

'Under the willow tree I see you
As if it was yesterday
You made my head spin.
I thought as if I had known you all my life
It took me by surprise'

They walked over to the willow tree and declared,' No one is touching this, do you hear?' Kathryn said, placing her hand on its old bark.

'Well, they could clip it back an inch or two, the branches, that's what was suggested,' he said, with a wink.

Kathryn took a large intake of breath. 'Sebastien you were teasing me, how could you?' Kathryn said, now realising he had been trying to goad her.

'Well, Kathryn, you have been avoiding me, and I miss you.'

'Sebastien, I haven't been avoiding you, I have just been busy!'

'Maybe you don't love me any more now I'm injured!' he said pouting.

'Don't be ridiculous, it's not like that between you and I and how is your leg?'

'Better thanks, and I will be able to chase you around once it's healed,' he said, now straightening it and pulling a face. 'Looks almost as good as new!'

Sebastien then grabbed some branches and showed what the tree would look like if they were cut by a few inches and thinned.

'So Kathryn, if you love me, could you love me, you know romantically?' he said, teasing her, hiding his face behind the foliage.

Kathryn went silent and stood still for a minute, wondering what to say to him.

'Sebastien, what are you trying to say?'

'I love you, Kathryn, I always have,' he said clearing his throat. 'With a passion!' he continued, with a glint in his eye.

'Sebastien stop it, you love everyone with a passion. You loved Dawn with a passion once,' said Kathryn, not taking him seriously at all.

'You are hurting me Kathryn. Every time I see you I can't take my eyes off you. It's always been like that. If Alexander Pillard hadn't come along when he did, I would have swooped off with you. Like a Hawk, and spirited you away.'

'And please don't bring Dawn into this. I don't love Dawn. I thought she was the most beautiful girl I had ever seen once but I think she is a terrible person, but you Kathryn are beautiful inside and out.'

'I think I'm flattered,' she said, laughing.

'You know you can't resist me,' he now said, teasing her again and making her giggle like a young girl.

'But Sebastien you are so much younger, really, stop this!'

'Well, I'm not going to give up.' And with that, he waltzed off back to the house and left Kathryn standing alone, feeling a little foolish amongst the willow tree branches.

She put her hand to her brow. All those years of knowing him and now he says he loves her romantically. She could see from the distance he had slammed the front door. She had hurt his pride. Not many women turn down Sebastien Comte-Wright, she was well aware of this.

In bed that night, her head was spinning. Had she really not been aware of his love for her? She had noted his flirtatious behaviour towards her when he first came to Dallington Place. She reminisced with a smile. She had had to warn him that she was not alone. Pulling the eiderdown over her and snuggling down, she remembered he had said, 'I would never imagine a woman like you, Kathryn, would ever be alone.'

When he had jumped to fasten a necklace around her neck at the Christmas Party and when he brushed past her, there was always an electricity. When they journeyed together in the train to London to meet Alexander Pillard and their trips in the motor car to Dallington Village, when he always wanted to talk to her alone. She always enjoyed his company. Smiling again, she had thought of the time he had picked her up excitedly in his arms at the races when her horse had been triumphant.

She was aware she often took his side and was protective of him when others were not. Perhaps it was because she had seen him as a small boy in Mesves-sur-Loire. Coinciding with a pivotal moment in her life, when Bertram had let her down and it was the end for her and Bertram as a couple. That moment on the path, the boy bouncing his ball along had caught her eye and then she had seen them, her Bertram with another women. She didn't want to think about that. It was history.

Now closing her eyes, she had to admit she felt terrible jealousy when Sebastien flirted with other women but she wondered did their differences make them worlds apart? Could she possibly think of herself in a couple with him? He was a lot younger after all. And what would Dawn say? Would people think them silly? The questions were endless and she couldn't sleep. She got out of bed and tip-toed to the window. There was a light dusting of snow on the lawn and the trees. It was a serene and beautiful sight. She looked over to the Nissen huts. Lights were out and it was calm outside. She felt like a walk to clear her mind, so she dressed, putting on her warmest pullover and some fleece lined boots.

After tying her hair back, which she had grown out from its marcel wave, she opened the door and went downstairs. Looking upwards on the stairs to the attic, she wondered if the girls were sleeping well and hoped they were warm enough. Perhaps she should have given them all an extra blanket, she thought.

She was just about to open the front door, when she noticed a letter on the side table by the study door. It was addressed to her and it was Dawn's handwriting. Kathryn, was surprised she had omitted to see it. Petra must have left it there for her. Taking it with her, she left the house shutting the front door quietly. She walked across the lawn, passed the willow tree and down by the Nissen huts. She wanted to look at The Tree Tops building to see how it was progressing, without the prying eyes of the men. The grass crunched under her boots as she made her way behind the orangery.

She thought she heard footsteps and stopped for a moment. There were some starlings beginning to go about their morning routine and she brushed the footstep noise off as the little bird's dawn chorus. The building was half completed. The timber was in place, and Kathryn imagined what it would look like finished. There was going to be a dormitory on the first floor that slept about twenty men, and a further two floors and an attic, which would sleep the rest. Windows were kept to a minimum due to building regulations. She walked around the back of it where a pool house would be built next. Then she saw him. A shadow near the trees at the side of 'Tree Tops.' Someone was watching her and smoking. She could smell the tobacco. It was Sebastien's French tobacco.

'Hello, you,' he called out to her.

'Sebastien, what are you doing here? Why are you not at Willow Tree Cottage?' she asked, flustered.

'I didn't go home last night. I fell asleep in the orangery after work and woke at midnight. It was quiet out so I thought I would just stay and go back to sleep.'

'In the wicker chair?'

He nodded.

'I didn't lock it. I was so busy I forgot,' she admitted, realising her mistake could have been foolhardy as any one of those prisoners could have barricaded themselves into the orangery.

Sebastien approached her, stubbing out the cigarette. Taking her hand he noticed the letter with Dawn's handwriting.

'What is that?' he asked abruptly.

'I don't know, Sebastien,' she said, rather abrasively, 'I haven't had the time to read it.'

'He raised his eyebrows as if to ask her to open it.'

'Come on let's go and sit in the orangery,' she said, realising she didn't have anything to hide from him. She may as well open it there and then.

'I have some brandy with me, I left my glass there. I will pour you a glass, I will take the bottle!' he said, smirking.

'Sebastien, it's three o'clock in the morning,'

'Kathryn, live a little, will you?' he said, putting a protective arm around her shoulder. They settled into the chairs and Sebastien poured her a small glass. He took a large swig from the bottle.

'You are not all right, are you?' she looked concerned at his pale face.

'I received a solicitor's letter yesterday, and she wants me to move away from Dallington Place. What with the divorce and everything it's beginning to get to me,' he explained, leaning back and resting his hands on the back of his neck.

'That's a little harsh!' Kathryn agreed.

'I want to see Lily. I have every right to see her when I want'.

'Yes, you do, and it's not like you are living at Dallington Place, you are at Willow Tree Cottage,' Kathryn stated.

Then she realised why he had slept in the orangery. She knew him. To him it was an act of rebellion.

Opening the letter, she quietly read it to herself first as Sebastien eyed her and waited patiently for her to tell him what was in it.

Sighing, she passed the letter over to him. She's gone to India with Rani for a while and she wants me to look after Lily. She's being sent for tomorrow. Her nanny is bringing her back from Norfolk.'

'I thought Dawn was going to London for a few days. She must have been planning this for a while,' he said, angrily.

'Well I have no fight with Rani. Ernest and he saved my life in France but I could sue her for a divorce,' he said bitterly, taking another swig from the bottle.

'Sebastien, then you will implicate Rani and well you are not without sin. I know you. You have to play fair,' Kathryn stated firmly.

'I will help you to be able to stay on here and work and live at Willow Tree Cottage but you must promise me not to get embroiled in a large fight. You must think of Lily and your future. We don't want scandal here. Get your divorce and move on with your life Sebastien. Take it from me, life goes fast and I for one like to keep moving on and not get bogged down with bitterness.'

Sebastien grabbed Kathryn's hand, and pulled her onto his lap. She could smell the brandy on him. It was intoxicating. He flicked his hair out of his eyes and looked longingly at her.

'Thank you, Kathryn, for being understanding,' and he buried his head into her shoulder. Looking up from his dark eyes and lashes, he looked adoringly at her face.

'Kiss me, Kathryn, I so want to kiss you,' he said, as she bent her head down and did as he asked.

Chapter Fifteen
Return from Guwahati

June 1941 Guwahati India

Dear Kathryn,

Rani and I are returning home on the 12th of June. We were married in Guwahati on his father's Estate and we honeymooned in Assam at the end of May.
I can't wait to come home to Dallington Place and see Lily.
Thank you for taking good care of her.
See you soon,

Much Love,

Dawn Singh-Hithop

Kathryn took in the good news that Dawn was returning. Lily had missed her mother and it had been too long. Kathryn, on the other hand, was taking in some news of her own. And rather shocked by it, as the news was a pleasant surprise. She sat in Doctor Laraby's surgery on the other side of Dallington Village.

Doctor Laraby had moved out recently into new buildings on the other side of the village and newly decorated, the paint was making her feel nauseous.

'You are quite happy with the news?' the doctor asked.

'Well I am surprised, with my age of forty-one and the fact I have never fallen pregnant before,' she said, suddenly feeling vulnerable.

'Some things are unexplained but you are a fit and active lady, there is no reason why the pregnancy shouldn't progress well,' Dr Laraby said, in a reassuring tone.

'And the gentleman, will he be equally pleased?' the doctor asked, without prying as to who the father was.

Sebastien and Kathryn had thought it best to keep their relationship to themselves for the last few months but now that was going to be impossible.

Kathryn nodded happily.

'Yes, the father is Sebastien Comte-Wright, we are engaged,' she said. Thinking she may as well expose them as a couple now.

Dr Laraby, didn't even raise an eyebrow. Kathryn was relieved. She felt rather embarrassed as it was.

'My dear, I must congratulate you, but you must rest in the afternoons. Plenty of tea, fresh air and rest,' the Doctor said, showing her to the door.

***

Kathryn and Geraldine sat in the sitting room. It was too hot to sit in the orangery. Kathryn patted her stomach.

'I'm going to shock Dawn when she returns,' Kathryn said, a little concerned.

'Oh I don't think much shocks Dawn, I wouldn't worry,'

'If Sebastien and I marry, we will all have the same surname. All three of us. What an alliance,' said Kathryn, thinking how strange this was.

'Did you know he was in love with me, Geraldine?'

'Yes, he was always at your side like a puppy. You know you told me the time when he had plucked that feather out of your hair and you felt he was going to kiss you years ago, I knew then. And of course when he rushed to do up your necklace at your Christmas party. He couldn't have got across the room any faster!'

'He's always been rather fast on his feet hasn't he?' laughed Kathryn.

'You know I am happy and I like the fact he shares an interest in Dallington Place. Always fun and thinking of ways to help me with it all.

'You look happy Kathryn, I'm pleased for you, really I am.'

'He is very attentive and never leaves my side, well apart from today.'

'Where is he?' Geraldine asked, picking up her handbag.

'He's gone to the builder's merchants with Mr Montgomery, he will be back soon.'

'How's Roberta today?' Kathryn asked.

'She is going to have the babies any moment, I should wonder,' said Geraldine, hoping to see her daughter before she had to leave.

'She and Ernest went for lunch. You know I'm so pleased they are here full time now. I worried for them in London,' Kathryn stated, seeing Colonel Shaddock wave at them through the open window.

'Thank goodness, I want to be near her when the babies come,' said Geraldine, standing up and looking to the window, sighing at the sight of all the uniforms.

'It's an unusual place to bring a baby into the world, with all this rabble here,' she said, sitting down and pouring herself another cup of tea. 'Dr Laraby thinks it will be only another couple of days until the babies arrive,' Geraldine said, happy she was going to be a grandmother.

'It seems funny that I will be having my baby only some months later!' Kathryn said, placing her hands on her stomach.

'Kathryn you will be a grandmother and a mother in the space of a year,' Geraldine said, laughing. Kathryn put down her cup and saucer, laughing too.

Holding her stomach, she laughed until it hurt with tears rolling down her face. Sebastien burst into the room wondering what the noise was. His face lit up when he saw Kathryn. Going over to her, he kissed her on her now very wet cheek.

'Can I join in?' he asked, sitting down next to her and holding her hand.

'Sebastien, we are laughing at the thought of all these babies in the house, and I'm just so happy Dallington Place is feeling like a home again,' she said, kissing him back.

'Talking of home, I'm going to collect my suitcases with Dawson this afternoon from Willow Tree Cottage,' he said, getting up again.

Geraldine gave Kathryn a look which she dismissed.

'Yes Sebastien, I have made room in my wardrobe for you, everything's ready.'

Sebastien kissed her on top of her head, and said goodbye to Geraldine.

'Do you know where Dawson is?' he asked, as he opened the door.

'Last seen pottering about by the orangery, he was arranging some plant pots,' said Kathryn, now getting up to look through the window, concerned where Ernest and Roberta had got to.

Sebastien blew Kathryn a kiss and went to find Dawson.

'Are you happy for him to be living here Kathryn? Do you know where Dawn is going to live with Rani?' asked Geraldine, looking puzzled.

'I rather thought they would be living at Endelwise Manor, but yes,

Sebastien won't like the fact that Lily will be living away from him,' Kathryn said, musing that Sebastien may have to travel back and forth to Norfolk.

'Kathryn, I think you are underestimating Dawn. I have a feeling she will want to stay put at Dallington Place,' said Geraldine, concerned that Kathryn had overlooked that Dawn could be difficult and stubborn. 'And she has a right with her claim on her cottage, the refectory now.'

'Really? I supposed I hadn't thought it through properly, this pregnancy has consumed my thoughts,' Kathryn said, now feeling worried.

Just then they heard a motor car and Kathryn presumed it was Ernest and Roberta and sat down again.

'I'm feeling tired again. I think this pregnancy is going to be a long one!' Kathryn laughed, lying down, kicking her shoes off and placing her feet on a cushion.

'I will go and answer the door,' said Geraldine, aware that Dawson was out with Sebastien.

'Ivy will go, you stay here with me, they will be in in a minute,' Kathryn told her, stifling a yawn. Geraldine slumped on the sofa and picked up a magazine.

'You are going to have to buy some maternity clothes soon, you know,' she said, flicking through some fashion pages.

Ivy knocked on the door and peeked in.

'Kathryn two things, the girls were wanting to know where they could go horse riding? Can I send all of them to the farm? Or will Milly be overwhelmed? And by the way, Dawn is back. She and Rani are out by their motor car.'

'What?' said Kathryn. 'Already? I thought I heard Ernest and Roberta.'

'They are back too, just seen them out front talking to Dawn and Rani,' said Ivy, waiting for a reply from Kathryn about the Lumber Jills.

Kathryn sat bolt upright and felt immediately overwhelmed.

'Tell the girls to all go to the farm, I need an afternoon off, Ivy. I can't think what else to do with them. Where's Petra? Do you know?'

'Petra's out with Jorie doing some campaigning in Brighton,' replied Ivy.

'Oh, yes, I forgot, she's campaigning for Giles to be put forward for MP there, Geraldine,' Kathryn said.

Geraldine looked impressed for a minute, then stood up to go to the door, seeing as Kathryn look agitated.

'Oh, by the way, Kathryn, Sebastien has just pulled up too. Do you want me to do something?' Ivy said, now disappearing for a minute as she went to open the front door.

'I will handle this Kathryn, don't you worry, hold on a minute,' said Geraldine, aware that Kathryn shouldn't be stressed.

Dawn opened the door and waltzed in with her hands on her hips.

'Kathryn don't tell me Sebastien's moving back in?' Dawn said, demanding an answer and her brow pinching, just masking her beauty for a second. Pursing her lips, she waited for an answer from Kathryn.

Kathryn stood up and then immediately sat down again. She felt light headed. Closing her eyes and then fixing them sternly on Dawn, who was looking impossibly glamorous in a white silk blouse and cream skirt and dripping in jewels up to her ears.

'First of all, Dawn, it's lovely to see you looking so well and secondly, no one is doing anything, without my permission. Now I am not feeling so well, so if you would please leave your discussions for later I would much appreciate it. I am going for a nap!' Kathryn declared.

'Fine homecoming this is,' Dawn said, storming off to find a drink.

'Come along Rani we are going out!' Kathryn could hear her say through the open door.

'Ernest,' Kathryn said, as she saw her son standing looking at her from the hallway.

'Can you help me up to bed, I'm feeling rather fragile, and where's Sebastien?'

'He has gone upstairs,' said Ernest, rather puzzled, as to what was going on.

Geraldine had her arm around her daughter.

'Kathryn, I think Roberta's in labour,' Geraldine said, catching Ernest's arm.

'What?' said Ivy now coming in through the front door with some luggage of Dawn's. 'I will telephone Doctor Laraby!' she said, rushing to the study.

***

'Simon and Rachel,' Ernest said, sipping his tea in the kitchen and chatting to Ivy.

Ivy nodded. 'Fine name those!' she said, waving at Dawson who was coming down the old backstairs adjoined to the kitchen, which used to be the servants' stairs. She could see him through the window as he tentatively took one stair, carefully, at a time. She wondered what he had been doing but presumed he had been cleaning the gutters. She shook her head. He shouldn't be doing that at his age she thought.

'Be careful,' Ivy shouted out through the open window. The man was now perspiring in the heat. He beamed a large smile at her, clearly excited by the news of the babies.

'Why is he coming down the back stairs?' Ernest said, with a smile on his face. The man looked so comical. He knew Dawson so well, and as soon as there was something exciting going on, the old man would suddenly get rather spritely and have a gleam on his face. But then he realised there was something more serious going on. 'Good grief,' said Ernest, knocking some of his tea into its saucer as he jumped up immediately to let Dawson in.

'Sorry to trouble you Ernest but can you come to the front door. I'm afraid Mr Sebastien and Miss Dawn are fighting something terrible,' explained the old man, looking strained.

'Good grief,' said Ernest, jumping up immediately.

Ernest rushed up the stairs to the hallway. He could see Dawn and Sebastien through the large bay window and he could hear Sebastien shouting for Dawson to let him open the front door which she was blocking

Ignoring Sebastien, Ernest ordered her to open the front door. Once in, Sebastien pushed past Ernest and approached the staircase, just as Kathryn appeared on the landing.

'Will you all be quiet!' her voice boomed down the stairs. For a small woman when she got angry, which was rare, she really could stop a train in its tracks!

Walking down the stairs towards Sebastien, she glared at him. He walked past her, up to their bedroom and slammed the door.

'Dawn, how dare you disturb the peace in my house!' she said, glaring at her.

'I am pregnant, I need my peace. Do you understand?'

For a second, Dawn thought Kathryn was joking, and then a thunderous expression took over her face.

'No!' she said, realising that Kathryn was in a relationship with

Sebastien.

Rani was sitting in the study and came out when he heard Kathryn's voice. He had never heard her raise her voice like this, before.

'This is my home and I want you to respect it and my decisions,' she said, glaring at Dawn. 'If you are to live here and I mean if, you are to get on with Sebastien. Dawn do you understand?' Kathryn said, now looking to Rani for support and understanding.

'Of course, Kathryn,' Rani said, respectfully, lowering his eyes at the embarrassment his wife had caused.

'Dawn, apologise to Kathryn, please,' Rani said, taking his wife's hand and pulling her towards Kathryn.

Dawn's expression changed and softened.

'You didn't say Kathryn, I didn't know,' said Dawn, now coming to terms with the news. Then her expression changed again and she smiled.

'You are brave Kathryn, I will give you that,' she said, picking up her own suitcase that was left by the front door and taking it upstairs herself.

Ernest smiled at his mother.

'That will keep Dawn quiet for a while,' he said, giving her a hug.

There was another knock at the door and Dawson came across the hall to answer it.

'Dawson, I don't wish to be disturbed. I will be in the sitting room,' Kathryn said, feeling worn out but relieved her news was out to everybody now, or it would be soon.

'Very good, ma'am' he said, answering the door to Colonel Shaddock who had heard the rumpus from the lawn and had come to investigate.

'Ma'am, it's Mrs Blomberg on the telephone for you,' Dawson said, taking over duties for this afternoon as it was Ivy's day off.

Kathryn got to her feet slowly. Smiling at Ernest she said, 'It's now or never, wish me luck.' And went into the study to let Jorie know the news was actually true. Now all of Sussex would know of her pregnancy!

Chapter Sixteen
The Honeymoon

3rd January 1942

'Do you like the tea?' Dawn asked Kathryn at the breakfast table. Kathryn put down her newspaper. She felt the baby kick again and she put her hand on her belly.

Bataan Completely Occupied by Japanese, the headline read splashed across the front pages of the Morning Herald.

'Sorry Dawn, what did you say, I was reading about the Philippines?' Kathryn said, engrossed in the news.

'I said, do you like the tea? Rani and I are thinking of importing it.'

'Really? That sounds interesting,' she replied, taking off her reading glasses and helping herself to the new loaf of bread that Ivy had freshly baked this morning. There was a knock at the door and a couple of the Lumber Jills came in.

'Kathryn, I can't find Sebastien. We were supposed to go with him and Officer Harding to start chopping down some of the trees near where the memorial will be placed,' said Lucy, one of the newest recruits who arrived last week.

'We have to hurry, as the monument is arriving back here tomorrow,' interrupted Elizabeth.

'If I knew where he was, I would tell you!' Kathryn said, knowing how Sebastien liked to rise early and go out for long walks. He loved the South Downs and they reminded him of the Champagne region of France, where the same type of chalky rock runs through the chalky hills of Sussex. Ivy had just come in and was placing some more scrambled eggs on a side dish when she spoke up.

'He said he was going to have a meeting at the Heatherley's this morning. I met him on the driveway an hour ago,' she said, pouring herself a cup of hot chocolate.

'Oh yes, you are right, I forgot!' said Kathryn, now rubbing her baby bump.

"I'm so forgetful with this pregnancy!' she said, smiling at Elizabeth.

'I have been married one month and I lose my husband all over the place!'

The girls started to laugh.

'Well, I suggest you have some breakfast whilst you wait for him,' Kathryn said, knowing her husband could be a little unreliable these days.

Since marrying at Christmas and all the excitement of the wedding Kathryn was worried that Sebastien had lost interest in the work that needed doing here at Dallington Place. He seemed distracted with one of his business ideas.

'May I have another cup of tea, Ivy? I do love this Assam tea,' Kathryn said, getting up for another napkin and smiling at Rani.

'Let me wait on you, Kathryn,' said Ivy, happily knowing the baby could arrive any minute. 'Please sit!' she ordered, passing her some buttered toast.

'So Rani, how would you go about importing the tea, how would it work?' Kathryn asked him enthusiastically.

'We thought perhaps once the war was over, that we could have a tea house here?

We could use the factories in India to supply just to us, a special combination that Dawn and I will create especially for Dallington Place and we can sell it here,' he explained.

'That sounds a romantic story but would it, could it really work as a business, I mean?' said Kathryn, loving the notion but could it be a viable business she mused.

'Well, tea is keeping us going through this war!' Rani said, proudly, leaning back in his chair and relaxing for a moment.

'Just think, Britain has bought up almost all the world's supply of tea and it's more popular than ever,' Dawn chipped in.

'I know, quite incredible really,' said Kathryn, interested in what they had to say.

'Dawn and I are thinking of travelling back to Assam for six months to begin the process, if you agree to it,' Rani explained, quietly.

'Six months. Really? That's a long time. But, as you say, it will be your business, you need to put the work in but maybe I can have a share of the profits once things get going?' Kathryn asked, knowing they could all do well financially from this. Kathryn reached for another piece of toast and thought about the idea as Ivy went to make them some more tea.

'If it's to be here, at Tree Top House, yes of course, it makes sense,' Kathryn said turning to Rani who had got up to adjust the radiator, as the room was cold. Kathryn knew that was going to be part of the deal, they would use her rooms, but why not, she thought.

Rani nodded.

'Kathryn, it is ideal, what with my father's estate and your estate here. It would be such a wonderful alliance,' he stated.

'I totally agree, Rani, if that is what you would like to do. We all need to find new ways of working throughout this war and after, if I may say,' Kathryn said feeling rather full. Ivy was worried she may just fade away or something!

'We will have to be patient because of the war, but, after, everything can be put into motion. This is the time to lay foundations,' he said.

Kathryn couldn't agree more.

'It certainly is, Rani, it certainly is the time to build foundations. As you can see the monument has been lain. New beginnings here, and we should toast to this literally,' she said, laughing at Ivy who was bringing even more toast and jam up from the kitchen with the tea.

'Well, when were you thinking of going back?' Kathryn asked them nonchalantly.

'Next week,' Dawn said firmly.

Rani nodded uncomfortably.

'Already? I really need your help here you know, what with the unveiling of the monument next week, I could have done with your support here,' Kathryn said, sighing and looking a little annoyed with Dawn. 'And what of Lily, will she go with you?'

Rani shook his head. 'I'm sorry it's such short notice but, you see, my father needs my help in the factories at present as I am off sick from the army so I offered. I am his only son and it is an opportunity as well for progressing this tea business and getting it off the ground,' he said feeling a little guilty, as he knew Kathryn could use his help and to leave Lily would be a difficult choice for Dawn.

Kathryn sighed again but they had clearly made up their minds. 'Well, I will miss you both, and for goodness' sake, hurry back,' Kathryn said getting up to hug them both.

'We need to celebrate but I cannot drink, perhaps, Rani, you would like something stronger?' Kathryn asked, mindful of his religion.

He shook his head.

'We will be back as soon as we can, won't we Rani,' Dawn said, hugging her husband then Kathryn.

Kathryn wanted them to be happy. It wasn't up to her to keep them here at Dallington Place, but she hoped they would come back for Lily's sake. She never really knew with Dawn. Getting up to peer at the clock on the mantelpiece, she beckoned to Ivy to clear the table.

'On that note, I really must find out what's happened to my husband,' Kathryn said, needing some air.

She decided she would walk to the bridge. She couldn't go far on her own, especially now, as the baby was due any minute and as she walked past the army trucks, she saw Officer Harding walking swiftly over to her from the lawn.

'Is Sebastien with you? We want to work on the ground where the memorial will be placed and he should have been here an hour ago,' Officer Harding asked.

'Yes, Officer Harding, I am aware of this, the land girls are waiting. Maybe, you could round them up and make use of the time until I find out where he is.'

'Right you are, ma'am. I'm sure he is on his way back soon,' agreed Officer Harding now walking briskly on.

The day was colder than yesterday and the willow tree's branches moved eerily in the wind, as Kathryn approached the bridge. She held on to its frame as she stepped onto its wooden foundations. She looked in the distance to see if there was anybody coming up the driveway. It was quiet today and she couldn't hear the Prisoner of War from here, or actually see anyone milling about on the lawn. They must all be working in the woods she thought.

She could feel the baby kicking and she put her face up to sun, that was now emerging from the morning's clouds. Her hair whipped around her face and then she felt someone behind her and she jumped. It was almost as if someone had put a hand on her shoulder, which made her swing around. But no one was there. She shrugged it off and thought perhaps the wind was stronger than she had first realised and she wanted to get off the bridge. The river was flowing fast today and although the bridge had been reinforced to allow the army vehicles to drive over it safely, she didn't feel safe. Finding her footing over the slanted, wooden panels, she walked slowly over it to the other side and as she steadied herself with the wooden railings, she looked up and she could see a motor car approaching from the distance to the left of the Matthews' farm.

A man and a woman were waving, and she could see it was Sebastien and he was with a young woman. They stopped just short of the bridge.

'Hello,' cried out Sebastien, 'I got caught up. Do you remember Karen, Mrs Jerobaum's daughter? I stopped off to buy some cakes for you, we got talking and she told me the story of you working at the Munitions factory. I didn't see the time.'

Kathryn stifled her anger. She didn't want to appear annoyed in front of Mrs Jerobaum's daughter.

'Hello, yes of course, I remember, how is your mother?' Kathryn called back.

'Very well thank you, and I took Sebastien's invitation to come up to the big house as I'm a seamstress now and Sebastien thought perhaps I could help you with a new wardrobe after the baby comes.'

'Really?' said Kathryn, rather surprised.

'Sebastien said...' she continued, uncomfortably as she was not sure if Kathryn had heard her, because of the wind in the trees.

'Well, it's lovely to meet you again,' Kathryn called back, holding her hair away from her face as the wind whipped it in all sort of directions.

Kathryn expected Karen to get out of the motor car and walk with her back to the house. But Karen stayed sitting and Sebastien called out, 'See you at the house!' before driving off over the bridge and leaving Kathryn just standing alone with one of her feet on the bridge and another on terra firma, leaning against the railing.

Shocked, Kathryn wondered if she had just imagined his rudeness, to leave his pregnant wife without a lift back to the house? Almost shunning her. She felt the baby kick again and she put her hand on her stomach. Then she saw Doctor Laraby's motor car in the distance. She knew it was him. He was the only person in the village who would have swapped his lovely new motor car for an older looking model. Its chipped blue paint and a bumper that looked as if it was about to fall off. Relieved to see him, she summoned up a smile as he approached the bridge.

'Morning! Doctor Laraby,' she said, feeling foolish standing alone on the bridge.

'Morning. I thought I would stop by and see how you are. Geraldine telephoned me last night and said she didn't like the way you were looking.'

'She did?' Kathryn said, now biting the inside of her lip with annoyance.

'Jump in and I will test the baby's heartbeat. Can't have you roaming about on your own out here, I think the weather's turning,' he said, in his comforting manner.

Smiling at his thoughtfulness she got in and they drove slowly up the driveway.

Sebastian was taking shopping bags out of the car when Kathryn and Doctor Laraby pulled up beside them. Sebastien shot Kathryn a sheepish look and she ignored him.

'I'm going to have a check-up with Doctor Laraby, Sebastien. The Lumber Jills are waiting for you to start work,' she said, a little too sarcastically.

'Are you all right, Kathryn?' Karen asked her, now looking embarrassed knowing she had intruded at an inconvenient time.

'I'm very well thank you, just heavily pregnant and perhaps we can have a meeting another time about my wardrobe? I would like that very much.'

Karen smiled back shyly and looked to Sebastien for a lift back to the village. He just raised his eyebrows and mentioned something about Doctor Laraby will be returning into the village in a while, implying she could wait for a lift if she wanted.

'Oh, Sebastien,' Kathryn called back. 'Could you let Ivy know, Ernest and Roberta and the twins, will be arriving back for supper from London. And could you please pick them up? They are arriving on the six thirty train from Victoria,' she knew this would get his back up. If he wasn't going to take his own wife back home, he could jolly well pick up his half-brother!

Later in the afternoon, Kathryn was in the sitting room going through some government correspondence when she saw Sebastien sitting, resting with a drink in hand on Bertram's bench. He sat with two of the land girls.

The other land girls and some of the Lumber Jills were working at the Matthews' farm this afternoon. They were helping with the horses and Kathryn thought it a good idea to mix up their duties so they didn't fraternise with the Prisoners of War too much, so that they didn't get too bored and tired from their forestry work.

A couple of girls who had decided to stay behind today to clean out the old stables, were on a break sitting on the bench and chatting to Sebastien who was speaking to them animatedly and dragging on his cigarette. She wondered what they were talking about, as they all laughed together. She watched him push his hair out of his eyes with his free hand and then take a jockey's pose and pretend to gallop around the bench. She smiled. He looked like the old, happy Sebastien today, not the irritable one that ignored her this morning.

She grabbed her coat and walked out to them.

'Hello, I thought I would come and join you,' she said feeling a little nervous.

The girls offered her the bench and then thinking it best to leave the couple alone, made their excuses to get back to work. Kathryn snuggled into Sebastien as he sat down and put his arm around her. Stamping on his cigarette, careful not to smoke around her and the baby.

He kissed her cheek. He smelt of musk and cigarettes and she moved in closer to inhale his smell and she felt comforted at long last.

'I've missed you today, he said, breathing in her scent too as he snuggled back and buried his head in her neck.

'I have missed you too,' she said, a little tearfully.

'Dr Laraby thinks the baby is on the way, next couple of days probably!' she told him.

'Good. It feels like forever!' said Kathryn in a jolly manner, realising her temper may have been rather too short with him lately.

'By the way, how did your meeting go with the Heatherleys?'

'Short and sweet. They want to sell the hotel to me, what do you think?'

'How much would we need to raise, if that is the case?' Kathryn asked him carefully, knowing Sebastien's frustrations were enormous, not having Sebastien's restaurant any more.

'If I can get the bank to lend me ten thousand pounds and you and I stump up another, it could be ours.'

Kathryn balked for a minute. 'Sebastien, I don't have much left now, maybe three thousand, you will need to raise the rest. Luckily the roof was funded by the government, at least they are doing the repairs here now. And I want it in both our names as I'm giving you the last of my savings!' she said touching his arm for reassurance. She hoped she was making the right decision here.

'Let's see what we can offer them then, they may come down in price!' he said, kissing the back of her hand. 'Let's hope,' he smiled confidently

Her Sebastien, always an optimist, Kathryn thought, as he got up to telephone the agent with their offer.

After a few minutes Kathryn saw Ivy at the door waving for her to come in. She went to see what she wanted. It was going to rain any minute anyway so she ran quickly into the house.

'Geraldine was on the telephone; she is coming in for tea. I said that would be fine as I didn't want to disturb you, you looked lost in conversation with Sebastien.'

'Thank you Ivy, yes we had some things to discuss, very observant of you.' Kathryn smiled, knowing Ivy had wisely picked up on Sebastien's moods too lately. I'm looking forward to seeing Geraldine and she can help me make some baby plans, you never know, baby could arrive tomorrow!' she said, thinking she needed to make lists.

Can you bring the tea out to the orangery for us? It's cooler in there now, and perhaps we could have a couple of blankets? Oh, and by the way, we have the cakes that Sebastien brought in. Geraldine loves Mrs Jerobaum's tea cakes.'

'Which cakes?' Ivy asked, confused as she didn't remember Sebastien putting any cakes in the larder. She narrowed her brow. Perhaps Sebastien had left them on the hall table and the officers had eaten them. 'You know, I haven't done a major shop recently. I thought I would wait until I knew which day the rest of the prisoners were returning this week,' Ivy explained, getting her notepad out from the drawer and hoping she hadn't made a mistake with the cakes.

'Didn't Sebastien put any cakes in the larder?' Kathryn asked Ivy, now concerned as the baby kicked furiously. She felt sick for a moment.

'No, I just saw he had some shirts that he had brought from Scarsdales, that's all that was in his shopping bags,' she retorted, looking for a pen. 'Mind you, he could have left them in the hallway. Those officers have such an appetite. Perhaps they took them thinking they were for them.'

'Perhaps,' said Kathryn, knowing this was unlikely.

Kathryn felt confused. Why did he go and visit the Jerobaums café then? Her heart was beating fast. She hoped she was wrong but felt, maybe, their honeymoon was over.

***

'Did you have a nap?' asked Geraldine, looking happy to see her friend. 'You look rested,' she said bustling past her and taking off her far too warm coat.

'I have to say, I have been exhausted,' Kathryn explained. 'Doctor Laraby thinks the baby should be here by the weekend.' Kathryn explained.

'You may need your coat actually, Ivy is going to bring our tea out to us in the orangery, Kathryn told her wisely.

'Is Sebastien looking after you?' Geraldine asked, taking her coat from the hallway stand, worrying for her friend that looked so hugely pregnant and vulnerable.

The ladies walked down to the orangery as Kathryn pointed out different sections of the land and what they were going to do with some of the trees and the plants. They nodded at various men that passed them and they hurried past lost in conversation, not waiting to engage in unnecessary chit chat with anyone today.

As they settled down in the blankets and cushions that Ivy had kindly arranged for them, Kathryn poured the tea, her back now aching and finding it hard to get comfortable.

'I think he is back to his flirting best, put it like that,' Kathryn said, looking down to her lap and straightening out her napkin nervously.

'No! already? And with whom?' Geraldine asked, looking unusually imperious.

'Oh, I don't know, just a girl from the village. Mrs Jerobaum's daughter actually.'

'Well, of all the nerve, you know what, I will go down there myself and put it straight, you can't have that going on and with you in your state,' Geraldine said, disgusted, and putting down the tea cake.

'Better still, we will have Petra go and put her ten cents worth in down at the tea shop.'

'Just nip it in the bud, Kathryn, as soon as possible, before anything serious happens,' Geraldine stated, sensibly.

Taking a long sip of tea, she then looked up at Kathryn's pale face. 'Do you think they are having an affair?' Geraldine wondered seeing as Kathryn seemed uncharacteristically resigned to the outcome.

'No, I don't but he seems distracted and short tempered with me and over friendly with her,' Kathryn said biting the tea cake with ferocity. 'We know Sebastien, give him an inch and he takes a mile.' Geraldine nodded in agreement to Sebastien's frailties.

'Well, once the baby comes, he won't have time for tea cakes and flirting, let's tire him out!' Geraldine said with a great triumphant smile.

Kathryn stifled a smile, her friend was such good medicine, but she wasn't in the mood for jokes. She felt terrible.

With a wave of her hand, Geraldine declared that Kathryn must be kept as stress free as possible. 'I will ask Petra to come and stay for a few days with you. She is the lady to deal with this.'

'I have to call her tonight anyway. I want to talk to her about Throgmorton Street before I'm preoccupied with the baby. Apparently there has been a lot of drama going on there with the Smithfields. Roberta told me yesterday, that Mr Smithfield has move out as Pearl discovered he was married. His wife was knocking. at the door one day last week and caused quite a fuss. Pearl threw him out straight away. Poor Brenda had no idea he was married,' Kathryn explained, glad to have a different conversation other than the one about Sebastien.

Did Petra not tell you this last week?' Geraldine, asked, concerned her friend was being worried with too much of these dramatics.

'No, you know she doesn't like to worry me but I telephoned the next day and the police were there.'

'Really? But I'm not surprised, he was a bit of a shifty character,' Geraldine said, never taking to the man when she had met him once or twice.

Kathryn closed her eyes for a second. 'I will brace myself for the next instalment of the story! Let's go in and get ready for dinner, Ernest and Roberta will be returning soon,' she said, looking forward to seeing them.

***

A week later

'I'm going to drive you both into the village to register the baby,' said Petra, popping into the nursery to find Kathryn. Baby Celeste was in her cot and Rani was cooing over her.

'She's very beautiful, Mrs Comte-Wright,' said Rani, respectfully.

Kathryn stood next to him as he rocked the crib.

'I will miss you both when you go to India, Rani, you have been good to Dawn.'

'I love her very much, you know, Kathryn,'

'Good, I am glad!' Kathryn said, pleased at least one relationship around here was going well. Sebastien had been quite attentive she had to admit, but she couldn't help but compare him to Devlin. Devlin was always there for her, and Sebastien was more attentive to himself she felt. But she knew it wasn't fair to do this and it wasn't as if she hadn't known what Sebastien was like before she married him. Perhaps she thought… then she dismissed the thought and then her mind was calmed by Rani. He was now singing in Hindu to the little girl, with the black hair and the black eyes. 'It's to wish all the wonderful blessings of life on a baby. My grandmother used to sing it to us.

'Indian Lily Moth,
Caterpillar to Butterfly,
On the lily plants,
They grow into beautiful butterflies.'

'That's lovely, Rani, is your grandmother still alive?'

'Oh yes, she is nearly a hundred years old!'

'My goodness, Rani, you better keep singing then!' Kathryn smiled at this nice young man. 'There hasn't been a lily here for at least two years. When will they return Rani?'

'Oh, they will, Madam, they will. We have to be patient, that's all.'

Chapter Seventeen
D DAY — Operation Neptune
June 1944

Another year had gone passed and the family were sitting around the kitchen fire listening to the radio. Celeste was trying to stand up and Lily was playing and laughing with her on the corner sofa by the window. Ivy was watching over them as Kathryn and Ernest sat together, fixated by the news they were hearing.

Petra was making tea and scones and washing up at the kitchen sink. It was Ivy's afternoon off but she had stayed in at Dallington Place as there was a reported storm coming and she wanted to catch up on her needlework. Petra saw Mr Montgomery come to the back stairs and rushed to find the lock to the kitchen door. He had popped in for a cup of tea after work while waiting for his lift home. He looked shattered.

'I was going to offer you a cup of tea but would you like something stronger, a brandy perhaps?' she asked him, noticing him slightly stumble on the stairs.

'We have been moving heavy logs all afternoon, I can barely move now, my back is seizing up,' he said as she watched him try to straighten himself up at the foot of the stairs.

'Come and sit down, I will get you a hot water bottle,' she said passing him a glass of brandy.

'Sorry, I would take my muddy boots off but I can't even reach them.'

'Don't worry about that. I've got to clean the floor anyway. Porridge thinks it's his playground now.' Petra smiled as Porridge was trying to get Mr Montgomery's attention and bringing a ball to him. 'Well, we just won't tell Ivy! She hates mud!' said Petra trying to avoid Ivy's eyes. Ivy had had enough of Porridge for the day.

Mr Montgomery smiled at her and then Ivy as he grimaced in pain as he lowered himself into the wooden chair. 'Down Porridge!' Kathryn shouted, fed up at the little dog, seeing the ensuing chaos of mud and poor Mr Montgomery in an awful lot of pain.

'I will join you in a brandy, Mr Montgomery.' Ernest said, turning up the radio so everyone could hear what was being said.

Porridge slunk off to his bed just as the words rang out from the broadcaster

She suddenly had a lump in her throat as she thought of Bertram leaving Dallington Place that Sunday night all those years ago, when he was her fiancé. As he had ventured forth to discover his fate in France, he was so full of life and ambition.

'Mamma, are you all right?' asked Ernest, as he watched her stare wistfully into the fire and seeing a tear fall down her cheek.

'Yes darling, I was just thinking of the Great War and the sadness it brought with it, I will be fine,' she said, patting her knee.

'Hello everyone,' said Sebastien suddenly at the door looking buoyant from a successful evening's work at Heatherley's restaurant.

Kathryn got up and kissed him on his cheek and Petra asked him if he would like a brandy.

'I think I will draw a bath and relax upstairs if you don't mind. It's been quite a day today, but I'm not complaining.'

'That's good, we need business to pick up,' said Kathryn, smiling at her husband.

'Cheers to that,' said Mr Montgomery, getting up to leave.

'I think my driver should be outside,' he said, swigging back the rest of his brandy and standing up slowly. Ivy took his glass from him and helped him to the door.

'Can you manage the steps or would you rather go out the front?' she asked him as he hesitated at the kitchen door.

'I will be fine,' he replied taking each step carefully and pulling himself up by the balustrade.

Locking the back door, she took her pinny off and declared she would be turning in too. 'See you tomorrow,' she waved at the family as Kathryn threw another log on the fire.

'Roberta is late back, Ernest,' Kathryn stated wrapping the armchair blanket around her shoulders as Sebastien passed her a glass of brandy. Hearing the window rattle from the wind, she gave Ernest a concerned look.

'Give it half and hour and then if she's not back, I will drive the motor car over to the farm to pick them up,' he stated, checking the mantle clock which struck 8.00 pm.

'I'm going to put the girls down for the night,' Kathryn said, feeling weary herself.

Calling to Lily to put away her toys, she scooped up Celeste who was patting Porridge in his basket.

Just then, Roberta came through the front door and the twins ran up to Kathryn.

'We were just wondering where you had got to,' Kathryn said, relieved to see them as she bent down for her grandchildren to kiss her on the cheek. Celeste grabbed a handful of Rachel's hair, making her wince and Celeste giggled. She was such a giggler.

'Sorry to keep everybody, one of the horses was in foal and we watched her give birth. The twins loved every minute of it and were transfixed. They both want to become vets now!' she smiled peering into the kitchen to find Ernest.

After taking the girls to bed, Kathryn went into the bedroom to talk to her husband. He was sitting on the bed in his dressing gown and was about to light a cigar. Smiling at her, he patted the bed next to him. She snuggled into him and told him how proud she was of him.

'I've missed you today,' she said, now holding his hand.

'Hold up,' he said, placing the unlit cigar onto the ashtray and reaching into the open bedside table drawer, he pulled out a very expensive looking jewellery box.

'What is it?' cried Kathryn, clasping her hands together. She loved surprise presents. She opened the black gift box and gasped at the beautiful diamond and ruby brooch. It was a diamond horse with ruby stones for its reigns.

'I love it, where did you buy it?' she asked, thinking this was something that would be for sale in a London jewellers.

'I had this idea to have a cabinet in the hallway of the hotel to sell some nice trinkets to the visitors. Obviously, I will mark up the prices. I bought it in London last week,' he explained, taking it from her and pinning it to her dressing gown.

'You went to London last week? I don't remember that,' said Kathryn.

A frown went over Sebastien's face. 'You were taking Celeste to the doctors and I thought I would go to London and buy you a present. I wanted it to be a surprise. You don't mind do you?'

'No of course not, but next time let's have a day together there soon,' she said, feeling guilty she had made him feel bad for taking the day off. 'I miss you sometimes,' she continued, feeling that her life was so preoccupied with children and work these days she could hardly keep up with her husband.

'Would you like me to draw you a bath?' he asked, kissing her on the lips.

'That would be nice, thank you Sebastien,' she said, thinking she was being over sensitive.

When he stood at the door and watched her undress, he said, 'I love you,' but Kathryn felt his words didn't sound sincere and when she got into the bath alone, she had never felt more lonely in her life. Tears fell down her cheeks. When she remembered the words he said when he first met her "a woman like you Kathryn, would never be alone", she couldn't stop crying. When he came to see why she was so sad, she said it must be overtiredness and thanked him for the jewellery. But in her gut she knew something wasn't right and she thought she knew what it was.

***

Christmas 1944

The summer and the autumn had passed in a whirl and the news of war still dragging on was depressing. They wanted to make this Christmas special and Kathryn hoped Dawn and Rani would be back. Kathryn had agreed with Petra they could have some of the evacuees from the village over for Christmas lunch. She was planning to have a huge table set up in the orangery, for at least thirty including family. Ivy had managed to ask the butcher to donate two turkeys, and Sebastien had managed to obtain a huge side of beef, on the black market, or so she thought.

There was going to be a roast pork for the Italians, from the farm, which was simple to arrange and easy to cook and would provide some Christmas roasts for their hotel too. She didn't ask too many questions about some of Sebastien's dealings in London. He had been frequenting the Gelding Club and he had befriended a chef called Francois, who was teaching him more culinary skills. He had decided to stay at Throgmorton Street as he had promised Kathryn he would sort out some accounts and gather revenue, which they would plough back into the hotel.

Ernest and Roberta were now safely ensconced back at Dallington Place so Sebastien had their rooms. He only went out when it was necessary. The bombings had made such a mess of London, and he wanted to be back in the English countryside. Sitting amongst all the toys left by Ernest's and Roberta's twins, he found he couldn't concentrate. Deciding to take a long walk in the City and then he would take a bus to the Gelding Club. As he walked past St. Paul's Cathedral on the way to the Gelding Club, he balked at the damage to the Cathedral's dome. It depressed him, thinking about what Mr Opperly had told him about the inside of it. The high altar in ruins, beautiful flooring and ceiling just obliterated. Hands in his pockets, he walked on slowly weaving in and out of workers rushing back from lunch hour to their jobs. A pretty shop girl smiled at him, clutching a Fortnum and Mason bag and it gave him the idea to go shopping and buy some presents for Kathryn. He could go to Harrods he thought, but he remembered he favoured the jewellery stores of Piccadilly. So, hailing a taxi, asked the driver to take him to the Burlington Arcade. Rain started to fall and he was happy he had made the quick decision to take the taxi. He checked in his wallet to see how much money he had, because he wanted to splash out on Kathryn. She had been really understanding of the late hours he was putting into the hotel. Maybe, he thought, he should buy the other women in the household a little trinket each, especially Roberta. He entered the shop whose little bell on the top of the door, rang out sweetly. The shop was Pritchard and Sons. A dark place, with black walls which he presumed were chosen to show off the diamonds and pearls in the cabinets and drawers. He had been there many times before.

An attractive assistant brought out a drawer of rings and Sebastien chose a garnet and ruby ring for Kathryn, knowing she loved to wear red at Christmas. It was an instant choice and one he knew she would love. It reminded him of the night he knew he had fallen in love with her, as he fastened the pearl necklace at the nape of her neck during the evening of the infamous Christmas party so long ago.

He took longer choosing a ring for Roberta but, in the end, he chose an amethyst and gold ring and he took a liking to a tiny sapphire ring, so he bought that too. The sapphire stones were tiny and really it was the yellow gold he was paying for but it was inexpensive and it was pretty, he thought, perhaps Petra would like it, he thought. Two brooches caught his eye from a glass cabinet to the left of the door as the shop assistant wrapped the other jewels.

I will take those as well, both of them,' he insisted.

Pleased with his purchases, he rushed on to the Gelding Club where he thought he would telephone Kathryn and ask her if she needed anything in London. Then a quick drink and a meal would be a good idea he thought and then he would make his return back to Sussex. Paying the driver, he was told that there was likely to be an air raid in the next few hours and perhaps he shouldn't hang around.

Thanking the chap for his warning he rushed up the stairs of the Gelding Club. Suddenly, he heard the taxi driver calling to him as he had left his hat on the back seat. Rushing back, he saw there was already a gentleman sitting in the taxi.

Sebastien put his hand through the open window to let the gentleman pass it to him, when they both recognised each other.

'My old chap, it's Alexander,' the large man said, smiling and extending his hand through the open window.

'Alexander, well I never', said Sebastien, shocked to see him.

'How are you, do you still live at Dallington Place?' Alexander asked him, to make polite conversation.

'Of course,' said Sebastien

'Give my regards to Kathryn and Dawn then, a Merry Christmas to you all!' And then he motioned to the taxi to drive away. Tipping his hat at Sebastien, he then settled back in his seat and left Sebastien a bit bemused by his rather brusque manner. He was polite but not particularly friendly. Perhaps he was late with his travel arrangements. Alexander was always travelling somewhere. Besides it was Christmas, he rationalised.

Picking up the receiver, Kathryn was happy to hear from Sebastien.

'I bumped into Alexander, he got into my taxi outside the Gelding Club!'

'Gosh, what a coincidence,' cried Kathryn.

'He sent his regards! I will be home by eight, I don't want to hang around because of the night raids,' he told her in a hushed tone.

'No, please don't, I miss you, and Lily wants you to play scrabble before bed!'

'I will try, love you!' he said, and hung up.

As she put the receiver down, the telephone rang again. It was Nora.

'Kathryn my dear, just a quick telephone call to check if you are coming to the W I Christmas Party at Judith Jerobaum's tomorrow night?'

'Oh, I had forgotten to reply, yes of course I'm attending. So sorry. I will call her now, see you tomorrow,' Kathryn said, realising she was forgetting all her appointments lately. Geraldine had mentioned it last week. Looking at the grandfather clock in the hallway as it chimed nine o'clock, Kathryn had butterflies in her stomach. Sebastien should have been home by now and Lily was waiting for a bedtime story. Celeste was already asleep, as were the twins. She telephoned Dawson and asked if a driver had been sent for him.

'No,' Dawson said, sleepily.

'Oh, sorry to have woken you. I just was a little worried. He promised to be back by eight.'

'I think he took the Rover, ma'am. I'm sure he can drive himself back from the station, don't fret. He will be fine.'

'Thank you Dawson. I didn't realise he took his motor car,' Kathryn replied, parting the damask curtain to see if his motor car was on the driveway.

Giving up on the night time read, Kathryn told Lily that her daddy was on the train, turned the light off and watched his daughter roll over and go to sleep.

'Night, Kathryn,' she said sadly, and Kathryn felt sorry for her. Her father was somewhere in London and hadn't returned when he had said he would and her mother was in India. She was going to have to make it up to the little girl this Christmas, if Dawn didn't get back in time. It wasn't fair and she thought her parents selfish. Sighing, she went down to her study to pour herself a brandy.

The grandfather clock struck eleven and turning off the light, she gave up on her evening with Sebastien and started to make her way up the stairs. Just as she got to the top landing, she heard a key in the lock and he opened the front door. He had a big smile on his face and he was clearly drunk!

'Kathryn my love, my darling,' he said, dropping his suitcase and umbrella on to the chequered floor. 'Kiss me!' he demanded.

'Where have you been? Lily and I were worried about you!' Kathryn said, going to pick up his umbrella.

'Darling, so sorry, the train was at a standstill at the Darton Crossing for two hours and we all had to get down onto the tracks and I waited at the Blue Bell Pub after, so it would be safe, and I had far too many drinks!'

'Really? Did the signal fail?' asked Kathryn, not believing a word of it.

'I don't know. Something about a raid so we came to a standstill and the lights were turned off. Simply frightful! I can tell you.'

'But Dawson or even I could have picked you up, you could have telephoned,' Kathryn said, feeling a headache coming on.

'Nope. No signal at the pub either. Lights and lines were down. There were five or six of us having a drink behind the bar while we waited. I'm safe, and here I am, see!' he continued. 'Look at my hands, my fingers, am I a ghost? I'm here silly billy!' he said, trying to grab her and kiss her.

'Don't be silly, Sebastien, I'm going up to bed. I'm glad you are safe, and by the way, Ivy has made up the spare bedroom for you tonight. Goodnight!' And with that, Kathryn marched up the stairs, turning around one more time to say, 'Turn the lights off, would you?' knowing he would probably fall asleep on the sofa in the sitting room. There was no spare room, every room was filled. And he certainly was not going to share her bed.

***

21st December

Geraldine passed Kathryn a small glass of sherry. Judith Jeroboam had decorated the café beautifully. Paper chains in red and purple were hanging across the ceiling and Judith's two waitresses were handing around plates for the mince pies. Nora was already there when Kathryn arrived with Petra, who was parking the motor car in the car park behind. Wearing a bright red frock coat, Nora was playing the glamorous belle of the ball and handing out name badges for everyone. A pretty tree with some candles precariously placed in the corner of the room, was laden with baubles and some presents underneath, making the room look very festive. A violinist was playing by the front of the café, serenading women, as they came through the door.

There must have been forty to fifty women there, mostly from the W I. Kathryn and Geraldine found a seat by the Christmas tree, as most of the women were milling about excitedly meeting each other or greeting the ones they were already acquainted with. After half an hour, there was a sound of a bell and Judith asked everybody to cease talking and listen.

'May I have everyone's attention, please? I am Judith Jeroboam if anybody didn't know and I want everyone to contribute to the injured soldiers fund tonight, even if it is a small donation. We have our envelopes here on the table and if everyone can please leave their donations by the door as they leave tonight.

My daughter, Karen, will collect them, however large or small. Thank you.'

Karen held up her hand so everyone could see her. Kathryn recognised her straight away, her impish face and newly-cropped, blonde hair, which she kept tucking behind her ears nervously. Karen looked over in Kathryn's direction and Kathryn looked away.

After a couple of hours and a few sherries later, Kathryn felt it was time to leave. It had been a fun party and she had met some new ladies who had moved to the village with their families, to escape London and the blitz.

Petra decided to stay on, so Geraldine and Kathryn said their goodbyes and headed towards the door to give their donations. Kathryn walked up to Karen and smiled, but Karen's gaze was frosty. Kathryn ignored her rudeness, placed the envelope on the tray she was carrying and left as quickly as she could.

William was outside in his Daimler, waiting for his wife and her best friend.

'Look at William's present to himself,' giggled Geraldine to Kathryn.

'It's beautiful. Do you remember when Devlin bought one and then he was too embarrassed to go out in it?' Kathryn reminisced.

Sitting in the back and placing a blanket over their knees, William made his way back to Dallington Place to drop Kathryn off.

'Did you see the way that Karen stared at your brooch that Sebastien had bought you?' Geraldine said, wondering why this woman would look so envious.

'Yes, I noted it, and she gave me such an icy stare,' Kathryn agreed.

'You know, Geraldine, I have made a decision. I'm going to put a private detective onto Sebastien. If he is having an affair I want to know,' and she lowered her voice, so William didn't hear, 'I'm going to divorce him. I want to catch him red handed though. And with a photographer!'

'What, when did you decide this?' asked Geraldine, shocked.

'A while back. I have had my suspicions about that women and I'm not normally wrong. I won't tolerate this sort of behaviour from any man, and I think Sebastien is going to be in for a shock. I'm not so gullible any more, Geraldine, and I'm not standing for any more nonsense. I'm not going to be made a fool of by anybody,'

Geraldine nodded quietly, resting her hand on her husband's shoulder.

'I'm tougher now you know. I just want it done. It's finished for us if he is having an affair. No second chances. A quick divorce,' Kathryn stated.

'William will know someone to help,' Geraldine said, patting her friend on her arm. William watched the two women from the motor car's mirror but didn't say anything, and pretended not to hear.

'No, I know someone, somebody that Devlin used to know. I will make inquires after Christmas,' Kathryn said, wrapping her shawl around her.

'Yes, good, let's get through Christmas, and don't forget we are coming on Christmas Eve this year, you have the room?' Geraldine asked, tucking Kathryn's hair neatly around the shawl in an affectionate manner.

'It may be a back bedroom, but it depends if Dawn is here or in Norfolk. I'm just waiting to hear some news from her. Ivy said she telephoned a few days ago, but then was cut off. I hope they will be here in the next couple of days! For Lily's sake!'

'As long as we are all together, that's what matters!' agreed Geraldine, hoping her husband wouldn't mind a smaller room. He seemed to have delusions of grandeur she thought these days, but secretly she loved his more ostentatious manner. She was seeing another side to him since he became a grandpa. The motor car pulled up outside Dallington Place and they said their goodbyes.

Kathryn could see Officer Harding talking to some of the prisoners who were confined to their quarters. It had started to snow and Kathryn shivered as she looked for her keys. Elizabeth and Lucy waved at Kathryn and she beckoned for them to come in from the cold.

Chatting to them, Kathryn omitted to see a letter on the marble table under the mirror, addressed to her with a stamp marked India.

'Kathryn, you have a letter,' the young girl smiled, passing it to her.

'Thank you and goodnight girls, see you in the morning,' Kathryn said, walking into her study and closing the door, wanting to be private.

Kathryn wasn't sure where Sebastien was and she didn't care either. She sat down at her study desk and ripped open the letter with her letter knife.

It read:

Darling Kathryn,

I hope this letter finds you all in good health and especially my beautiful May Lilian. I know we promised to be back for Christmas but the business is flourishing here and we have been exploring the whole of Assam, looking into teas that would suit Dallington Place, as you know.

The time has flown and we didn't make our plans to return in time. Then Rani had some ideas to tour the plantations by horseback and we have been camping out for nearly a whole month, since the beginning of November. We rode on horseback, staying in six or seven towns from Bangladesh to Assam. We slept under the stars and during the day we made enquiries and explored more territories that we could perhaps purchase in the future. It will all pay off in the end. Rani has convinced me.

Please don't be angry with me, forgive me, and look after Lily for us. I will telephone you at Christmas so we can talk to everybody.
All my love, Dawn and of course Rani.

Kathryn sighed. She knew that Lily would be disappointed. Christmas 1944 was going to be a tough one. She just hoped the war wouldn't drag on much longer.

Chapter Eighteen
Armistice 1945

The land girls and the Lumber Jills sat in the sitting room, with their suitcases neatly by their sides, waiting for their lift to the station. The excited chatter could be heard from the kitchen below and Ivy was making hot chocolate as their lift was caught up in the armistice celebrations in the village. War was officially over. The Prisoners of War had finally left and Kathryn should have been in the mood to celebrate but she wasn't. She was in the middle of a nasty divorce. She sat at the kitchen table with Porridge on her knee and was quietly making some notes to give to her solicitor. Although life had gradually grown quieter, it wasn't less stressful for her.

Geraldine and William were coming over for supper to give her some support and she wanted to seek their advice on a few things. Spending most of her morning yesterday with her solicitor, he told Kathryn she would have to negotiate a better deal for Sebastien. But she wouldn't budge. She wanted him out of Dallington Place for good!

'He wants to stay you know and he even had the cheek to say that Dallington Place was more his, than mine, as he married Dawn and her family owned it first!' Kathryn said, to the couple.

'That's ridiculous!' cried William, looking for his napkin which had fallen under his seat.

'He wants to take Dallington Place away from me, Geraldine. I am absolutely appalled!' Kathryn stated, with her hands on her hips as she watched the oven timer for the apple pie to rise. They were sitting in the small kitchen, because it was warm and cosy and Kathryn wanted to be private. It was a rainy day. The officers were still milling about and she didn't want anybody else knowing her private business. She didn't want any scandal. And for once, she was pleased that Dawn was away and couldn't sneer at her, as if to say I told you so!

'Well, where is Sebastien now?' Geraldine asked her, sipping her tea.

'He is at Heatherley's but all his clothes are here!'

'He wants a foot in all the doors, doesn't he!' said William enjoying his apple pie but stabbing the crust angrily.

'Would he not negotiate?' asked Geraldine, sitting back in her chair.

'Well, I spoke to him a couple of days ago and he said he wanted the hotel and a chunk of the land here at least,' Kathryn said, slamming the oven door shut.

'The lawyers unfortunately agree with him. After all, he wants access to Lily and Celeste. He has to be near them. I told him, over my, well, you know… body, that he would ever get possession of Dallington Place.'

'Well, you are going to have to find a compromise. Do you mind giving up your share of Heatherleys?' Geraldine asked, looking worried.

'No not at all but I don't want him to have a share here. After all we were married only a few years. It's like he planned it, you know,' Kathryn said, close to tears.

'How about Willow Tree Cottage, with a couple of acres of farmland?' suggested William, helpfully.

'Could that not work?' asked Geraldine, cheering up for Kathryn's sake.

'Willow Tree Cottage is dear to me, it was where Devlin and I were first together as husband and wife. I don't want to. Devlin would have been appalled.'

'Kathryn you are going to have to give something away. If this drags on, you may lose Dallington Place,' Geraldine said to Kathryn, but looking to her husband.

'We have a hearing next week. I will suggest it then, maybe he will agree.'

'Do you want me to talk to him?' asked Geraldine, kindly.

'I don't think it will do any good but you could try,' Kathryn answered, shrugging her shoulders.

'I will go up to Heatherley Hotel tomorrow, then,' she said, determined to help her dear friend.

'I will come with you my dear. I don't want you getting involved in a hot-headed scene,' said William protectively.

***

Heatherley's were holding a party for the soldiers and their wives and girlfriends. It was a beautiful hot day and Sebastien had been cooking in the vast kitchen all morning. The hotel was attracting a lot of interest as a wedding venue and Sebastien was enjoying the attention and the business possibilities, now the war was over. Many couples were so happy to be reunited they couldn't wait to get married, and did so, as soon as possible.

Geraldine and William walked into the pretty hotel reception with its red carpet and red and white curtains Sebastien had had brought over from a contact in Paris. Sitting down on a red, velvet chaise longue, they waited nervously to speak to him on Kathryn's behalf. A waitress asked them if they would like a glass of wine or a soft drink. Geraldine knew that Sebastien was behind that, a glass of wine to soften them and to cajole them into agreeing with him, she thought.

Sebastien joined them after a few minutes, rushing up from below stairs still wearing his chef's apron and stepping forward to shake their hands. They both declined and sat back in their chairs, looking at each other awkwardly.

'Listen. I haven't long, my guests need me. We have a wedding party to cook for tomorrow, as well,' he said, feeling the weight of the couples brush off.

Geraldine spoke up first. 'I'm here on behalf of Kathryn and she wants to know if you would be willing to close your case for the rights to Dallington Place, in exchange for Heatherley's and Willow Tree Cottage, plus five acres of farmland that backs onto the Matthews' farm,' Geraldine said, nervously reading from the notes Kathryn had given them. Then she handed him the outline plan of the acreage, not looking him straight in the eye.

'I would be willing to discuss this, yes,' said Sebastien, taking off his apron and sitting back in his armchair.

Geraldine smiled with relief.

'But on one condition,' he continued.

William raised his eyebrows.

'I will drop all claim of Dallington Place, and it's five hundred acres. I will take Heatherley's and Willow Tree Cottage and five acres of farmland, but I want a third of Throgmorton Street! Otherwise, the deal is off the table,' he stated, untying his apron and rising from his chair.

***

Spring 1946

It had taken a year for everything to almost go back to normal. It was late March, and Kathryn was walking with Celeste and Lily to the stables. Holding on to her little girl's hand, Kathryn pointed out the trees and their names to the girls.

Some rooks who were nesting in a stable, flew out and encircled them, making Lily squeal with delight and made her half-sister laugh. Lily ran on ahead following the rooks as they foraged in the branches of the trees. Gone were the cuckoos, the Italian prisoners of war and gone were some of the Nissen huts. They had been removed to recover some of the lawn.

As they walked past the orangery, they waved to Mr Montgomery who was giving Tree Top House a new coat of paint. It had been made ready to be a tea house by Kathryn who had meticulously designed the interiors with Rani and Dawn's influence, from their travels through India. Kathryn had just finished completing the menu, consisting of different teas and teacakes.

Dawn and Rani had perfected a perfect brew now and the importation of the tea was going really well. Ivy was busy perfecting her lemon sponge and an anniversary chocolate cake to sell.

She hoped the Tea House would bring in much revenue as there were some much needed repairs to the refectory now. Kathryn thought perhaps now she should convert the refectory back into cottages. But she couldn't decide.

Would it ever be a race course again she wondered? Should she burn her bridges? She had much to think about. There was no more government funding and she had to put her business hat on once again. She should really come up with other ideas too, but first she had to get this off the ground.

Sebastien had been keeping a low profile as he had been busy up at Heatherley's, except on either a Saturday or a Sunday afternoon when he drove over to Dallington Place to pick up Lily and Celeste. He would take them out for lunch or tea at the new 'Sebastien's' restaurant, at the Heatherley Hotel which they loved.

The other guests at the hotel always admired them and the girls loved the attention. Everyone always saying how much the pretty, raven-haired girls, looked so much like him.

Ernest and Roberta and the twins were spending more time in London as Ernest's political career was taking off. He had been working as a political aide for the home secretary, and his good work was being noticed at the privy council. He and Roberta were enjoying London and Throgmorton Street again now the war was over. Roberta was helping with quite a few charities, especially the Family Welfare Association, which helped aid poorer families in cities effected by the war. London was being slowly rebuilt and the camaraderie and pulling together served London well. Roberta now had a nanny and she was finding the time to work and serve charities which were close to her heart.

People loved her warm nature and soon women's institutions were flocking to her, to support them in their causes. Enjoying the freedom of London and the making of new friends, both of them decided to settle at Throgmorton Street for the foreseeable future. Knowing Sebastien owned a third of Throgmorton Street made Ernest and Roberta even more determined to make it their home for the time being. Sebastien wasn't going to move in any time soon, as he was busy at the Heatherley Hotel and they thought it a wise decision to put down roots there, mainly to prevent Sebastien from taking over so readily and easily if he wanted to live in London.

On the morning of the opening, Kathryn was in her study going over some accounts from a large Assam tea factory when she was just about to telephone Dawson for some help with a last-minute change of plan to the seating arrangement at the Tea House. Looking over her list of the VIPs who were attending, there were more than she had first anticipated. Excited by the prospects of all the good advertising this would bring in, she reached for the telephone but Dawson beat her to it. Dawson sounded out of breath.

'Ma'am I have just come from my morning walk and I saw a motor car on the white bridge. There's a gentleman broken down on it,' he said in a whisper.

'Who is it?' she asked, thinking perhaps it was someone to do with the refurbishments of Tree Top House.

'I believe we all know him well ma'am, it's Alexander Pillard,' he replied, clearing his throat. Kathryn took off her glasses and sat down on hearing this news.

'His chauffeur and I were looking into the engine and I fear the motor car is not going to start. May I have your permission to ask Mr Montgomery to have a look?' he continued. 'He is rather a whiz at that sort of thing and may Mr Pillard see you ma'am? He wants to know.'

'Of course, Dawson,' she answered, wondering why he was here.

'Yes, Dawson, show him up to the main house, I will wait for him in my study,' she continued.

Kathryn's heart started to beat fast. She hadn't seen him since that day in Harrods. As soon as she placed down the receiver she rushed out of the study almost bumping into Ivy.

'Ivy could you fix two whiskies for me and bring them to my study in five minutes? I'm expecting a guest,' she instructed her and then ran up to her dressing room to change.

***

Alexander knocked at the door and Kathryn sat nervously at her desk. Smoothing down her hair, she waited for Alexander to open the door and stand before her. The door opened and he paused for a minute, looking at her. Kathryn was rather surprised by his appearance. He had lost a lot of weight and his hair had receded and gone was the large moustache. But as soon as he spoke, he was like the old Alexander that she had known.

'My dear Kathryn,' he said, walking briskly over to her and he lent over the desk to kiss her cheek.'

'Sit down please Alexander,' Kathryn said, rather imperiously passing him a whisky. The flash back of the day she caught him talking to someone else in this very study made her purse her lips and clear her throat nervously.

'My Kathryn, you look so well! Beautiful as ever,' he said, with a jovial glint in his eye.

'And you my dearest Alexander, are as charming as ever!' she said pleasantly, if not a little sarcastically.

'What brings you to Sussex? I'm sorry about your motor car but the men will get it repaired for you. We have been crawling with mechanics here for years!' she said, smugly.

'I can't believe Dallington Place was a prisoner of war camp. Dawson was telling me all about it. That man goes on and on, so much energy!'

'Yes, he is my rock!' said Kathryn, again a little harshly and not meeting Alexander's eye.

'Kathryn,' Alexander said, looking up nervously,' I have apologies to make to you.'

Kathryn stayed silent and let him speak. She sat back in her chair to listen.

'Kathryn, I made some terrible mistakes, some terrible decisions,' he said, paling. 'I regretted leaving you, the moment I married Pearl,' he said, pausing.

Kathryn was just about to speak but he put his hand up to stop her.

'Please let me continue.' Kathryn nodded back at him, clearing her throat again quietly, and resting back in her chair again. Sipping her whisky, she listened, gesturing for him to do so.

'I figured I'd made my bed so I should lie in it, but we only lasted a year and then I moved out of the apartment in New York we shared. I want you to forgive me.'

Kathryn looked surprised and pushed a piece of stray hair behind her ear and sipped some more whisky. She cleared her throat.

'Alexander, I'm in no mood for romance. I am just figuring out my divorce settlement from Sebastien,' she said, shocked at his admission.

'Yes, I heard,' he said.

'Ever the journalist then!' said Kathryn, rather annoyed that he seemed to know a little too much about her.'

'No, Kathryn, I wanted your forgiveness. It's plagued me all these years throughout the war and I thought if anything happened to you, I would never forgive myself,' he explained, genuinely looking remorseful. There was sadness in his eyes. Even tears she thought.

'Why now?' she asked him sternly.

'I decided to move to England for a while. There are projects in London I'm looking into and I'm writing for the Telegraph. I have an interview later today with a chap from Texas, working as a horse whisperer funnily enough. I suppose they knew I was involved in the horse racing business here,' he explained.

'I have tried to contact you a few times throughout the war and I didn't have the courage until now. I saw you in Harrods one day, I called out to you,' he said, slightly embarrassed. Kathryn then realised perhaps it had been him that had been calling the house periodically with a silence on the other end of the line.

'Yes, I remember, I think I saw you,' she said, nodding. 'I went over to Riley's and they said they had seen you,' Kathryn said, her voice softening.

Alexander took a large swig of his whisky.

'I saw Sebastien not so long ago outside the Gelding Club and then I decided then and there, that I would come and see you. It was time.'

Ivy knocked on the door and peered around the door.

'Ma'am, Mr Pillard's car has been repaired, it's in the stable ready for him. His chauffeur is waiting.'

'Thank you, Ivy,' Kathryn said, relieved of a pause to their conversation.

'I suppose I should be on my way for my meeting,' Alexander said, feeling the coolness from Kathryn. He stood up from his chair.

'Kathryn, do you miss the horses?' he asked, looking across to the large photograph of the opening to Dallington races.

'Of course I do Alexander! They are all gone now except for the few they have at the Matthews' farm.'

'Kathryn, may we salvage a friendship, do you think?' he asked, placing his hat on his head. Kathryn paused and walked around the desk towards him. Normally she would have said no, but there was something different about him now, almost as if he had been humbled by her. His eyes were so sad when he looked at her so earnestly that she couldn't help but say yes.

As soon as she had agreed, his eyes lit up. Showing him to the door, he touched her arm.

'Kathryn I was wondering, would you ever go back in business with the horses?'

'Well, I have new businesses here, but yes, I miss the horses. But it's not the time for the race track, too soon after the war. I don't think people would like it,' she answered, reaching for the door.

'I just had a thought. This man I'm interviewing today is a horse whisperer for an American polo team but you know, polo would work here now. On a small scale at first,' he suggested.

Kathryn could see Ivy opening the front door for him.

'Polo? Goodness now that's a thought,' she exclaimed.

'I don't know Alexander, this has come out of the blue,' she said, with her mind racing.

'Think about it, it could bring in quite the revenue, the Sport of Kings!' he said, relieved he had got things off his chest.

Kathryn was about to let him go and then she decided to walk with him to his motor car.

'Thank you, Ivy. I will be back in a minute, I need to take the cakes to

Tree Top House,' she said, taking a dozen of the cream slices carefully wrapped in a large box from the table by the door, that Ivy had just placed there.

'Let me help you with that,' offered Alexander, taking them from her.

'My, the place has changed Kathryn. I would love to see your Tea House, Dawson was telling me all about it.'

'Was he now!' Kathryn said, sternly.

'Well, as I said, Kathryn, it's just a thought, and if you need the revenue, it may be quite lucrative. I would enjoy getting back into business with you. I have some money saved.'

Kathryn smiled back. He was always a good business man, like Devlin. She could never fault his business skills.

As they walked past the willow tree as Alexander greeted Mr Montgomery, something caught her eye. She walked over to the edge of the grass and there bobbing in the wind, was a small clump of Orange Lilies. Her heart lifted. A large grin spread across her face. As they reached the motor car and Alexander passed her the cakes and clambered in, he caught her happy expression.

'What?' he asked, curious as to what had brightened her up suddenly.

'Alexander, I might even take you up on your offer if it's business with the polo you are after,'

'Really?'

'Maybe, but Alexander!' she called, as his chauffeur turned the keys. 'Strictly business!'

'Strictly business, Kathryn!' and with that, he was off motoring down the drive passed the bobbing lilies.